FLIPPING
RICH
BASTARDS

AN ELEANOR ALBRIGHT EDWARDIAN P.I. MYSTERY

JULIE G MURPHY

FLIPPING RICH BASTARDS
Copyright © 2019 by Julie G. Murphy

ISBN: 978-1-68046-801-4

Published by Satin Romance
An Imprint of Melange Books, LLC
White Bear Lake, MN 55110
www.satinromance.com

Published in the United States of America.

Cover Design by Caroline Andrus

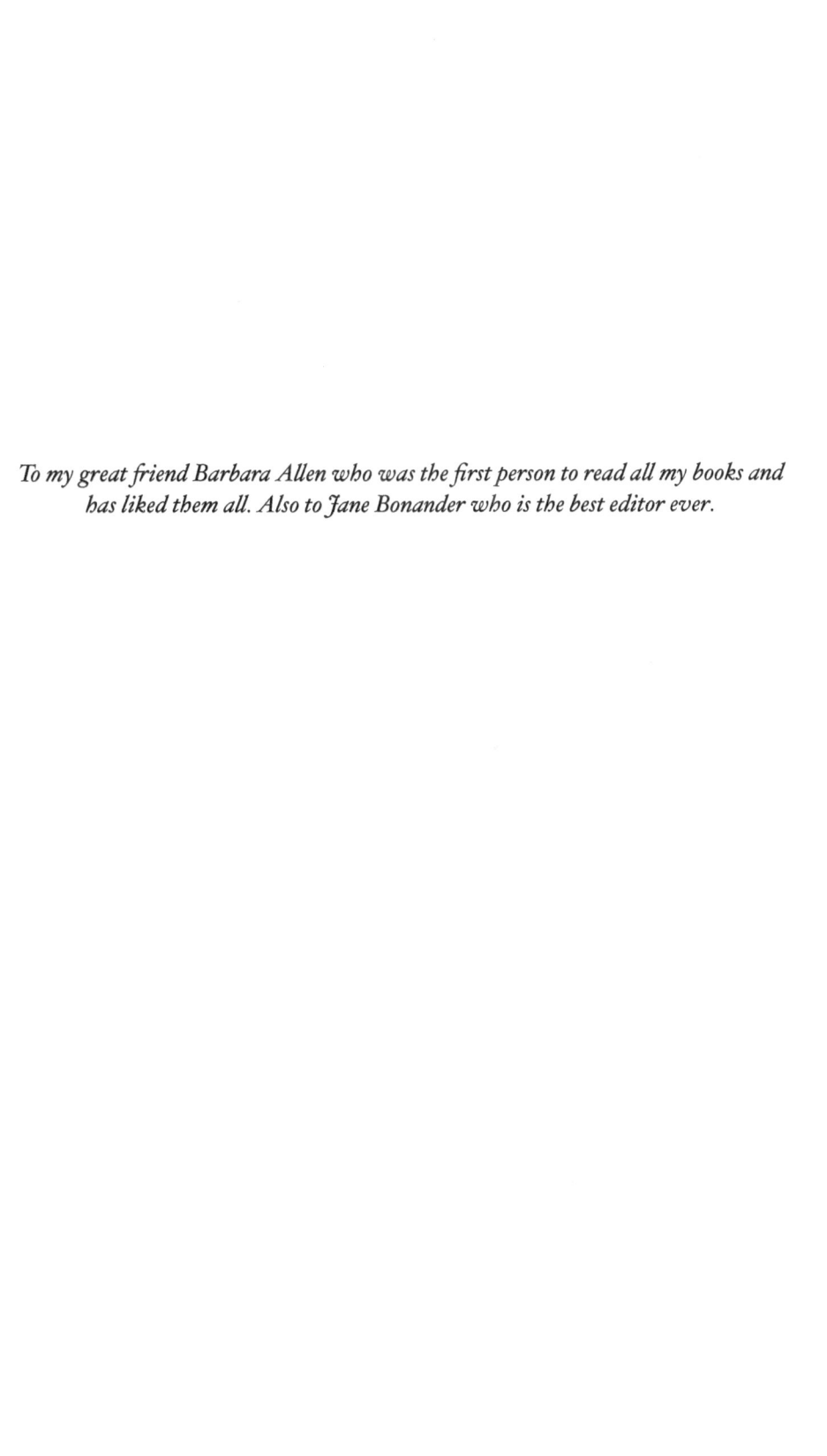

To my great friend Barbara Allen who was the first person to read all my books and has liked them all. Also to Jane Bonander who is the best editor ever.

The baby doesn't understand English and the Devil knows Latin.
—Monsignor Roland Knox

L ady Eleanor Albright shifted on the skinny cross-end of a polished shooting stick that was folded open. A beautiful day in the Cotswold ruined. She turned her head from the shot red grouse that rained from a deep blue sky as if Maxim heavy machine guns were the weaponry of choice instead of breech-loading shotguns. Again, she adjusted her skinny behind on the damnable seat. Trying to ignore the pain from a blossoming bruise of the derriere, she pulled at her corset. To breathe some air in this heat!

Irritation picked at her last happy thought as downwind she heard her brothel-loving, twelve-year-old-girl-seducing, entitlement-inflated, estranged husband, with whom she couldn't believe she'd ever had sex, laugh. A desire to rip a gun from any nearby loader and shoot the man was making her nauseous. She hadn't really processed that Lord Flipping Albright would be here.

"Dear Lord, and I bloody insisted on coming."

She sat behind the long line of gentlemen standing in their crescent-shaped shooting-butts. Why the hunters call the place they perch themselves "shooting butts" she had yet to understand. Maybe because they are shooting, and because she could see their butts—some were larger than others.

Eleanor's blistered thoughts also wondered why only the birds were being killed and not the beaters. The beaters were the men out in front of the guns who wandered about and hit at the brush to get the birds to fly. Which was even more insane than attending the shoot. Granted, the beaters resemble the king, queen and jack in a deck of cards, and they are much brighter and much, much bigger than the birds. Still, with some of these shooters, regardless of the red tunics, size mattered.

Just in front of her, size seemed to matter to the host of the event. Lord Haversack. He was shooting—*bang, bang, bang, bang, bang*—and then swearing like a man possessed. He needed really big fowl.

Possessed, that's what I must have been when I decided to get out of a soft bed in the middle of the night to scramble through a barley field in a long skirt. She picked at her blouse. Her undergarments were sticking to her like a depilatory. She pulled at her corset again. Damn thing. It was like being in the clutches of a drowning man. She fanned down her neck. Who would have thought October to be so hot? She wanted to raise her arms and let perspiration dry in the wind.

Her heart ached for the birds. They seemed forsaken. Oh, dear girl, ridiculous "forsaken," maybe defenseless. Whatever they were, she felt one with them.

She poked cotton wool farther down her ears and tried not to flinch at the incessant sound of exploding powder across the golden stubble of the area. Her narrow shoulders seemed permanently lodged against her ears. She felt like an egg-bound hen. All this because she had left her husband and was back living with her mother. Mutiny. Damn it.

The dogs piled limp-headed birds at their masters' feet.

"Just keep remembering who you are not sitting next to at the lodge, your mother-in-law...your mother...and Lady Pillock," Eleanor said to herself, again.

She pictured Lady Pillock striding room to room, searching for any immobile person with two ears. Lady P had never been much of a philosopher even on her sober days. The woman was upheld most evenings by the stays in her full dresses. She always woke early, probably from her snoring. Lady Pillock was a hard female to avoid. She had just moved to Minister Lovell. She attended every party, was never ill, and her weight was in relation to how much she drank. Tons. The problem was, Eleanor did feel sorry for the woman and was an easy target for conversation.

Eleanor blew her nose and sighed. Her picture of Lady Pillock, wrapped in massive yards of seemingly armor-plated fabric, moving down the hallways like a river barge blasting a foghorn, made Eleanor smile, but it wasn't enough. The air smelled bloody and smoky. As Eleanor watched clouds of birds rise like a fog, only to fall back to the ground again dead, she wished for a dram of what kept Lady P afloat.

She glanced next to her at Lord Louis Montfire and at the flask of whiskey he had in his hand. The Baron of Tweedmouth's son had propped himself and his stick against a young tree, for support. A veteran of the carnage no doubt, he had brought refreshments.

She noticed that Louis looked pale and vague. He held his handkerchief to his nose and mouth. Now and then he wiped his eyes. A gentle soul, like a plump cherub, Louis Monfire tended to be a little soft around the edges. With birds dying everywhere, he was here, no doubt, in an endless attempt to please his father. What was it like to be the sweet son of a think-from-the-crotch type of father? Eleanor couldn't imagine. Louis just kept covering his eyes and wiping his nose and leaning against the skinny tree.

She patted his shoulder, and then her nose seized. She sneezed and sneezed. Damn, what a world. They were both miserable, but here they were. It was like an Irishman's raise, a foot forward, two back.

Louis handed her a fresh handkerchief. "I bring loads to these things."

Lavender scented, she noted. "You here for your father?"

"Absolutely, and I believe it is more peaceful here than at home. Here, I have the beautiful countryside. There, I have a house that's a stage for a cast of bad actors. King Lear and his wife. You?"

"I have Lady Pillock. I'm too kind to shake her, and she knows it. Talk about a performer."

He smiled—a little.

It was the most she had gotten out of him all morning. He was usually such fun. Talking, talking, talking like a female, a good-natured one. He was a hugger and a hand-patter, and his hazel eyes always shone in instant sympathy. He was everyone's best friend. Today, though, he seemed leaky, like something had let the air out of his soft body.

His pallor worried her. She always had concerns for Louis.

Eleanor glanced at her still-legal husband. She realized Louis had a million more reasons to do in his father. She placed her hand on Louis's shoulder again. With the other hand, she dashed a tear from a corner of her eye. "You hate this sort of thing." Eleanor waved out to the dying birds.

"I used to shoot, you know. I'd just shoot into the air, pretending, until I hit one. Now I watch. In a few more years maybe I can just show up for the wine at the luncheon."

"How is your Father anyway?"

"Noisy."

"The asthma not any better?" Or any worse, she thought to herself.

"I don't ask." He turned toward her. "Why are you here?"

"I couldn't listen to one ounce more advice on being a good wife. He isn't a good husband. I needed some air." As the man she had promised to love and obey waited for more birds, she could hear him laugh.

"He doesn't have a care in the world. Why do I feel so guilty, like I could have done more...or less? I'm so angry at the world that I'm snapping at everyone. It's safer for them all if I'm here. I forgot he'd be here, and now this." She waved her arm at the scene again. "They kill so many. It's like they feel entitled to, to everything. I should have brought seed or something to feed the ones who live."

Louis patted the back of her hand as she gazed again at the exponentially increasing number of dead birds. She tossed Louis a we're-in-hell look, and then averted her eyes to the plump hills. Lines of beech trees quilted the fields in a patchwork. Red grouse had escaped to the branches. Probably the ones Haversack had been shooting at. Amen.

The beaters in their colorful, medieval tunics flushed another round of panting birds. The gracious host once again shot like a madman. His loader sweated at his side. There was a yell from the field, and then more yelling. Eleanor stood, letting her shooting stick fall to earth. She shaded her eyes. The butts were emptying; all the gentlemen had rushed out, all but the maniac shooter. At least Haversack had gone quiet. Her sanity felt better already.

With Louis beside her, Eleanor hurried forward. A beater was yelling. Someone was down, a beater in a purple tunic. She thought she knew the fair hair. Early that morning, he'd helped her over a ditch.

She walked faster, concentrating on missing any ankle-turning holes in the ground. Anger pushed her steps. Stupid. No one should walk in front of half of these lords especially with said lords' guns loaded and half-cocked.

Louis got to the man first.

"Just a grazing," he called out. "He's breathing."

Just a grazing, as in what a great shot to have just missed?

At the information, the lords about-faced in one movement, except Louis who took out his flask and another of his endless supply of handkerchiefs. He wet the cloth and pressed it against the man's blonde hair. Patting either side of the beater's jaw with the flat of his hand, Louis called, "Hello...hello?" Louis glanced up and down the body for another possible pooling of blood.

Eleanor knelt just as the beater's eyes opened.

"Good man," Louis said as he helped the man sit up, and then he gave him a drink from his flask.

Eleanor had been wondering about the flask. Louis never drank hard alcohol and didn't like beer because it bloated him, but he had been sipping from the flask all morning.

Louis stayed with the man. "Scotch is just the thing," he said as he offered what was left in his flask to the beater.

"Jesus," the man kept saying as he scrutinized the field of shooters.

Louis and Eleanor helped the beater stand and walked with him to a wagon. He had been kind to her, and, well she stuffed some silver into the man's hand.

Louis left the man in the charge of the other beaters. As Eleanor ambled away with Louis, she said to him, "I'm glad he is well. How do you get people to be beaters? It seems so dangerous."

"It's something men do."

Eleanor attempted a deep breath. "I've been telling myself that a little fresh air is good for me. All this fresh air has done is clog up my sinuses."

"We should trade," Louis said. "I need your mother to say, 'Stay at the lodge, darling, and let's have a good chat,' and you need my father to say, 'Go out and make your mark.'"

She smiled at his observation. "Maybe it's more interesting if you shoot? Not so damn many, but one for dinner."

"It's decent, until you hit something."

Eleanor used her finger and thumb to make the shape of a gun, and then she aimed it at the backside of her husband. "Bam, bam." She blew pretend smoke from the end of her finger. "See, that could be fun, and I wouldn't mind hitting him." She continued to stare at him. "Not at all."

Louis laughed and then coughed and coughed.

She laughed and then sneezed.

"You are angry." He handed her a fistful of handkerchiefs.

"Livid with an added drop or more of bitters." She took the proffered linens.

JULIE G MURPHY

"It's good to have you and your finger here." He laughed again. Now he was sounding more like himself. She also felt her mind lighten. Maybe this had been a good idea.

Louis and Eleanor ambled toward the rest of the shooters who were slapping each other on their backs and drinking whiskey from their silver flasks. The gentleman hunters were talking of traveling out of the area to the next shoot, and of joining King Edward at Sandringham. They talked about Sandringham, and how three hundred thousand pounds had been spent on it, thereby making it into a first class venue. The King had been talking of introducing Virginia quail and red grouse.

"Shooting may be the opposite of a hen party, but both have plenty of bloodshed," she said to Louis as he continued to walk beside her. "Is it necessary, do you think, that they all shoot like maniacs?"

"According to the Great Lord Ripton, 'Aim high, keep the gun moving, never check.' At least that's the advice I've been given"

She shook her head. "No wonder Haversack is out of control."

"He's not the only one. He's just the most obvious. He shoots his foot every time; the others can at least miss their feet. There are some who are very good shots."

"Three thousand five hundred and eighty," a man called from the line of dead birds.

"Yes, I suppose there must be," she said.

Eleanor left Louis to the men and walked to the luncheon tents. She thought of the very large glass of wine she was going to drink. To toast the health of the beater, and to Louis—a kind, suffering man. She couldn't celebrate all that in just one glass.

Louis had joined the backslapping of the men. He seemed to enjoy that part. The other men liked him like they liked their favorite dogs. Better than their wives.

Eleanor wandered to the Windrush Creek to freshen a bit. She brushed hard at the straw imbedded in the fabric of her new skirt. The yellowed bits annoyed her with their tenacity. The great outdoors she thought with irritation, and then she dipped Louis's handkerchief into the stream and dabbed at her neck and face.

She always left the house looking impeccable; somehow, she never returned that way. Louis on the other hand was always turned out. His thinning black hair always in place, his long hands always manicured. She must get some pointers.

The water felt good on her neck. Louis's smell of lavender was soothing.

6

The third-day-of-October's bright sun had probably reddened her cheeks. Then, no one would notice if she had three large glasses of wine. Her Irish ancestors were right. Drink helped. Time to forget her husband and his fetishes; forget nearly dead beaters, and dead birds, and smoke, and blood.

As she was sweeping escaped locks of reddish-brown hair back into pins, she heard Lady Pillock's booming voice. Oh God, the women were arriving —like beautiful, feathered parrots disgorging from their opened cages. The sound was increasing.

Women are noisy.

The fish were rising. She wished she had her pole. Now that's a sport. It did involve dead fish though. Maybe she could learn to shoot. A brace of birds, not a mob of the things. Not enough to wipe out the species for all eternity.

With that thought, Eleanor strolled through the servants who moved about the picnic area like insects while they finished unpacking the luncheon and arranging the tables in the tent with linen and silver. She bribed three full champagne glasses from the busy butler with a winning smile and felt good that she had done it. The first of the wine was going to Louis who still looked ghastly. If Louis was coming down with something, he should be in bed.

"Three? You are a darling," he said. He took two, one for himself and one for Lord Charles Wallingford, and then kissed her on the cheek. She rolled her eyes. Of course she should have anticipated Charles would be with him. His fondness for Charles was legendary. She paused to take her own deep drink, one meant to wet the beater's head, and then she looked for another waiter. Stocked, again with two glasses, she walked toward the long line of carriages, and wondered who had injured the beater. As Louis had said, most of the shooters could at least manage to miss their extremities. Still, she could think of at least one who would be challenged to even hit the slow moving Pillock woman, and she was an ample target. With some shooters, the field was dangerous for everyone but the birds.

❧ 2 ❧

Father!—to God himself we cannot give a holier name.
—William Wordsworth

E leanor took the third glass of wine toward an impromptu avenue that lined the middle of the field, and to the singular motorcar in a mix of wagons and carriages. It was easy to find, being painted bright red. She gave the champagne to Lord Henry Faraday who balanced it on the bonnet of the car as he reached onto the buttery leather seat to get his cigarettes.

Eleanor liked looking at Faraday. In his company, she felt lighter from constant laughter. She inhaled his outdoor scent of wool and acidic powder.

"May I?" he asked.

Eleanor pushed at the damp hair at her brow, lifting it to the breeze. Faraday leaned against the motor as he lit his cigarette. She wanted to ask him for one, or at least share his, but the women—more importantly her mother—were here, and Eleanor couldn't commit two sins in one day. The shoot had been her limit.

"Get many birds?" she asked. "A thousand or so?"

Faraday smiled. He was a tall, lanky man, as fair in coloring as his name suggested. He was the youngest barrister at the Old Bailey. He was also the

8

youngest in a long line of males and his mother's favorite. Eleanor had known him since childhood. Their fathers had shot together. He was an anomaly in a very sober family. Faraday was lofty in height and agreeable. His mother said that he had smiled at birth, as if he found the rush of air on his naked, wet body refreshing after such a closed womb. Anyway, she thought him a breath of fresh air. He rented a manor house in Minister Lovell for the shooting season.

"A feast of birds in every pot in every house in the village tonight," he said and then he plucked a bit of tobacco from the end of his tongue.

"Hum. I'd say there's enough to feed the world."

He reached over and straightened her hat. "Can't stand a rotting pile, what?"

She lifted her hand to where Henry Faraday's fingers had been. Her husband's less-than-baritone voice, annoyingly squeaky really, hurt her ears and brought her back reality. Eleanor dropped her hand. She squared her shoulders.

"How well does Lord Flipp———I mean Albert shoot? I've always found his aim a little crooked."

Faraday cocked an eyebrow and then the ends of his mouth turned up. Oh, she had sounded too acidic. Still, his eyes were merry as he said, "I can't say from your point of view, but in the field, your left-behind husband is a crack shot. Absolutely ringing, I'm afraid." He stamped out his smoke and put his arm around her shoulders. He hugged her to his side.

"I suppose in the field his performance is bound to improve as there he gets to shoot at anything that moves, jaded or innocent, two legs or four."

Laughing, Faraday said, "He's not worth all the anger."

"Anger is all there is left."

He changed the subject. "Did you enjoy the sunrise?"

"I did, but shooting? That's another potential interest shot down," Eleanor said as he released her.

"It's not for women, what?"

Eleanor had to hide her face from Faraday. She hated it when, on occasion he was just like the other men. To stop her eyes from tearing, she opened them wide and pulled at the corner of one as if a grain of sand grated there.

"I'm sorry," Faraday said.

"What? Some women like it," she stammered.

"About the idiotic comment, what?"

She touched his shoulder and shook her head. She groaned when she heard a, "Hey ho." The host of the shoot, oh good—the bright auto was always a huge draw.

As Haversack sauntered over, she noted that his face was less red, and his eyes were resting easier in their sockets. She thought of wandering off as Faraday began his litany, that the car was an 1898 Panhard-Levassor racer, that it uses a clutch pedal connected to a gearbox—away from the heads of the two men that would soon be bonded together while looking into the depths of the engine, but where else to go?

Faraday moved from her side to lift the bonnet to show Haversack the Systeme Panhard. "It has a front-mounted engine with rear-wheel drive." Faraday polished a little at the carriage lights with his sleeve, and then he offered Haversack a cigarette. He finished his speech with: "It finished the Paris to Bordeaux race in two days of twelve-hour driving at a speed of fifteen miles-per-hour."

"You're racing it, yourself?" the man asked.

"God, yes. Wouldn't let anyone else, what?"

"Hear the vibration of the chassis gives a lad a start, heh, heh." Haversack elbowed Faraday in the ribs.

Eleanor decided that she needed much more bubbly. She straightened from leaning against the car just as a quick-walking constable called Faraday's name. The policeman threaded through the crowd and the line of carriages.

As the breathless constable approached, he pushed wheezing words from his taxed lungs, "My Lord, there's been a death—"

"The beater? I was there," Faraday called back. "It was an accident."

"No...no...after a long fall...a peer in his nightdress." The bobbie's air gave out and he stopped and bent over. His hand pressed in at his waist, probably to relieve a stitch in his side. While stubbing out his second cigarette in the dirt, Faraday moved forward. He glanced at Eleanor with a what-more sort of look. She flowed in behind him.

A hand at the end of a strong arm pulled her back. Her mother, Lady Alannah Darnley, had found her. In leaving her husband, Eleanor had gained back her mother, every neurotic inch of the woman. Her mother was a middle-class Irishwoman from County Cork who was posing as an English Peer. Over the years, the woman had developed some bizarre mannerisms and an even stranger accent. With the breakup of Eleanor's marriage, her mother acted as if she were Eleanor's best and only stalwart friend. God, maybe she was.

"There you are, and with Lord Faraday again. Your husband *is* here after all. Come and sit for God's sake." Her mother's tone had a perfected whine to it and the sound reminded Eleanor to find that champagne refill. She wondered if anyone would notice her a bit tipsy. Probably not. They all already thought of her as just that side of odd. Her mother, the soul of effort, was trying to keep them acceptable—a hard job by anyone's standards. In deference to society, Alannah had been sitting for the last thirty odd years. She had plenty of unspent energy, so Alannah performed her job relentlessly.

"There's a problem," Eleanor said.

"My dear, Lord Faraday's a barrister. The other is a policeman. They don't need you. What do you think? That your less-than-a-lady's interests are of value to them?"

She bristled. "Chemistry is not just an interest."

Her mother made a sour face and then tugged Eleanor into the ebb and flow of the rest of the guests from the lodge. Eleanor paced herself alongside the older men who were too ancient to shoot and were arriving with the ladies. She meandered with the men at their meager speed, an amble on old feet. All sexes were mixing, with the men dotting kisses on the women's cheeks.

"Champagne!" Eleanor called to a waiter.

"And don't drink too much." Alannah was like the thorns on blackberry bushes—a woman protective to small mice, nurturing to birds, beautiful in flower, but prickly all the same.

Eleanor eyed her mother's back while thinking of arsenic poisoning and the cadaveric alkaloid defense. It would be so easy. It was so easy with arsenic being an alkaloid. *Your Honor, cadaveric alkaloids, the chemicals found in decomposing, dead bodies, resemble arsenic alkaloids. Once the body has begun decay, it's difficult to prove the presence of arsenic.* Would her mother decay? That was the question.

Eleanor entered the luncheon tent. It stood in a grassy place, next to the river where the last of the toothwort bloomed along the bank in between the beech trees. Under the big top, the sugar bees had turned their backs on the local flowers in favor of lavish, floral centerpieces. Water-beaded, red roses perched on linen-covered tablecloths. The fragrance mingled with snipe and tongue and with ham and caviar. All so peaceful and in contrast to the constable who was still talking, his hands gesturing in constant motion.

A peer, she thought. Sure, weren't they all mostly here? Glancing around, Eleanor noted that, only the occasional face in the crowd was giving the policeman a second glance. Everyone had his or her champagne. Eleanor appraised the grouping. She knew most of them didn't care for each other, except in theory, including her mother who was chatting like a bird greeting the sun. Lady Pillock was attacking some lord or other, talking about the Transvaal War.

"A Fff-french journalist wrote that our Bbb-british soldiers are bringing in trained apes from Australia to fight the Bbb-boers in South Africa," she stuttered. "What is the www-world coming to? We are bringing civilization to these people, and what do we get for our effort? Bbb-bad press."

Phew, that was a mouthful, Eleanor thought. Completely over the woman's head. So it goes. The Pillock's voice grated on her like the shrill of a mynah bird.

"Maybe we should all visit Earl's Court to fire at the pop-up South African savages at the shooting gallery," Eleanor snapped. It was like her brain had been stretched too thin and had tightened back into place. Damn it! She shouldn't take it out on Lady Pillock. The woman drank enough to indicate that she was probably also a tortured soul. Besides, she was working with a pickled brain. It was just that the day had been full of dead birds, and a wounded beater who had been sent off in a wagon. Layered in were her mother's insanity, and her estranged husband's laugh. And somewhere deep in her heart, her husband's mother, the damn dowager, who gave Eleanor her monthly stipend during luncheons of turtle soup and salmon. 'What a silly and ungrateful girl you are, Eleanor.'

"My Dearrr, there you are. I was looking for you, and then I heard that you'd taken up shooting. How brave. Is it going to be one of your new hobbies?"

Speaking of the dowager-in-law...Eleanor winced. It was payback for taking out her frustrations on the weak and innocent.

"It's not a bad thing to have a heart," the dowager added while reaching with her palm across the table toward her son. "Of course going to a shoot for the sole purpose of watching birds die seems a little heart-less to me."

"You would watch them and then skin them," Eleanor mumbled, "after your son had shagged them first."

Alannah glared at her.

Arsenic. Eleanor could understand the temptation.

Eleanor moved to the food without much hunger. She'd better eat though, a little cushion for the champagne. She waited for her mother to spoon fruit onto her china plate, the process being done strawberry by strawberry, and then grains of sugar sprinkled with a silver, slotted spoon over each berry. Her mother had developed delicacy as well as manners. No one had worked harder to reinvent herself.

Lady Pillock was now talking about going to Paris to see a dirigible fly around the Eiffel Tower.

Eleanor laughed to herself. Her roll fell off her plate onto the ground. She punted it out the tent flap—for the birds that were left.

A baron dead from a fall. The words reentered her brain as she noted the cop and Faraday again. A baron...the barons were all here, except...Tweedmouth! She closed her eyes, so easy to kill an asthmatic.

Her head snapped to Louis at the table. Her Irish grandfather would say that Louis had looked all day like a man who needed a priest and a saint that specialized.

Faraday was on the move. She wasn't surprised when he put his hand on Louis's shoulder, but Louis startled.

"May I speak to you a moment?" asked Faraday.

Louis lifted his head, and then as if by the sheer intensity of her scrutiny of him, he found Eleanor's eyes. She glimpsed fear. She wanted to shake him and have him tell her that he hadn't...hadn't given in to temptation. He broke off his glance and straightened with effort.

All the picnickers were now watching. Under the tent there were no clinking tableware, no voices. Everyone strained to listen. She sensed communal joy and the wait for good news. Hallelujah! Hallelujah indeed. If the Baron of Tweedmouth were dead, everyone here would be over the moon.

Eleanor understood breaking points; the moment when you can't stand another second and action is survival. So tempting to get rid of an overriding, ailing man. She placed her hand over her lungs. Louis. She sensed that she was no longer inhaling.

Aim high—keep the gun moving—never check. Tweedmouth is dead. The police are involved. How easy to smother an asthmatic. Poisoning with prussic acid produces quick, gasping breath. Someone has sent a man for Faraday. She gritted her teeth to stifle tears as Louis walked away.

Remembering breath, Eleanor inhaled somber air. She couldn't sit like the rest of them. She knew chemicals. She'd apprenticed in the local chemist's back room to know what could go right and what could go wrong for Louis. Eleanor put down her plate and glanced at her mother. *Of course you glanced at her and of course her hard eyes are digging into you like a well digger's spade. What is that, Mother? Oh do, go grope around a corpse, you say? That will help us remain respectable within society.*

Eleanor wondered if she were too old for a temper tantrum. She lowered her head to hide her angry eyes. The fingers of her left hand strummed the food table. She could still see Louis's face, the disquiet there. Poison was a woman's revenge. Lady Tweedmouth was not here.

Eleanor tried to never openly cross her mother. She understood the impossible position her mother was in, in society, and her mother tried so hard. But this, Louis! Faraday and Louis were now some distance away. She'd have to walk to them unaccompanied. And Lord Charles was there, he'd have something to say. Her heart thumped like a startled bird. Two sets of eyes were stuck in her mind, her mother and Louis's. Someone laughed. Damn it, she thought, just go. With the first two steps, she felt as exposed as the red grouse had been—flushed for sighting. *Bam.*

Knowing that they were on the path of supreme regret, her feet were reluctant to take proper steps. She tripped, of course she tripped, and a man snorted. She knew that sound, her husband. There was a light cry out, maybe her mother pretending to faint. Don't look back. Faraday walked toward her. Her feet didn't feel like blocks of stone anymore.

"I'm glad you're here," Faraday said. "I thought of asking myself, but I wasn't sure of the timing, your mother and all."

"I know." She took his arm. She needed and wanted his support and felt silly for it. His arm felt sure and warm. She almost clung to it.

"Will the constable have me?"

"You're with me." He covered her hand, the one on his arm.

"Will that be enough?"

The look of pain in his face exaggerated, Faraday walked her forward. "Where will the west wind blow?"

"Where?"

"Where it pleases. Come make the best of it. I'll tell them you're me sister what's come to bring me lunch."

She wanted to rest her head on his shoulder. Instead she asked, "Is Baron Tweedmouth dead?"

"Fallen from his balcony."

The words jarred her. She had, they all had, assumed his manner of death. She blurted out, "Fallen! From his balcony! Not dead from the asthma, or smothered? Not in his bed?"

"There's the rub of the thing, what? You can ride in my auto. There's adventure afoot."

"Poor Louis."

"Poor Louis indeed. I'd say he's the favored horse."

She and Faraday joined Louis and the constable. Faraday clamped his hand on Louis's shoulder again. "I've asked for your driver, Louis. Will you be coming, Charles?"

Olivia, Charles's fiancé, was heading toward the group. He knew that look on her face because he then said, "I'll stay and come later. Louis? I'll be there soon as I can."

"Yes. It's fine. It will all be fine. I'll see you later." Louis turned and walked alone towards his arriving carriage.

Finally, Eleanor sat back in Faraday's auto and breathed a lungful of velvety, country air. She refused to look back. Louis had already left, sitting all balled up on black leather upholstery, looking very alone. Seeing him like that, she remembered that none of this was about her, or her mother, or her husband. Eleanor had wondered what to say to her friend. Very little had been said, as congratulations wouldn't be appropriate, though that was what everyone was thinking.

For the day, there had been one death, one near miss, and by the official count, three thousand nine hundred and one deceased birds. She wondered if birds went to Heaven, and if so, were they now perched in large numbers on Heaven's gate? The red grouse pooping on Tweedmouth's head, with the handsome, blond haired beater still on earth, maybe it hadn't been a bad day all round. Except for the look on Louis's face as his carriage passed them and sped down the lane.

No man ever believes that the Bible means what it says: He is always convinced that it says what he means.
—*George Bernard Shaw*

I n life, the Baron had borne down on society like the Pillock's low-flying dirigible with the same shape, towering height, and combustibility. The peers avoided him whenever they could for reasons more than his new money. He never kept his opinions to himself and had become more religious than God.

After the long drive, Eleanor observed the man as he lay broken on the stone flags.

The Baron of Tweedmouth is no longer alive. He slipped; he fell; he can't be revived.

The Baron did resemble Humpty Dumpty in his gown with his round, white tummy. She looked away.

Tweedmouth's balding white head had smacked a stone patio floor. His skull now resembled the cracked and oozing egg of a large, ugly bird. He'd never been pretty, but now, the outside of him matched the ugly inside. His unattractive nature appeared to be inside out.

The skin under Tweedmouth's nails was as blue as a baby's blanket. His blue body lay tucked inside his boiled-white dressing gown. According to the rigor of his body, he'd died before dawn. His body lay cold in the shade of his castle, but his conscience had always been colder.

"What's she doing here?" asked Chief Constable Owens, moving his full muttonchops, a hangover of the eighteen hundreds.

At about the gatehouse of the Tweedmouth stronghold, Eleanor had been wondering the same thing. As a rule, sane people avoided Abbey Leix Castle, the home of the Baron and his French-fetished wife. Eleanor knew at the entrance gates that this wasn't going to end well.

The lane to the house, once trod upon by Henry the Eighth, was sharp-edged and straight like the neck of a sword. Planted on either side of it were lines of maturing lime trees. In flower lore, lime trees meant convivial love. Eleanor coughed out a laugh, no love at Abbey Leix.

The castle had long Tudor windows. It epitomized the dilettante fashion of living in and with antiquities. The building seemed its age by being neither as tall nor as pretentious as many of the newly built mansions, nor as crisp in the corners of its stone. It was smooth and had been rounded by centuries of wind and rain, and of humans in it—living and dying. She was surprised that Tweedmouth had had the taste to choose Abbey Leix rather than build some new-money monstrosity of his own.

From the side of the house, where Tweedmouth lay, she could see the burnt-out section of the castle that had not survived the last English civil war. The towers of scarred stone were like a black skeleton in the bright light, so much death. Abbey Leix Castle smelled of ghosts from its basement to its attic. They'd have to move over and make room for one more, Eleanor thought.

Around her nothing stirred. There was no wind, no voices, just light, bright light. She listened to Faraday answering the Chief Constable Owens's question of why she was here. She was glad to have her hat to hide her eyes, *murder you say?*

At the body's side Faraday was explaining Eleanor's presence. "Lady Albright is a friend of mine, and I assure you, she will be an asset here, with your permission."

"I can't have women about my business." Owens crossed his arms over his chest.

"That's all right, Chief Constable, I understand," Eleanor began. "Even in serviceable wool, better-bred women in a crisis are expected to pout or pour."

Owens's back stiffened. Faraday coughed. The others shuffled. Oh damn, wasn't she always saying just the wrong thing?

"Don't believe in women detecting," Owens said. "Too much emotion and intuition. Too much trouble, have her keep out of the way."

She knew she should have left it at that, but it was a sickness that she couldn't resist saying, "My grandfather used to tell me that crime is in direct relation to men and women preferring an easy morning, and an evening stout."

"That so," Owens mumbled. "And just who is your grandfather?"

"A police detective in Dublin. He is the only Catholic officer in the Dublin Metropolitan Police. He caught James Toole who cut the throat of his girlfriend."

Owens smiled a wicked grin. "That's why you think you need to be here, 'cause your grandfather sat you on his knee and tol' you all about detecting. And Irish to boot."

The nerve of the man, she was here to help. What did he know about poisons, or anything for that matter? She was about to retort when Faraday cleared his throat. He nodded her back a bit from the body. Where the wind blows. Ha! More like, where the whine blows.

The ass, satisfied at his win, returned to the dead man's head. He talked over the Baron's face, low enough to keep Eleanor from overhearing. "Nothing to hear anyway," she muttered. "He's afraid of making a mistake. That's why Faraday is here." Pigs are smarter than this chief constable.

Eleanor felt glassy. She wanted Faraday's easy acceptance.

After some minutes, and since Owens had had his sliver of flesh, and no one was paying any attention to her, Eleanor edged in. The Baron's feet were bare, and his legs were swollen at the ankle and feet. She gazed up to the balcony. It had the appearance of being more recent than the house. The balcony must have been constructed to match the visual line of the castle. That's probably why it was built so wide and with such a low railing. He wouldn't need to be lifted, just pushed.

"Let's take him, boys," Owens said. "Where's the wagon?"

"Nigel's waiting at it," the constable who came for Faraday said.

"Well, for Christ's sake whistle for him."

Faraday walked to Eleanor.

"So that's it?" she said.

"Appears so."

"Won't they let us check the room? The balcony?"

"All the Venetian glass is upright, and the babe is in his cradle."

"They said *that*?"

"'Nothing is messed, nor neither broken' would be more exact. That constable over there has a drinking glass in his pocket." Faraday patted down his own pockets and took out his cigarette case.

"Don't they know about fingerprints in the country?"

"Owens is a relative-in-law of a relative, and a very good fisherman, can almost smell the pockets of coarse bass. The fish fear the sound of his voice. He's convinced that the Baron stopped breathing and passed out while walking near the railing. He's afraid of Lady Tweedmouth. Sort of an anti-climax you," said Faraday.

"Ah well. I suppose the glass is empty if it's in the constable's pocket?"

"Clear as a well-hammered, crystal bell."

"No tonic, then?" asked Eleanor.

"Not through Tweedmouth's pious lips."

"I suppose tonics are alcohol. He is a virtuous man."

"He exceeded the word," said Faraday.

When Owens walked away from the body, Eleanor crouched over the dead man's face. She smelled his mouth, and peered past his teeth, and scrutinized his tongue and gums. She opened the lids of his rigid eyes. She lifted the unbuttoned neck of his nightshirt to peek under. She touched The Baron's skin to measure its heat. Fat bodies hold heat. Exposed bodies lose heat. Both factors need to be considered in time of death. She tore strands of still-black hair from his head and wondered if he dyed it. Holding them in her fist as she crept away from the body, she hid them in her bag.

Eleanor sashayed to the side of the constable with the tumbler and produced for him a blinding smile. "May I smell that glass?" she asked in the tone her nemesis, Lord Haversack's daughter, the wonderful and talented-with-men Olivia Haversack would use, and damn it, it worked. He handed it to her. Being a woman did have some plus points. She'd be a fool not to try harder to take advantage of them. The vessel was as Faraday had said, as clear as a bell. No obvious residue, no smell at all. A tumbler of this sort was for whiskey, and the Baron was reputed to be as dry as an over-baked soufflé. She licked her finger, wiped at the bottom of the vessel and smelled again. Nothing.

The constables lifted the body. They cursed at its corpulence, as they tried to keep body and clothes together. Tweedmouth would have hated the streaks of dirt that lined the back of his white dressing gown. As the men manhandled him, the body stiff as a plank, Tweedmouth's nightshirt inched up over his behind. She thought of all the self-proclaimed and virtuous—in the end exposed.

She walked back to Faraday and said, "The twenty-four-hour rule in the case of chronic disease. The attending physician must state that the illness is the cause of death. Will Owens bother to contact Tweedmouth's physician to sign off on the certificate? I mean, you don't like Tweedmouth, and you like everyone." Eleanor noted the castle's elegant stone side. "Didn't Saint Paul live with only the sandals on his feet?"

"Not at home," said Faraday.

"I think Owens is beckoning you." She couldn't catch the Chief Constable's wordy, last instructions that still floated to earth as the man and his whiskers strode away.

Faraday walked back to her. "Now, to the Baroness, a show to which I have gained your admittance. He asked me if I would reassure them—ask no questions, just answer them."

"Owens is off like a scared hare. There should be a post-mortem. The chronically ill are sitting ducks, especially the ones with golden eggs."

"Did you notice the beads around Tweedmouth's neck?" asked Faraday.

"Yes, blue glass to ward off bronchitis."

"I thought women wore those."

Eleanor shrugged. "They obviously didn't work for him either."

"I expect Tweedmouth's source for the beads forgot to bow to the new moon."

"Should have chosen his gypsy more carefully. What will you say to the Baroness?" asked Eleanor.

"Natural death, as I've been instructed, and then I must ascertain if everyone in the family is satisfied with the verdict."

"I can't imagine any dissenters. Who's staying here at the moment?"

Faraday gazed at the house. "People come and go from Tweedmouth's like bees from a well-honeyed hive. Tweedmouth's been ill, so no doubt his stinger has been sharp. That probably means just the brave and the bold, some of Louis's friends, and Monsieur Renard, the castle's Standard French poodle. Of course, we must also think of servants, and locals, and passersby," said Faraday.

"Now that Owens has left, let's have a gander around—as long as I'm here. Do you think Tweedmouth died...naturally?"

"How natural is it to fall off a balcony, what?"

Eleanor considered Faraday. "Natural causes, then."

"The man didn't look atal' well," he said.

"Aren't the ill surrounded by tablets and powders, tonics and whatnot?"

"There's usually East-ender original Beeman's Tonic at every bedside." As

Eleanor began to survey the immediate area Faraday added, "Do you know that London's East Enders cut the hair of a sick child, put it into a sandwich, and then feed the sandwich to the first available dog? The illness then leaves the child, and enters the dog, thereby the phrase: eat yourself sick...or is it silly? Maybe that's why Renard is still here," said Faraday as he lit his cigarette.

Eleanor laughed as she stepped off the porch. "Hair is always telling. Tweedmouth had an empty glass. So why was it there?"

"Water?" Faraday asked toward her back as she scrounged through bushes.

"Speaking of charms or maybe portents, there are mushrooms in a number of places here."

"Meaning?"

Eleanor plucked one and held it out to him. "Meaning suspicion."

"Or bog. It wasn't a water glass."

Eleanor tossed the mushroom toward a privet hedge and then brushed her hands together. "I had to listen to Lord Haversack all morning at the shoot." She thought of Haversack's red face, his bulbous nose, his quivering jowls, and his yellow teeth that had clamped a cigar between them all morning. She rubbed her arms as if she was cold. "The man's conversation and sweat were more than I could bear. Among other things, he was talking incessantly about Louis's father. I believe he said," Eleanor's voice went husky, "'going to be over five hundred birds per hunter—*bam*. Christ—*bam*. My stock is going to be indefinitely depleted—*bam*. Damn that Tweedmouth. I've taken his refusal to host and shoved it up his backside. *Bam— bam—bam—bam—bam*. Damn new money.'"

Faraday was laughing so hard he dropped his cigarette onto his lap and had to jump up and brush it to the ground.

"If Haversack shut his mouth when he shoots, he might hit something," said Eleanor.

"He's harmless," said Faraday while still smiling.

"He's an idle sort of man, given to flights of fancy of his own superiority. According to Lord Haversack, the hunt today was supposed to be Tweedmouth's hunt—his birds, his beaters, his land. Haversack is never going to forgive the Baron."

"Very good, Holm—"

"I didn't smell alcohol on Tweedmouth." She wouldn't let Faraday tease her. "If he was close to death. He might have taken up the drink again."

"Not dealing well with chronic illness, what? Can't smell all of them though. It would be another explanation for his teetering over the brink. Hard to think of the man drunk, what? Goes against his and Saint Paul's core principles."

"He's got a broken nose," she added. "He didn't land face down. It's a straight drop."

Faraday sat onto the garden bench and watched her.

"We are talking about Tweedmouth," Eleanor said in an irritated voice. "The man reputed to make his house guests attend early morning-prayer."

"I've been to one of those dawn services. They made the road to heaven impassable."

"One man's interpretation of Hell?" Eleanor asked, giving up on him and turning back toward the lawn.

"Two men, both Tweedmouth's and mine, though from different points of view. I doubt God pays much attention to the rhetoric."

"How often did you stay?" asked Eleanor over her shoulder.

"Once. He didn't brace his fall, by-the-by."

That felt better, Faraday taking the thing in a little more serious manner. After hunting in silence some minutes more, Eleanor returned to her friend. "His bruises are after-death blows. I couldn't see, or smell vomit around his lips. No smell of garlic."

"Doesn't sound like arsenic then. Natural causes what?"

"The nose though. How can we say that there was no foul-play?"

"It was a long fall. Let's see how the family reacts. We'd better go in." Faraday offered his arm to her.

"Humoring me?" She couldn't resist even as she hated the lack of confidence.

"People also die from chronic illnesses. Even mean ones."

She didn't believe a word of it.

"Let's go in," he said.

She gathered her skirt and stepped down and onto the stony path. "Even if he wasn't to the point of sainthood that he was throwing dirt in his lentils, maybe his death should be investigated."

"I remember him being a fussy man about what he ate."

She walked close to Faraday but felt farther apart from him. It was all too lighthearted. He wasn't thinking murder any more than Owens had been. "Medical jurisprudence manuals insist that physicians of chronically ill patients should never sign death certificates if they haven't seen their patients within twenty-four hours of said patients' demise. Tweedmouth's specialist practices in London," she insisted again. The shift of gravel under

Faraday's shoes was the only sound. It seemed loud in the conversation gap. "Tweedmouth's organs need to be examined. There's a tight constriction in the pupils of his eyes."

"If we find murder, what then?" he said.

"What then?"

"Yes, what then?" He regarded her, waiting for an answer to some moral question presented within those two words.

"You mean, if Louis did it." She felt the painful stretching of her heart. What in fact...if he did.

"Yes. What if he did?"

"What if he didn't?" Mutiny sparked the words, Eleanor dug into what she believed her friend capable of. "He couldn't have done this, not Saint Louis. So we let it go; what then? Someone else did this."

"Just because you believe something doesn't make it true. Sometimes the finer points of an argument should be sidestepped."

The philosophy of a lawyer, she thought. "He didn't do it." She heard the lack of conviction and hated it. Mutiny diluted. "Oh, for pity's sake, all I know is that in four days Tweedmouth will be in the ground and forever covered by a heavy blanket of dirt." She didn't go on. She couldn't. He was a cherished friend, but he was being a man explaining to a woman, and there was a distance toward him she'd never felt before. For the first time she felt disappointment in him. *Push through. This is Henry.*

"Actually, you know," Eleanor began a few minutes later, "it's not so much about who did it as it's about conscience...whether or not you can stand up under a lie. You know that Louis is a terrible card player, and together with his best friend Charles, they have lost fortunes. Charles is, I don't know, entitled, and not very smart; and Louis can't bluff. The truth always comes out of him. The truth always comes out of Louis, and he is naïve. I mean look at his choice of friends. Charles introduced him to gambling. That's what we need to be prepared for, if he did it, and if he didn't."

"Louis owed money, and that's a great motive. Once again, the cards are stacked against him," Faraday said as he and Eleanor rounded the front corner of the house.

She passed under one of the stone angels Tweedmouth had put on the roofline. One angel seemed to point at her with her mother's finger. *You will mess this up.*

Guilt, Eleanor knew it, and also Louis knew it all too well, and being squishy, he never won.

🎐 4 🎐

The devil is most devilish when respectable.
—Elizabeth Barrett Browning

Alannah Darnley couldn't feel her feet. She couldn't move her fingers. She couldn't inhale. The hubbub of voices around the picnic table sounded indistinct, but loud as the hunting party digested the drama. Louis taken away to his father's...well was the man dead? And Eleanor! Alannah felt stiff and incensed that Eleanor, her own daughter, would do this to her and in front of her closest neighbors. Mad-brained Irish...they were all thinking that. Bad ancestry. Alannah clutched at her heart. It was surely failing. She was so dizzy. She had to go home. It wasn't very often, when in society, that she didn't want to go home. If Tweedmouth had been murdered, any one of these that sat at the table with her had the basic character to do it.

As if to prove Alannah's thoughts, Olivia, daughter to Lord Haversack, leaned across the table. "How comforting to think that Lord Tweedmouth's stomach will be in Eleanor's capable hands. We can all breathe easier." She took her eyes off Alannah and winked at her father.

Miss Olivia Haversack had been holding court the whole afternoon. The girl inhaled gossip for breakfast. She liked to talk about gossip for lunch, and she poked fun at the unfortunates involved in the gossip for dinner. She'd blather the daylong and never gain an ounce. She was never short-breathed. She had exquisite lungs.

All afternoon, Olivia had been on the hunt. She was a catcher of men. She didn't realize that she tossed her blonde hair like a flag on a gusty day, or that she laughed like the blast of a horn, calling riders to the hunt. She enjoyed sport. She pursued men. Men were her sport. The ring on her finger was a trophy.

In spite of being engaged, and her fiancé, Charles, at the table, Olivia had been sitting smack in the middle of a group of males. She had developed the trick of reading the headlines of a newspaper (on her way to the societal column and court pages) in order to repeat the headlines into a group of men. She'd then pause just so, waiting for someone to pick up the conversation. Olivia then sat as if she too were part of the discussion. She was as good at it, as Lady Pillock was bad. On all sides of Olivia, men appreciated her intelligence.

Smoke and mirrors, Alannah thought as she watched the girl laugh. Alannah took in a deep breath. Had she been breathing? She had never really liked these people. Worrying a button at her chest, she popped it from its moorings. "For God's sake." She curled her fingers around the button in her palm.

Alannah felt her friend's hand cover hers. "Shall I send for our driver? The salts?" Letty whispered.

Alannah shook her head no. She forced herself to chew food that had lost its flavor. She drank a little more than usual. She waited for the moment in which she could leave. The cheese had arrived, the last blessed course in a long lunch. The party could break soon.

With Olivia's mother, the hostess, up and moving, Letty said to Alannah, "I'll get the driver."

Merciful words thought Alannah as she followed the rest of the party from the tent. She walked like exiting a stage. She didn't want to seem hurried. Letty passed Olivia's shoulder. "Olé, Miss Haversack," she said. "Well gored. Not squeamish at the sight of blood yourself, I see."

Flayed by the best. Thank God Letty was here. The women were walking to their carriages in packs with their heads connected at each other's hair-roots, and their conversations at a dull roar. Alannah walked behind them. She knew that all her work to be in society, all that sitting and all that tea, had been undermined. Damn it, Eleanor.

Lounging opposite Letty on her carriage bench, as the brougham rolled forward parallel to the line of carriages, Alannah closed the curtains in spite of the heat. She was grateful to be hidden. Her bones shivered. When the carriage had the road to itself, she pulled back a curtain and opened a window. She stared out at bristled, untamed hedgerows growing over old stone walls. The air smelled of sheep. Alannah put one hand over the other to stop the emotional tremor. Possible conversation passed through her mind as broken sentences that began from nowhere and ended there. She held back tears like the seasoned socialite that she was, but hopelessness pushed at her heart threatening its regular beat. She wondered again why she cared so much.

The carriage began lurching. When the bouncing had become more frequent, and she had braced her legs against the opposite seat, Alannah asked Letty, "Why is the road so rutted?" she asked with an acid that still churned in her stomach.

"It's a short cut."

"We won't damage a wheel?" she said with her head against the back of the seat and her eyes closed.

"John's a good driver."

"Today, we'll probably break something. The world has gone to the dogs. Oh, I'm sorry. It's just that, that girl will break me," Alannah muttered.

"Compassion avoided her at birth?" Letty suggested.

"Compassion and kindness."

"Not at all. Eleanor is both compassionate and kind."

"Humpf." Alannah thought that the evening was more peaceful than it deserved to be. The track was narrow. Dark trees grew close, and black branches hung over the road, shuttering the bright light. Still, she tried to let the serenity of the countryside relax her.

"What awful road is this?"

"We turned off the main road at Church Handborough. Over this side is Bladon Heath."

"We are close. Oh, Letty, here I am on the worst road in Christendom under a canopy of blackened trees pondering the idea of moving back to Ireland. After all my struggles, has it has come to this?"

"It's not far now."

"Yet, how far it has become."

. . .

A t her home, Alannah lounged opposite Letty in a Queen Anne wing chair wearing her favorite tea gown with her slippered feet on a footstool. The garden room was cozy. It had no crisp edges or dark stained wood. This room was golden. Light seemed to pour from the yellow embossed wallpaper. Alannah had arranged ivy over a mantle as a symbol for friendship. A fire crackled. Fabric, decorated with intertwined fern and lilac, for sincerity and modesty, adorned the sofa slipcover. Lavender, for distrust, scented the air from open crystal bowls. Red pomegranates had been put in the lengths of ivy. The pomegranates signified foolishness, her daughter's.

Alannah had worked for years to earn even a modicum of respect. It had been her life's work. She had fashioned herself from clay into fired china. Eleanor had lived as china all her life. She didn't appreciate its luster. Alannah felt fragile and thin, overused and cracked. Parties had always been hard—all the subliminal words, and winks, and knowing glances. She'd been brave. She deserved her rewards.

Letty lounged on the sofa next to Alannah. She'd met her American friend within the margins. Letty was a person who thrived there. The woman defined the Marlborough Set. With her blonde hair down, she danced with maracas. Her round face was always sunny, even when she hotfooted people that irritated her, especially then. Letty's light hair always had a lock left loose in the front as if she didn't want it all restrained. She was drawn to people who smiled well. There were only a few. Most smile as a social necessity rather than an extension of a happy interior.

"Would you bring us a repast, maybe the Bavarian crème from yesterday's dinner?" Alannah asked a servant.

"And a full bottle of brandy, please," said Letty.

The brandy smelled sweet. The Irish in Alannah drank about two fingers before she felt she could breathe again. "I'm sure that I was flushed."

"What's wrong with her leaving and with Lord Faraday? I like him."

"He's too young."

"Too young for what?"

"What?"

"He's too young for what?" asked Letty.

Alannah laughed without energy. It felt good to laugh. "He's a baby to her thirty years."

"How very young is he then?"

"Twenty-two."

Letty lifted her eyebrows. "Well done Eleanor."

"You see, you see. Even you. Where's the brandy? I tell you what we don't need more of: notoriety."

"I love notoriety. Take your mind off it. Redecorate," said Letty.

"So says my daughter. Only she says that it should be something Greek with an oracle from whence I can prophesy her doom, or some such nonsense. Ah...I think a little music would be soothing. What do you prefer, opera or classical?"

"Anything."

"Now, this is an invention I can endorse," said Alannah.

The phonographic cylinder began with white fuzz, and then a Bach pastoral blared at them. "Sorry," she said as she turned down the volume, "my favorite." Alannah wandered the room. She picked up a photogravure of a man with no smile, but rascally eyes. "I should have kept my father away from Eleanor. He's a slippery man who conforms to the widest version of truth. The ocean is less broad." She put the picture down hard. "He follows his own conscience and expects everyone else to do the same...his not theirs. He is catholic by nature and protestant by affectation."

"Good Lord, what does that mean?"

"He is general in a very specific sort of way."

Letty chuckled. "Darling, you are delightful. Now, have I ever told you how much I adore your paintings? These are extraordinary landscapes. You are very talented. I must have one."

"My husband loved my paintings. He loved my father for that matter." Alannah sighed. "My father told me that it wouldn't work. I should have listened. There have been so many times I wish I had stayed away from the self-absorbed person my husband was. My name was O'Sullivan, his favorite pub in Dublin. He married me because of a pub," Alannah scoffed. As she lifted the cut-glass container to slosh a bit more drink into her glass, she heard a thump outside the window, like a rock falling onto a dirt bed. She continued pouring. Nature had its noises.

"Darling, what else do you have for that phonograph?" Letty walked to a stack of cylinders. She pushed through them. "You're living in the past. We need livelier music."

Alannah inhaled some Courvoisier. "Three years ago, I encouraged Eleanor to marry Albert Albright. Her father had died. We were on a very tight income, but she had a good dowry. It seemed a fantastic match. She was getting on, and he a first-born son. He was older, but she seemed to like him. She did you know. He was so pleasant and attentive. He replaced her father, I suspect. Who knew that the awful man loved brothels and eleven-year-old virgins? I should have guessed it when he didn't marry until he was old enough to be impotent."

Facing the window, Alannah rubbed her finger around the rim of her glass. Another thump. She glanced out the window, but then let her eyes go vague. "It was a strain on Eleanor. This awful interest of Albert's." Alannah liked the way the brandy warmed her blood. She drank another good bit.

Letty paused over the records, and after taking her own hefty dose of alcohol, she began changing the music.

"Faraday arrived then, like a brilliant sun at the end of many damp days. They are together like peas in a pod. He's rented a house here. All they talk about is medical jurisprudence and poisons. I can't sleep at night for worrying. My in-laws are going to quit calling." She took in a long skipping breath and drank again from her snifter. The big gulp of brandy tingled along her lips and burned down her throat. The music had stopped. She turned her head to the gramophone as something hit the window with a louder explosion. Five more aggressive shots hit the glass, one on the heels of the other. Alannah dropped to her knees and Letty screamed behind her. Brandy irrigated the carpet.

After three more direct shots, Letty said, "Good God," and crouched.

Alannah crawled forward, stopping to pull the fabric of her dress out from under her knees. She had to lift them to hitch her gown up. Just under the window, her head telescoped up as she said, "Jesus, Mary and Joseph, Jesus, Mary and Joseph."

Something sticky was sliding down the pane.

"What is it?" Letty asked.

"I don't know."

Letty stood and stared out. "Over there, movement."

Alannah peered through the glass her face pressed against it.

"Can you see? Can you see?"

"Just the bushes moving."

"Go out. Go out." Letty pushed Alannah toward the French doors and then sprang through them herself.

As Letty hared out for the brush, her tea gown flapped behind her, Alannah inspected the window. Eggs. The whites still dripped. She was overwhelmed for a moment. The hateful aggression, the action of the attack shocked her sensibilities, and then shame curled around her mind. She felt as defaced as the house. She heard a mixture of laughs and then a scream. She too ran into the dark. Tearing through the rhododendrons, her best tea gown ripped, she found Letty on her hands and knees. In front of her was the sound of horses thundering off.

"Jesus." Alannah dropped down.

"No, no." Letty tried to ease the moment with a wave of her hand. "I was trying to get to one of them and stepped into a hole. Just wasn't watching my step. My nose is bleeding. Stop clucking. I'm fine."

Still she allowed Alannah to ease her to her feet. She walked back while limping and leaning on her friend's shoulder. Alannah didn't wait for Letty to ask. Once inside, she picked both glasses off the floor and refilled them. Tears bubbled into her eyes and not from the hot shot of alcohol. Inside her hard anger had surfaced.

"I saw the back of one. A woman. Skirt flying. Remarkable. It's eggs."

"I know its eggs. They've left a trail on the window," Alannah snapped. She paced the rug and drank. She stopped and contemplated Letty. "Didn't you say once that Eleanor left Albert under the best of reasons? You said that."

"I did? Well, yes—"

"You said that it was reasonable...."

"Yes, but...."

Alannah turned and stood glaring at the assaulted window. "I will have Reverend Peacock speak to her."

"Eleanor? Oh, for heaven's sake." Letty refilled her glass from the emptying bottle. "You think this has to do with Eleanor?"

"Who else?"

"Maybe if the Baron was murdered and someone thought Eleanor a threat."

"A threat!" Alannah shook her head. "Anyway, there's a difference between not wanting to sit next to the man, ever, and wanting to kill him."

"Isn't Olivia's father in some Scottish feud with Tweedmouth, over land or something? I wouldn't put it past that girl to take no prisoners, or her father either." Letty dabbed at the slowing blood loss.

"Do be serious."

"Oh I am. Disagreeable girl, disagreeable family. Sic Peacock on them if you must. Speaking of The great Reverend Peacock, he has been sitting with Tweedmouth. They could have had a disagreement on moral theology."

Alannah snorted. "Sure...and Eleanor the great detective...fear in the hearts of all."

"Well you have just been egged."

Gaping at the window, Alannah knew a humiliation that shook her. "She should divorce. With a new husband and children, all this lollapalooza would end. I need more drink to even think about it. Who would have her after a thing like that? Like all this." Alannah waved her hand toward the window, stilled, and then walked to the bottle of alcohol. She tripped on carpet fringe on her way back to the settee. The room smelled of spilled brandy.

Alannah fell onto a flowered sofa, next to Letty who said, "That Lord Bennett would have Eleanor. He looks good from the back, not so good from the front." She giggled. "No brothels though. I don't think the man's ever had sex."

"Be serious. I need Reverend Peacock's patronage."

"The man who just killed Tweedmouth?" Letty laughed at herself and then at Alannah's glower. "Yes, yes I know. I know. The best thing is to thumb your nose at them all."

"I think I could talk her into divorce. As you said, she left her husband under the most credible of circumstances. She'd be relieved to move on. On to whom?"

Letty made a tsk, tsk sound, checked her nose again, and then leaned forward to spoon some Bavarian crème into her mouth, and always more gesticulate when drunk, she waved her spoon toward Alannah. "That Noel Phillips is ripe for the picking. He spits when he says, 'This party is simply outrageous.'" She laughed throughout her whole body. "He's available, no doubt."

Alannah knew herself to be drunk when she smiled. "He is already smitten. I saw him the whole afternoon talking with an unfortunate female with a plastered smile."

"One tête-à-tête with him at close quarters and the enamel on her face would be running into her eyes," said Letty, following up on that smile.

"Don't be daft."

"Have you ever been to Berners Street or better yet, to Whitechapel? There are wax figures there of the victims of some of London's most notorious murderers. One of them, I can't remember the name, stands like this." Letty stood and posed with her hands together over her head as if holding a knife. She swayed and laughed, and then she fell back onto the sofa. Her nose began bleeding again. Her voice muffled through the handkerchief, she added, "Berners Street is the first place I went to see after coming over. Go on a foggy day. The people next to you are distorted in the thickness, and every hand seems to come out of nowhere. The terror simply thins one's blood. Two women fainted."

Letty settled with one hand at her nose and the other with her drink.

"Who could it be Tweedmouth's killer? Everyone was either at the shoot, or at the house. Olivia was atrocious tonight. She could take someone out... with her tongue. I heard her insist that her fiancé accompany her to the dance instead of getting drunk with Louis, his best friend, as he should have. She is a Haversack. Tweedmouth and Haversack gamesmen have been shooting at each other."

"Olivia? Kill someone?"

"Well, I wouldn't put it past her to put some cog into the works. Didn't Eleanor's husband, Albert Albright's father and Tweedmouth have some financial fallout just after God arrived? Not enough prayer, I expect."

"Oh, for heaven's sake, do think about the Reverend. How can he be brought in?" asked Alannah.

"How can a Peacock be influenced? By even the slightest word of praise." Letty drank a last sip. She eyeballed her glass and then glanced around for the bottle.

"Who would talk to him...discreetly?" Alannah said and then burped. She couldn't think of anyone—names were fading. "I don't want Eleanor painted as desperate."

"She's not desperate, you are. Have we finished the brandy?"

"For good reason." The anger in the words was magnified by liquor.

"How about your husband's cousin? The one with the mole."

"Which one?"

"I don't know. The woman with the mole," Letty said as she poured from the hunted-down bottle. "I like her, and she must have some interest by blood to rein Eleanor in. Maybe a better outsider...good Lord, I missed the glass." Letty giggled as she licked her fingers. "I suppose it all depends on when he died."

"What are you on about now?"

"Who did it depends on when he died."

"From the asthma?" asked Alannah.

"God, have you no imagination?"

"My mind is numb." As if to prove it, Alannah poked at her temple.

"Someone followed us home, you know. I found this in the rhododendrons." Letty held up an egg basket. "I expect I surprised them. Old thing this. Bit of putty or something in here—"

"Let me see that. Oh, for Christ's sake, this is our basket. They egged us with our own eggs. I need to lie down," Alannah said as she gave the basket back to Letty and lay back on the sofa. "I feel sick. I'm going to pay a call on Reverend Peacock first thing tomorrow."

An Asse at a Harp.
—Greek Proverb

An upright and hushed butler opened the heavy oak door of the Abbey Leix Castle. It didn't creak. It wouldn't dare, Eleanor thought as she walked into the hall behind Faraday. Curiosity tingled in her fingertips. She'd never been inside; Louis lived in London except for shooting season. She'd asked about visiting once, but vague excuses had been his answer, and now she knew why. The walls were newly plastered covered old stone. A ceiling-to-floor, religious wall mural colored one wall. Sculptured figures of saints reclined over the pillared doorways. Gold trimmed the creamy room like a cloudy dawn or heaven. She stopped like she'd hit glass. The religious air was too rarified for breath or easy movement. Guests that came never walked in comfort on this marble floor under the scrutiny of so many holy men. Tweedmouth was *noncompos mentis*. Her heart went out to Louis.

"You've never seen this?" Faraday whispered to her.

"You have?"

"Indeed." Faraday indicated with his eyes and a tilt to his head the mural that had a likeness of Tweedmouth in the face of one of the apostles watching the Ascension of Jesus. Eleanor peered at the painting. Glancing at Faraday, she opened her eyes wide.

Tweedmouth didn't have himself painted on bended knee before the Lord but standing feet from the savior's side. So many motives, so little time, she was eager to meet with the Baroness. The woman was the very strange wife of a very strange husband. If anyone wanted the Baron dead, she would and could.

Eleanor glanced at the painting again—Tweedmouth against the sinful world. How God-awful for his family, poor Louis. Haversack was Tweedmouth's closest neighbor. The man's tirade seemed more credible now.

The butler pressed open a set of mahogany doors. He stepped into the drawing room and announced the visitors to Lady Charlotte Montfire, the Baroness of Tweedmouth, and to Louis Montfire, the new, second Baron of Tweedmouth. Their faces, one controlled, distant, and gracious, the other flushed from drinking, turned. The Baroness opened a beaded bag, took out a vial, and perfumed her wrists and her buttoned-up throat. She added more fragrance to the already scent-strangled, overheated air. As if she'd pressed her face into a box of pollen, Eleanor coughed as she entered the room; *Lavender. Forget me not, Lady Charlotte?*

"Remember, it was an accident," Faraday whispered to Eleanor before strolling over to bow over the Baroness's hand. "I'm so very sorry," he began. "Owens has asked that we inform you of the findings and answer any questions."

"Ah, good, Lord Faraday. So good of you to come," said Louis. "And my friend, Eleanor. Take the bull by the horns and all that, or maybe the birds I should say."

The Baroness ignored her son. Eleanor arranged a helpful smile on her face, the best that she could manage. In the room, a William Kent table flanked a green chair. On the table was a gilt-bronze, table lamp of Loïe Fuller in full flowing dance, rather naked, not a religious bend to her body. It was very fashion forward and plugged into the updated and wired castle. There was more ivory and faded gold on the walls. Portraits of Himself and Herself faced each other at opposite ends of the room. Squaring-off. She thought of the lime trees.

"Chief Constable Owens thinks that your husband passed out or quit breathing and fell," Eleanor heard Faraday say.

She watched Louis stand, walk to a Rococo side table, and refresh his whiskey straight from the bottle. It was a label that lived in servants' halls—cheap whiskey, no decanter, no decanters in this house.

"They ask you to be available tomorrow if they have any questions, your guests and staff as well," Faraday finished.

The Baroness opened her perfume again and retouched her wrists. Eleanor wanted to rip the vial out of the woman's hand. Instead, she eased a handkerchief from her bag and dabbed at her nose. The Baroness stared at her framed husband. She either was trying to cry or trying not to. It was hard to tell. The woman's features seemed immobile, as though she'd had the slight upturn in her lips drawn there. Charlotte's large green eyes balanced her square jaw. Large orbs or not, she was having trouble producing tears.

Eleanor remembered the Frenchman, Antoine Renard. Faraday had said that he lived here, the Standard French Poodle of the house. Eleanor had last seen him under the luncheon tent at the shoot. He had seemed abnormal there without the Baroness of Tweedmouth, as if she had been surgically removed from his side. It seemed he had a permanent bed at Abbey Leix Castle, so that Charlotte could speak her few French phrases to him, while in her French gowns, and under her French hair.

French men were legendary, and Renard's externals were fit for his advanced age. He had eyes that showed intelligence, an interest in life, and an aging, but once succulent mouth. She couldn't imagine the Baron liking the Frenchman or his wife's attraction to the man.

She wondered how Renard managed to stay. Why he was so attached to Charlotte was another mystery. Charlotte moved through life as though in a display case, far removed from the everyday and always being decorative. It was hard to think of sorrowful words for such a stiff woman. Again, Charlotte reached into her bag for her perfume bottle. Fresh scent, she was wearing her perfume like a nervous tick.

"The coroner will examine your husband tomorrow. If he says natural causes, as Chief Constable Owens anticipates, a man will be sent over to let you know, so you can make arrangements," said Faraday.

"Why do you think he was on the balcony if he was so ill?" Eleanor had to ask.

The Baroness' face closed. Louis guffawed.

Eleanor felt like the biblical beggar at the rich man's door—crust of bread. She hadn't expected the Baroness to be welcoming, even on Charlotte's best day, but the outright snub miffed her.

Ignore me then. Can't say that I'd blame you for a little arsenic in his milk. Still, the last reprobate standing.

35

"He will be available for burial tomorrow, Lord Faraday?" asked the dragon.

The words were a statement not a question. She ground her servants like nutmeg.

"Yes, tomorrow. I haven't the exact time," said Faraday.

"Did he seem close to death?" asked Eleanor.

Rearranging her face into a small smile, the kind of smirk Letty hated...without heart, the Baroness contemplated Eleanor. "How good of you to come, Lady Albright. I'm sorry that we have inconvenienced you so."

"When I heard the Baron had died, I wanted to help in any way that I could. Such a loss for you, I'm so very sorry." She was making sure that her eyes were full of concern, both real, and placed with precision.

"Thank you." The Baroness's dry face moved.

She isn't going to open that vial again? Good, bloody Lord. Hasn't she nostrils?

The Baroness turned to Faraday. Her anger concealed. Well, an effort to. "He's been ill, of course, everyone knows that. He should have died in bed with his family at his side; it was unexpected to find him in pieces at the doorstep. Had I been with him...you know...he may have not fallen. I should have been with him."

The Baroness wiped a tear that she'd been working to produce. The speech and the speaker had been brave. Eleanor clapped in her mind.

Where were you? The question was in her thoughts about to be said, when Faraday's piercing eyes shut down her tongue.

"I'm sorry I wasn't here," Louis blurted out. "I missed the ascension. It would have been quite uplifting to see the angel Gabriel himself on that very balcony. Hallowed ground now I expect."

Louis's round face was flushed up to the roots of his early receding brown hairline. She'd never seen Louis drink whiskey by the glassful. It didn't appear to be a celebratory drink, more like a dive-in-the-vat drunk.

"I'm sorry," Eleanor said and meant it.

He refused to meet her eyes—anyone's eyes—least of all his mother's.

She's gotten to him. "What, ah, was the Baron doing on the balcony, Louis?" asked Eleanor.

"Ha! The balcony! We've lost more servants because of his specter-like wanderings on that balcony. 'Tain't natural,'" Louis mocked, sounding like a maid in his high falsetto.

Then again, maybe not. While he was livening up, the Baroness was adding more perfume to her wrists and behind her ears. Close up, Eleanor couldn't see any gray in Charlotte's hair and wondered if the Baroness touched-up as well. It was easy to see that Charlotte thought she needed to shut down her son. "I should have told you, Lord Faraday,"—Eleanor noticed the pointed reference—" that when the Baron couldn't breathe, he felt shut in. He needed fresh air all around him."

The Baroness stood and faced Faraday and with full-throated authority said, "Now it is finished." She pressed the servant button. The butler swept the door open. "See Lady Albright and Lord Faraday out. Make sure the porch is cleaned."

"But the constables might be back tomorrow." Eleanor wanted to put her hand over her mouth.

"And that much they have seen. I will not meet with that place again." The Baroness walked out in full stature—her head stretched toward the ceiling. Eleanor could hear the swish of her six petticoats.

That left Louis. "Here's to you, Da." He downed the contents of his glass, the same type of glass that had been in the constable's pocket, and then he pounded it onto the table. "That'll have him rolling in his grave. Good of you both to come and all. Mother's right. Nothing to see here. No one liked him, did they? Well, what a night. Can't take it all in. *Ignis fatuus*, isn't it? We must live foolishly. That's it isn't it, old chap. It's the fire that drives us all. *Ignis fatuus*, we'll all burn in hell."

Eleanor fell in behind Louis as he left the room. She couldn't leave him like this. It's like his world was crashing around his feet. He couldn't be mourning his father. She stopped by the infamous mural.

"That's as close as he's ever going to get. He had to paint himself in, but they know, they know."

"It's a very good artist," Eleanor said.

"But not a good likeness." Faraday offered his elbow to her.

With the door closed behind her, the heavy feeling of extreme religion and incense lifted. Eleanor breathed again.

"By God, that motorcar of yours, Faraday," Louis commented. "It's a beauty. You must come by again, and we'll go driving. Father hates them."

Eleanor stood in front of the house in between Louis and Faraday. Night's shadows were creeping onto the horizon. The moon shone a shadowy, white orb; its edges not yet defined by a crisp brim of light to dark. Distant trees, hedges, and bushes made irregular shapes that followed a drunken line against the sky. An owl hooted, an earthy echoing sound.

"I hate the country," said Louis. "Long lanes of nothing. Can't stand the quiet. Can't take it all in. Thought he was dead so many times...lying there like he was dead. Hard to tell...sometimes."

"I could stay. Do you need someone to stay?"

"Good and kind Eleanor. Always so good and kind. My friend. So very good of you to have come this far. Couldn't impose an ounce more. Anyway, not staying myself."

"Where are you going?"

"God knows in this God-awful place. Charles will be at The Crown."

"Come to my home." She wanted to drag him there, make him talk. She'd never seen him so hard.

"Oh, no. I mean, not unexpected and all that."

She wanted to take him by the shoulders and shake him and ask him, did he do it? Did he kill his father? "Is there anything we can do?"

"You've done enough. We wouldn't have expected so much attention."

"Are there many guests that will be returning tonight?" asked Eleanor.

"People may wander in or not. Renard has nowhere else. He'll let himself in. I mean who won't know?"

She felt she needed to console him or make him courageous. "Owens says that the asthma did it," said Eleanor.

"That's right. It's about time. Well, goodnight." Louis stepped into his carriage.

Back at the auto, Eleanor said, "It's like he's been un-stoppered."

"I would be. They both seemed happy one way or another," said Faraday.

"They're going to have to hire professional mourners. The Baron was insane. I mean really tottering. I had no idea. Poor Louis."

"Louis is going to be more of his own man now. Where shall I drop you?"

"Home" she said. "He's gained precious little...with a mother like that. He does seem guilty. Do you think so?"

Faraday sighed.

"All right. Where are you going next?"

"It's rumored that Haversack is going to open a case of ten-year-old Noires at the dinner tonight. I plan to be there." Faraday helped Eleanor into the Panhard. He then climbed in himself. "When are you going to try a motorcar?"

"When my mother is senile."

Faraday used his whole weight to sit. "That was interesting. We must do this more often." He adjusted her skirt out from under his feet.

She noticed more this time than any other that in the small sportster they sat shoulder to shoulder. She felt the movement of his arm as he drove. The point of contact was warm. She should talk.

"Who else might have wanted him gone?"

He kept his eyes on the road. "The Women's League."

"Do be serious," she said and then laughed anyway. "It's true, though. He treated women badly."

"Saint Paul and his disciple, Lord Tweedmouth, never dipped their fingers into the dark, deep well of women's issues." Faraday slowed for a rut. The car pitched, throwing her body toward his.

"So, as you say, we women did it," she said grabbing his arm.

"The evidence is irrefutable."

"And Haversack is a crack shot."

Faraday chuckled. "A thousand roses to thy shrine."

"She wears lavender perfume like a poultice against the croup."

"I'm so glad you came." He took her hand from her lap and kissed the back of it.

Eleanor closed her eyes. She was too old to crave Henry Faraday. Don't encourage him, she thought. "Do come by early tomorrow and distract my mother. If you don't, I will have to come up with something by myself."

"I think I will be oil on the fire."

"You will be an old family friend."

At her home, Faraday jumped out and opened her car door. He helped her to her feet and then pulled her into him. He kissed her with a light touch and then said so close to her that she could feel his breath on her lips. "Albert is an idiot."

She gazed after the trace smoke from the car that was disappearing. All of it foolishness, a foolishness that was Faraday, but her heart pounded, and her lips tingled.

❧ 6 ❧

There once was a man who said, "Ayer
Has answered the atheist's prayer.
For a hell one can't verify
Surely can't terrify—
At least, till you know you are there."
—Wordsworth Wordsworth
Book of Limericks

Toward midnight, Louis arrived back at the Castle and fell while trying to tiptoe upstairs. "Christ," he said while righting himself. He held onto the banister while his body rocked like a canoe in the light swell. He brushed at his jacket with a global motion. "Sh-s-shit."

Starting up again, he missed another riser and tripped, and this time he gave his nose a crack. "S-s-son-of-a-bitch. S-s-shhhhh, be quiet." Remaining on the stair, he took out a handkerchief. He could taste the blood at his lips and at the back of his throat. He needed another drink. Only four stairs to the bottom, he eased back to ground level.

"You are dead," he yelled at the walls as he passed. "S-s-shhhh. You will wake her." Holding his sore nose, he headed to the drawing room.

"She is up, and you are drunk." Charlotte descended the last tier of stairs one slow foot at a time. The sash of her royal-blue robe was loosely tied.

"And you, for a change, are not...drunk," said Louis.

"I'm going to ignore that." She raised her hand toward him. "Just look at you. People will talk."

"What more can they say?"

"This needs to stay out of the papers. Our lives laid out daily in the Penny Press? People will need to forget."

"If society is our new God," he began, making a grand sweep of the entrance hall with his arm, "we'll need to repaint." Louis finished walking to the drawing room.

"You've had enough." His mother followed him. She'd been shouting at his head since he could remember. He swatted the buzzing sound of her voice. Her resonance had been in his ear since before his birth. He very much wished for his mother's silence because in his whole life he couldn't remember her having said anything worth saying or shutting up.

She was behind him, and when he turned, she tried to take the glass. He squeezed it harder, hanging on. The glass crushed. Scotch, fragments, and blood dripped to the blue carpet. Neither mother nor son dropped their gazes.

Louis backed down first. He turned from her as she laughed at him.

"You are a miserable drunk."

"I'm the new Baron of Tweedmouth."

She poured herself a drink. She sipped at it while looking at him over the rim of the glass, measuring him.

He waved her away, but she would never go.

Suddenly the room had no air. He struggled to stand. He made it to the foot of the stairs before he vomited.

"The new Baron of Tweedmouth," his mother scoffed, leaning against the door jamb with her whiskey.

He left her, intent on his own rooms. Her words stayed with him, and hate boiled though him as he stopped at his father's room. Voices, he hadn't heard the sound of his father's for hours. The house seemed to sleep.

Louis pushed open the door, and it banged on the inner wall. He walked all the way through to the bathroom. It smelled of his father's hair ointment.

Louis returned to the bedroom. There was a hint of his mother's perfume. She had been here. He was never going to get the smell of lavender out of his nostrils. He wandered the big room, lifting silver brushes, and godforsaken, pious statues. Letting a saint fall from his hands, he watched it bounce on the carpet, indestructible. He pounded on it with a brush until it broke. Louis panted. The broken figure on the carpet reminded him of his father, and he kicked the pieces across the room.

He still held the hairbrush. It was in his hand, as he climbed onto the slippery satin covering on his father's bed. His weight dented its pristine surface. He bounced a bit messing it further. Leaning against the carved headboard, he saw himself standing meekly at the footboard taking brutal, verbal blows from a man who was stronger than he, even when bedridden.

You weak fool.

Jumping off the bed, he stripped it of its coverings as he went. With all the bedding in a heap on the floor, he stamped on it. With his eyes burning and dry, Louis stepped into his father's dressing room and put his father's shirt over his own, and then his father's jacket. Without wide, thick shoulders to support it, the outfit caved at his chest. It hung at his arms. He'd never fill it. Louis ripped off the ill-fitting thing, and then he pulled down all his father's clothes, throwing them onto the pile of sheets and blankets. As Louis tossed, he called for any passing servant.

"Here you, get the others up here, and get all this carried out. I want it out of here. I want all of it out of here." Louis passed back into the dressing room. "All of this too. Take the whole bed," he called. "Take it out. Burn it. Get everyone in here. I want this room cleared. Pull up the carpet."

Servants rushed to and fro as if a fire had broken out. They bumped into each other. Broken things were kicked into corners.

"What should we do with all of it?" one hazarded to ask.

"Keep it yourselves, put it in a cart at the gate. I don't care. I don't want to see any of it again."

Charlotte arrived. "Louis, stop this!"

At her clipped voice, the domestics froze like a children's game.

"Keep going," Louis commanded. "I am the Baron of Tweedmouth." He was the Baron of Tweedmouth. "Damn you all, move, and keep moving. Do as I say, or you'll all be sacked by morning."

"No," Charlotte yelled. "Louis, my love." She crossed the room to him. "What are you doing?"

"Say it in French, mother, the language of love."

"This is insane. You must stop."

"Insanity? Insanity is what we do."

Charlotte stopped dead in her tracks. Her female smile faded.

"Stop this," she hissed. "You are drunk. The servants."

"The king is dead, mother, long live the king. What are you all waiting for?"

Charlotte took shirt collars, frames from servants and held them to her breast.

"Leave mother, why don't you. Go put your head on Renard's flabby lap."

Sheets, pillows, and clothing were carried past Charlotte as she stood with that stricken-queen formula to her face. He saw that look for what it was, meant to produce guilt—guilt, guilt, guilt, or was it real, this grief of hers? He laughed, he crowed, and he turned his back on her, something he'd never done before. She hated men rejecting her. He felt glorious as she left in a huff.

Louis stood in the middle of the chaos until the room lay bare, and he could breathe again. Still, the faintest odor of his mother remained. It will pass, he thought. He listened to the sexton ringing the bells at the village church to commemorate his father's passing from the earth. Louis staggered to his room. He got sick again, and then fought tears, and tried to keep his father from seeing them.

He had done it, only he didn't feel liberated. Now, his father could penetrate walls. He'd pay for it. *Ignis fatuus*. If only Charles were here now. He'd help laugh the night away. He'd poke fun at the Baron. Charles would say that Tweedmouth had died and he, Louis, hadn't. Louis had the feeling that his father couldn't die.

Trying to hear Charles's laughter, Louis jumped when a knock sounded at the door.

"Yes."

"Anything you need, my lord?"

Gillette. "No, I'm fine."

"Are you sure, my lord?"

"Quite fine...."

He listened to the fading steps of the servant.

Louis hated quiet. His mind roamed in the quiet. The castle would be quiet forever now. No, his mother would fill it. If only he had been born a girl. The pressure in his head would be easier.

Crawling on his own bed, Louis nestled into his down pillow. Let his own eternal sleep find him.

.   .   .

E leanor remembered the hair sample. She'd better get the work done on Tweedmouth's hair tonight. She lit a gas lamp and went down a narrow staircase that had a painted lumber banister. The smell of mold indicated a slight damp. She lifted the hurricane glass and lit two lamps and wished for electricity. In the middle of the basement, the concrete floor had been carved out, like a pond, as a gathering place for seeping water. She walked across the now dry space to the small corner of the manor that Alannah would allow Eleanor's pungent chemicals.

She aired Tweedmouth's hairs from her bag. Some arsenic in the body would be expected. Arsenic stimulates growth. Eleanor grabbed beakers and put them together. The test had to be closed bottle, and then she searched for her sulfuric acid and some arsenic-free zinc.

Eleanor had to first treat the hair in a solution of distilled water and hydrochloric acid. After filtering the mixture, she rummaged through a stack of papers until she found the one titled *Marsh's Test*. She read through it, using her index finger as a guide, and then put on an apron and sleeve covers.

Grabbing a double-mouthed glass vessel, she combined the zinc and the sulfuric acid to make a hydrogen gas. Oh, she hated that smell. The reaction consumed Tweedmouth's hair. In an adjoining tube, Eleanor watched as the gas dried over a pumice stone that she had moistened with more sulfuric acid. The gas passed through hard German glass. As it began escaping through the end of the tube, Eleanor prepared to light a jet. She had excluded air from the glass, so the thing wouldn't explode, hadn't she? Yes. This is what she loved about chemistry, the anticipation of an event. As the fire burns the gas, a black deposit should form on a white piece of porcelain held over the fire.

Nothing. Disappointment deflated her or gave her hope; she wasn't sure which. The porcelain remained clean—no deposit, no arsenic. She turned off the gas and wiped her hands on her apron. She was glad that she hadn't told anyone about the hair. Feeling foolish, she put her chin in her hand with her elbow on the worktable. It had been a long shot.

The result wasn't conclusive. Tweedmouth had been ill for months. They all must have been waiting for him to die, day by day, by day. It was true. If any of them had known anything, they wouldn't have picked arsenic. They'd want to mimic the asthmatic symptoms. He'd fallen off that balcony. It didn't make sense. If he hadn't fallen, no one would have taken any interest in his death.

The clock struck one, and Eleanor realized how late it was and how tired she felt. She washed her beakers, letting the sound of water in the basin sooth her. Something had constricted Tweedmouth's eyes. She needed his stomach. Apron off and rubbing her own hand cream into her knuckles, Eleanor climbed the stairs. She needed an autopsy. She thought of going to the coroner. Ha, doubtful he'd be of any help.

She paused at the noise from the garden room. Her mother snored when she'd been drinking. Well, at least the firing squad won't be rising at dawn. Small mercies.

The noise from her mother's throat reminded Eleanor that maybe she should let things be. Faraday thought so. The village probably did too. As much as everyone wanted Tweedmouth dead and buried, Eleanor sensed that the man wasn't going to settle into the grave—not Tweedmouth's style.

She was glad to see her bed. Her mother had put fresh lavender in her room. "Yes, mother, loneliness," she muttered as she picked up the vase and put it in the hall.

Louis had been bizarre himself. Louis as a murderer, preposterous! He just didn't have the heart to do it. He'd never be able to plan it. She paused with her hand on the bedroom doorknob. Oh God no, she thought as she realized that Louis was just innocent enough to think, under the right circumstances, that he had killed his father. So easy to set up an artless man.

✤ 7 ✤

Hell hath no fury like a noncombatant.
—C.E. Montague

Eleanor opened her eyes, stretched a little, yawned and when she turned, she almost hit a wall of black crepe. The wall was her mother in full dress. Eleanor nearly crab-walked backwards. The waking view of her mother holding a cup of hot chocolate in her hand numbed her to the core. It took a moment to recover her will to live. The rising steam in front of the body seemed less to do with the cup of hot chocolate her mother held and more to do with her mother's angry face. The sparkle in her mother's eyes made her seem more devious than ever.

Eleanor sighed. This was happening earlier than she had hoped or imagined. Her mother's color was like gray felt, the bags under her eyes like drained cheesecloth, yet she was here. The woman had stamina, and from the slight smirk, Alannah had been planning. Planning meant prolonged suffering.

"For God's sake." Eleanor moved to accept the drink, but when she saw the almonds in the saucer, she met her mother's eyes. "Indiscrete and thoughtless? Again? And before breakfast. That must be a record. My romp is rolling through the shire?"

46

"Without doubt, galloping. I haven't been out." Her mother's lips were so pressed together as to be nonexistent. "When we needed eggs this morning for crepes, we just scraped them off the side of the house."

"Been drinking?" Eleanor regretted the impulsive words before the last syllable had been uttered. Even the birds outside seemed to quit singing, leading to an unnatural calm. A tempest was gathering on her mother's brow. Eleanor closed her eyes, the only place to hide.

"The words you say, the things you do...what were you thinking? Do you think?" The tension in her mother's body exploded into motion. She put down the cup and began pacing. Eleanor could feel a breeze on her face. "The man was dying."

"Aren't we all?" Eleanor added to amuse herself.

With her hands open in a kind of imploring gesture, Alannah seemed to be struck speechless. Not for long, her daughter thought.

"How you can joke about something like this? Tell me, how the world will be for you with just me to talk to, daily, Eleanor, monthly, yearly. You're giving up a comfortable position in life for what exactly? I'd just like to know that if you please, because I'd be amazed if you can tell me."

"How often do people who are very ill fall from balconies?"

"People die in all sorts of ways."

"My point exactly." Eleanor paused and then said, "Last night Faraday more or less asked me, which was more corrupt, the man or his death?"

"Faraday!" Alannah plopped with a resigned sigh in an upholstered chair. She hadn't given in. She never gave in. Surrender not was her mother's every inclination, even in spontaneity it was there; *ex mero—motu*, Louis might say, out of one's own head. Alannah's long face made Eleanor livid. A lack of living was no compensation for comfort.

"Don't you think," Eleanor began, pulling back her covers, and forcing her feet into slippers, "that odd deaths should be looked into? Wouldn't you expect him to die in his bed? Charlotte did."

Alannah glared at her daughter. "Odd people die oddly, that's what I say. Why didn't you say to yourself that for him, the unusual is the usual? You have a glossy view of the world, justice, fairness, the contentment of poverty."

As if to prove her mother's point, Eleanor rang for the upstairs maid. She stepped into her dressing room and pulled her nightgown over her head. She knew her mother would not follow—thank God. Her mother's voice seemed blessedly distant. She opened a lacquered wardrobe with doors of painted garlands. Ground glass panes let in plenty of light—so important to a good dressing room. Walls of lilac next to *point d' esprit* tulle curtains served as a good backdrop for her dresses. A table draped with satin and framed in a ruche of lace held twinkling bottles of scent. Eleanor picked one up and admired its beauty. Her mother wasn't all wrong.

She got dressed while wondering what the devil was in store for her now. If ever there were someone who needed something to do in life, that person would be her mother. She was almost gleeful she'd asked Faraday to come, serves her mother right. She sifted through dresses from her wardrobe.

She thought about murder. It seemed it was a convenience—more common than water and less clear. She wondered how few people outlived their welcome. Probably plenty of forgery in the signing of death certificates.

"How fortuitous of Tweedmouth to die and not to get better," she mumbled to herself.

"It is stupid for you to get any more involved," Alannah called to her. "Everyone is pleased he is gone. No one will care. No one will want it to be Louis. Better unsolved than to be Louis. What are you doing now?"

"Dressing."

"For Faraday? Oh yes, a note came from your *amant*, earlier this morning."

Eleanor came from the dressing room in her first layer of clothing. "My *amant*? My lover? You are giving me too much credit. Why didn't you tell me?"

"How surprising that I forgot in all this intrigue."

Alannah held the note at the tips of her fingers. Her face showed disdain in an I–told–you–so way. Eleanor grabbed the paper from her. Her mother sniffed and arranged the folds of her skirt.

"He can't come."

"Now that is a surprise."

"Haven't you something to do?"

"Not a thing."

Eleanor sat on the edge of her bed in the beginnings of her morning dress, and scanned the note again, reading more into it with post-kiss attention. Over-riding the fluttering in her breast, she chided herself for looking for something more. She wasn't a schoolgirl. She was just lonely, and she liked him. The whole thing was becoming sad. Older, pining, separated woman kissed by younger man, pathetic. She wondered why he had done it.

"What?" asked Alannah.

She had a nose like a bloodhound.

"He had too much wine last night."

"He's too ashamed to put his face through my door," said Alannah.

"How much did you have to drink last night?"

"Can you blame me? I didn't leave you behind with Olivia Haversack. Oh, how could you, Eleanor? How could you do this to me? What have I done to deserve such treatment? Isn't my life hard enough?"

Hearing silent violins, Eleanor walked back into her dressing room. She'd heard it all before, her mother's plaintive speeches, and she'd hear it all again —*ad infinitum...ad nauseam*. She needed to move to her own house. The old thought was discarded, again. Alannah would take to her bed, leaving all that outdoor energy unspent. It would have to hiss out in some way, somewhere. Center on the task at hand—Tweedmouth—shift the bulk that was her mother's fears and aspirations onto constructive things. It was a long shot for both.

"Pretend you're the Baron," she called to her mother. "Hold your breath. You've got seconds to live...moments before you're to pass out, what would you do?"

"This is ridiculous," Alannah barked.

"What would you do?"

"For heaven's sake, fine, I'd pull the servant's bell."

"Or head for it. I wouldn't be walking about or leaning against a very low railing."

"He could have panicked," said Alannah. "Humph. I can't see the Baron panicky, actually. He used to fight in duels, once an illegal one with Albert as his second, and you can't suggest that someone pushed him. Why bother, for heaven's sake?"

"He could have gotten better!"

"You—" Alannah started just before a knock at the door.

Eleanor strode into the room, grateful for the interruption. "Come in." She was expecting Letty. Hoping for Letty. Hoping for anyone. She got a constipated-looking servant.

"Madam, we have run out of vinegar to clean up the eggs on the window."

"Eggs on a window?" Eleanor asked.

"I told you, but your detective mind didn't seem to grasp it."

"What about eggs?" Eleanor asked the maid.

Her mother answered. "The side of the house. Last night a chicken-coop 'full' hit the window just at my head while I was standing there. I was going to save the mess for you, for your sleuthing skills. Brown eggs,

Speckled Sussex breed. Anything in that for you?" Alannah tapped at her forehead.

"For God's sake." Eleanor threw her dressing gown back on.

Alannah held up her hand. "There's nothing to see. We were egged with our own eggs. Letty found our own egg basket at the scene of the crime. "All of them, by the way. We had none for breakfast."

Eleanor paused. Her mother had the upper hand. To gain the advantage she had been waiting at the side of the bed, a planned stratagem. She had probably nudged Eleanor awake just for this scene. Her mother had played it out beautifully. Let the nighttime events unfold. She'd probably told the girl just when to knock at the door. They probably had buckets and buckets of vinegar in the house. Worst of all, Eleanor did notice guilt creeping up the ladder of her spine.

"Louis had looked so unhappy, all day. It tore my heart."

"Ask cook to give you money for more," Alannah said to the girl. After the servant left, Alannah said, "She'll probably leave us. They all will probably leave us." Alannah sniffed. "My garden room egged." Real tears fell. "The tongues will wag like an idiot dog's tail."

"I suppose they will. I am sorry. Believe me, I am." She put her arms around her mother and kissed her cheek. There is a sort of shock and real shame in being egged, she thought. To what purpose, for God's sake? Just because she had the gall to help Louis? What about the eggers gall? "Let's put it behind us. I saw something amazing that might interest you. The drive down to Abbey Leix Castle is lined with lime trees."

"Hardly news, the Baroness planted those when they moved in. She was besotted. It was Samuel this, Samuel that—"

"So the trees do mean conjugal love?" Eleanor had risen and her maid had begun the process of putting on Eleanor's corset. Eleanor shouldered her blouse. Her mother was calming, so Eleanor asked, "Do you want to know what happened last night?"

Alannah just clucked her tongue, but didn't bluster, so Eleanor continued. "The constable that came to the luncheon said that Owens had been notified by his wife's sister's husband, who is a groundskeeper at Abbey Leix, that Lord Tweedmouth was dead after a fall from a balcony. I mean the Tweedmouth's would never tell. The locals passed on the information because they've always thought of the family as a bit touched. The locals here are very superstitious." Eleanor turned in front of her mirror. "What do you think of this blouse?"

"I thought you'd sworn off black?" Alannah asked.

"But the blue of this waist goes best with black." Eleanor looked over her shoulder at the back of the outfit.

"Fine then, and a cameo, and black boots." Fashion was an extension of the artist in Alannah.

"Which hat?"

"That one with the black feathers."

Eleanor tried the hat. She thought her face more pleasing in hats because of her high forehead. After turning this way and that in the mirror, she gave the top piece to her maid.

"Yes, that one." The craft of dressing relaxed her mother. She was herself within it. "You know, I never liked the Baron, and not because he was a pompous ass," Alannah drawled. "He was a bad loser. Everyone must lose from time to time."

"Like Charles?"

"Does he ever win? I mean, isn't he's going to be shackled to Olivia until death? Anyway, I say allow someone else the pleasure of winning, which Tweedmouth never, ever did. Poor Louis."

Eleanor returned to her dressing room and sat at a vanity table. The maid began her hair by securing the pompadour frame to her head.

"Letty told me that you're lucky to have such thick hair. Her maid has to save all her hair combings," Alannah said.

"So with the lime trees, was Owens, you know anticipating a muddle, or hysterics or something, he wasn't off the mark? She really did love him?"

Her mother, sitting on the fainting couch, considered the question. "Not hysterics, not now," was all she said.

"There isn't really much more except that he had fallen from a balcony, and was quite broken and blue," said Eleanor who gazed at her mother over her shoulder through the reflection of her vanity mirror.

"The asthma," said Alannah.

"No one knows. He was dead before impact. Heart failure on the way down, dead from asthma, poisoned—who knows? Owens had decided that Tweedmouth quit breathing and fell."

"How reasonable."

"Louis is acting strangely. He was drinking whiskey." Eleanor hazarded a glance at her mother. At the window, bright light whitewashed the front of Alannah's mourning dress and outlined strands of black hair. Her shoulders slumped. "No one is going to let anything happen to that boy. Just stay out of it. I mean it. It's not ladylike."

"Ladylike!" Eleanor exploded. She shouldn't have, but damn it she was tired of the word from her mother's lips. "Look at the rest of them. Lord Mountbank is feverishly writing his biography for money. Lord Rolls is selling cars. Strutt is in dairies. Lord Montague is publishing Car Illustrated. Lady Winthrop is a member of a ladies' poisoning society."

"We are not as well entrenched in society as is Lady Winthrop," Alannah flared. "You have your little advertisement in the Illustrated London News. 'Millions of women use Cuticura soap.' Isn't that what it says? So, do not tell me that I am not allowing you to express your interests. You also have an advertisement for your Sulpholine skin lotion. It's all quite enough. You spend every other afternoon in the basement concocting God knows what, and you come up smelling like who knows what. Do be satisfied. More would just be too much."

"Grandfather—"

"Do not—" Alannah closed her eyes, peering inside for patience no doubt. "Do not bring your grandfather into this."

"*Cen fáth nach.*"

"Stop it. First, you don't know enough Irish to have a conversation much beyond the words, "why not." In the second place, I forbade him to teach you, and beyond that you know very well why not, not to mention his joining those clubs. Every visit, he meant to make me miserable. I will not have you a party to it." Alannah stopped speaking. She inhaled. She let her face and her temper cool.

"Eleanor you are as unassuming as Louis. Charlotte is as mean as a rabid cat. The egging is nothing compared to that woman. You have always gone about your life with your head in the clouds. Your father encouraged you and left me rearranging and picking up the pieces. You don't realize that, do you, that I smooth things for you? Your father's gone. That makes it all harder. What do you know about Charlotte?"

"Isn't she French?"

"Absolutely, not. She has some distant, Huguenot ancestors that came to England in the sixteen or seventeen hundreds. Her Frenchness, if you will, is the affectation of a very irritating nature. She is the much younger sister of Sir Louis De Crespigny, the Mad Rider. He was a dreadful businessman, and he, we all thought, sold his sister to the highest bidder. He sold her to a man like himself who drank and dueled. They were both wild to the bone. He sold her to his good friend, Samuel Montfire, the first Baron of Tweedmouth. Charlotte was crazy about him. The sun and the moon about him. Do you see?"

"What about Renard then?"

"Oh, for God's sake. Truly religious men, like Saint Paul, Eleanor, are celibate." Alannah delivered the last line with a flourish from the center of the room—as the center of attention—being the woman of the moment. She was a detective's daughter, after all.

Eleanor rose and gave her mother a peck on the cheek. "I'm going to see Tweedmouth's doctor. I want to know if he'd sign off on the death certificate."

Alannah's eyes widened with disbelief. "Oh for God's sake, why wouldn't he anyway? The man was sick."

"Because Charlotte is a rabid cat," Eleanor said and then watched her mother's face change to surprise as she realized that she'd been one-upped.

8

What, after all, is a halo?
It's only one more thing to keep clean.
—Christopher Fry

Eleanor paused to look at the empty egg basket that was for some reason now perched on a table by the front door. No almonds in it at least. It looked ratty by the silver card salver. She sighed, picked up a grey mass, like a bit of hardened putty, from it and then put it all back. Leave it to her mother to deal with. It was here as an object of guilt.

She decided to go see Faraday first and refused to think about the decision. A few locals were about the White Hart Inn as her driver turned the carriage onto the main road to Whitney. Again, the day was fine and cloudless. The square window openings of the carriage glowed. Sunshine striped the upholstered seats and lit the disturbed dust. The boards of a wooden bridge sang like an abused piano as the carriage crossed the droughty Windrush River. The brambles lining the road were heavy with blackberries. Pale yellow fields of the Wold were whitewashed in the bright daylight. She breathed autumnal air as she thought about Tweedmouth. That he used to be wild amazed her—such breathless extremes, and Albert had fought in duels, hardly surprising.

54

Albert was boringly consistent, but Tweedmouth—well few people lived their lives within two absolutes like that man had. Maybe his actions were two faces of one extreme personality. She couldn't wait to tell Faraday. It occurred to her that he might not be up.

Whitney came into view with its slate roofs supporting creeping black lichen. Eleanor knew she hadn't much longer to Faraday's rental. She gazed out the window and watched the buildings pass: the defunct Blanket Hall where dirty children and toothless women had rocked loom shuttles back and forth. Now it was a meeting place for suffrage groups. A dressmaker's, next door, was livelier. Men loitered at the livery. As the carriage passed a millinery shop, she saw the Haversacks with hatboxes, yet with them it was the same old hat. Olivia noticed her passing and glared.

The uniform village of matching blonde limestone and peaked roofs with its smells of horse manure and trade slipped behind her. Eleanor thought about Charlotte. She had married an intemperate man. He had changed. Her resistance, defiance really, had been Renard. Why didn't Tweedmouth throw him out?

She was too early for Faraday. She decided to visit Owens. She was still thinking of the death certificate and whether the Chief Constable would contact Tweedmouth's physician. The attending doctor should be informed, but Owens would figure that an autopsy would suffice.

To have her driver turn around, she tapped the roof of the carriage with her closed fan, and then she called Owens's name from the window. She hoped the Chief Inspector would not be in. That way, she could speak to an underling. Feeling confident that if Owens had given instructions to have the glass tested, she'd be able to charm the results out of a constable. She opened the station door without hesitation. At the sound of the Chief Constable's voice she stopped. Her feet felt fastened to the floor by fast drying glue.

Owens seemed to purr the words: "Well, well, well, if it isn't Lady Albright. You're up early."

"So are you," she shot back and then backed down. Charming women never belittled small men. She was disappointed though. Owens was a late drinker, and late riser and not much divorced from the scoundrels he was supposed to catch. He shouldn't be here.

He stood behind his desk, and over arms that were propped, hands fisted, on its surface, he leaned in toward her. The overpowering smugness that radiated from the man surrounded and squeezed her charming intentions. It was almost a physical blow to her that he was just a few feet away.

Damn it. He should still be in bed with all the other unshaven, hung-over, under-active men.

"I'm glad you're here," he said with an attempt at a smile. The tone of his voice suggested that she would not be pleased to be here; that he was working toward a good verbal punch-up. "The coroner says that Tweed-mouth died from suffocation, from asthma. There was enough mucus in his lungs to choke a horse—thick with it, if that's what you came for."

"And the fall?"

"He didn't die from that. As I said, just standing too close to the railing...an accident. Nothing for you to further concern yourself with." His smile was atrocious—ugly teeth behind ugly lips. She felt its mocking brilliance. Two weasels watched her, one stuffed and dead on a shelf, one alive and teeth bared and behind a desk.

"We all know that he's been ill. Of course his lungs would be full. Did the coroner open the stomach?"

Owens smile grew even broader, his pinkish gums showing. He had forgotten to offer her a chair.

"No arsenic there either. See? We aren't stupid. Whims have no place in an investigation...whatever the fiction books with women detectives. I'm telling you, no, warning you, if you'd care to listen, that the coroner has said that it's suffocation, asthma." He opened a drawer, lifted out a glass, and placed it with a thud between them on the desktop. "Smith analyzed this, along with the stomach. Nothing in it."

"At all?"

"At all."

"Then what was its purpose?"

He recoiled, as if punched. To recover, to further press his point, he passed the coroner's report to her. Delighted with herself, she read through the pages as she dropped into a chair by his desk. All was as he had said. The arsenic test had been done right and it was negative. Smith was a good man.

"See? Nothing there." He snatched the document from her hands. "We aren't stupid here. This is not my first death. I had one where a rose had been shoved up the lad's backside. Straight in. Hell of a thing." He nodded his head toward some talcum powder and a brush, as if, 'See? We are competent here.' "We tried to get a fingerprint off it."

"Did you use gloves?" She was beginning to smart from Owens's rough treatment—small hearts hurt others. It was time to think of something else, the fine weather, the birds, another day. There was no point in irritating the man.

Owens' pinkish gums were still seeing the light of day when he said, "On the other hand...if you want to go there...the coroner said that a fist smashed Baron Tweedmouth's nose. A fight may have caused his asthma to get worse. Could've caused the death, the drill into his face. I should bring in the new Lord Tweedmouth for questioning. What do you think?"

I think that you are an ass. What was it with men needing to best women? Eleanor walked out with his laughter as a drum roll. She swooped the door closed behind her and managed to catch the hem of her skirt on a nail in the doorjamb. Owens was practically doubled over watching Eleanor struggling with her skirt and a constable with fat fingers helping her.

"A little snag, Lady Albright?" The Chief Constable was sick from laughter.

"Hammer home all your nails, Inspector Owens," she growled back at him. A closing door never sounded so sweet.

F araday had rented a manor just outside Whitney between Eynsham Park, where Olivia hung her hats, and Little Minister's Manor House, where Alannah held court. The house rested on a slight rise. Eleanor always found the sight of it dear. He had never hired a gardener. The roses here were becoming leggy, with brave weeds at their feet. Eleanor picked a flower as she passed—last of the season. She'd have Dunn bring them all in. The door of the house needed paint, as did the windows.

She'd never been inside, officially.

"Where are the dogs?" Eleanor asked the valet who appeared. The man's thin lips made him seem disapproving. A trick of nature—a kinder soul there never was.

"They've gone with the trainer. Their barking was doing his lordship's headache no favor."

"That bad, is it?"

"Yes, but he's up now, and I'm nearly finished cooking the breakfast. I'll tell him you're here."

An unshaven, pale Faraday arrived in his robe over shirt and trousers. His world seemed headachy this morning. He smiled abashedly at her, as he leaned against the doorframe. "Sorry about this morning. Was your mother very bad?"

"Brutal."

Faraday threw himself on a worn leather sofa. He looked like a hung-over, good-natured, great Dane. She pulled off her gloves. "All from the wine?"

"Haversack was being magnanimous. Celebrating the death, I think. It was fabulous. In spite of my state, I do have news. Owens's sent a man. The death is going to be ruled asphyxiation.

"Caused by a boxing match if I don't leave off. I know. I stopped by to see him on the way here. If he were being thorough, he'd go to London."

"Why, the King and his Queen are absent."

"You know why," Eleanor said.

Faraday rubbed his face trying, she supposed, to invigorate his thoughts. "Do you know that ninety-six percent of all cases are solved by finding that one person who knows who did it?"

"We should go to London. Do a little shopping. Owens didn't comment that Tweedmouth's pupils were not right, and it wasn't the sun or the shade. He only checked the stomach for arsenic. What invalid is not taking any medications whatsoever?" She leaned toward him to take a cigarette from his case. He reached over to light it.

"Oh, I know," she said after blowing out smoke. "The coroner's report was thorough. His lungs were full of mucus. The test for arsenic was accurately done. You know it would be very easy to place a pillow over an asthmatic's face. There would be no broken veins in the eyes, no indication of violence, except in the dead man's glare. Just shut his eyes. No worries about arsenic traces in his stomach."

"Tweedmouth did end up over the balcony. Not a necessary thing to do if you've just smothered the man," said Faraday.

"He could have broken his nose in the fall," she mumbled to herself, not believing it. She inhaled a good bit of burning tobacco. Spent, the smoke escaped slowly through her lips before she said, "There's just too much hate and too much money that surrounds Tweedmouth. Owens talked about bringing in Louis. It's starting."

She watched out the window. There had been no vomit. His eyes had been peaceful. No medication bottles. Nothing in the glass. If the glass had had water in it, it must have been at Tweedmouth's side to chase a dose of something. Maybe he was refusing all medications—waiting to meet his maker that much sooner, but then the glass would be full. Tweedmouth liked himself too much to want to see God early.

"What if the fall is a red herring? Come with me to his doctor to check on his medications...and to see just how sick the patient was. Are we expecting him to die as a part of wanting him to die?"

Faraday inhaled smoke and then exhaled it. "I remember once, Tweedmouth yelling at the cook at the club over something on his plate. 'I can't eat this!' That scene was a bit excessive what?"

"Expectation, our unruly mistress in this death."

"I suspect that the duel between good and evil, or maybe between evil and good, is set. The gauntlet thrown, blood will be drawn," said Faraday, rubbing his temple.

"Let me make you the constitutional I used to make for my father. Speaking of the gauntlet," she said, putting out her cigarette in a Waterford ashtray. "Mother said that Tweedmouth was very wild in his youth. He drank and fought in duels. He was the perfect ass. Did you know about Albert, seconded Tweedmouth in an illegal duel?

"There was some gossip, but no proof. You thought of leaving it be...last night, didn't you? You still want to." She flicked ash into the ashtray.

"I thought what we all were thinking. What if Louis had had enough?"

"I think he'd hesitate in the final act long enough to reconsider and then walk away. I have no confidence in his ability to commit murder. Then there's Charlotte. You have to admit Saint Paul and Jezebel wouldn't make good bed partners. Do you think Tweedmouth has been trying to save Charlotte?"

"He's been working on everyone else. Why exclude her?"

Eleanor bit on the tip of her thumb. "The coroner had only tested for arsenic. There are numerous ways to poison a man with other substances. Homemade toothpaste, for instance, has been inadvertently contaminated with belladonna in the past—why not on purpose? Belladonna is bitter which doesn't speak well for toothpaste. I should go see Patricia McGlynn for information on life at the castle. She used to work there. As a matter of fact," Eleanor added, as she gathered her gloves and stood. "Where's Dunn? The constitutional, and then I'll go. Will you meet me at the train station in two hours?"

A frisson of joy lightened her when he said yes. She felt it high in her chest and in her lips.

The McGlynn cottage had always been a favorite haunt of her grandfather's when he visited. Eleanor used to come with him when her mother was in a swoon and locked in her bedroom. Cottage tea had a distinct flavor. It was strong, with five heaping spoons of tea in the pot, and sweet. Leaves floated on top. No saucers—just mugs. The strength of the flavor could be smelled in the steam. When she thought of Mrs. McGlynn's brown bread with honey, Eleanor remembered that she hadn't eaten anything all morning. The bran of the wheat tasted wonderful slathered with butter and lemon marmalade. Sometimes the rough parts of life have more flavor.

The McGlynn cottage was just out of the village and had a small vegetable garden overgrown with marrow. Mother and daughter were picking large amounts of it. "A good year, I see," Eleanor said.

"Tis yourself. Welcome. 'Tis always a good year for the marrow." Mrs. McGlynn wiped her hands on her dirt-tracked apron. "We haven't seen ye for some time. How's your mother? We miss your grandfather. He was always one so to give us a good laugh."

Eleanor remembered his laugh, like a braying mule. Since Eleanor's marriage, her grandfather hadn't returned to England. His disgust could be felt in the choppy waves of the Irish Sea. He'd said that the devil himself had more about him than Lord Albright. Her grandfather had been right.

"Mother is fine."

"She'll be grateful for a basketful of fresh vegetables. I've got a good soup recipe for it. I'll send Pat around to your cook," said the mother. She picked a spider off a leaf and squished it between her fingers.

"Both are welcome. Thank you, Mrs. McGlynn."

"Hold on there, Pat, let me add some tomatoes to that."

"You're all well?" asked Eleanor.

"As well as can be expected with my joints aching something fierce at night. I'm not one to complain, mind ye," said the mother.

"I shouldn't take you from your work, but I suppose that you've heard of Lord Tweedmouth's death?"

"We have, so. Desperate. The poor man." She leaned toward Eleanor and said, "I bought a pair of the Baron's breeches just this morning for me oldest lad. The quality of them, like they were never worn. He'll look fine on a Sunday. Would you ever think it was all put on Jack the Tinker's doorstep in the wee hours, like a thief in the night, bedclothes, undergarments, socks? It's turning a fortune for him, so it is. I wished they'd dumped the lot here." She winked at Eleanor.

Mrs. McGlynn had one more bit of gossip, before she carried a basket, brimming with fall, green marrows, and red tomatoes to Eleanor's carriage. "Pat was told that the son had the room stripped, as bare as a pig's arse, even the carpet off the dead man's floor." Mrs. McGlynn made the sign of the cross over her bosom and then kissed the thumb of the hand that had done it.

Pat straightened and watched her mother walk off. She pushed back a bit of dark hair that had fallen over her forehead. She was a fair, trim woman, probably from years of service, not earthy like her mother. Her hands were firm, and Eleanor guessed that she could wring the neck of a chicken with easy grace.

"What was it like to work there?"

"Well, it wasn't a comfortable house like, but few are."

"How did he treat Lady Tweedmouth?"

"Himself? He was forever hissing at her, 'vanity thy name is woman' when she'd even so much as glance into a mirror; or when she'd come down the stairs, you know, as she does."

"How does she?"

"He wasn't far off, so he wasn't."

Eleanor and Pat followed Mrs. McGlynn toward the house. "What about Renard? Did he stand up for her, help her?"

"That one? He'd bring in the wine that the two of them would drink from teacups."

"What about Lord Louis? Did he ever take on his father?"

"You know, they all just seemed to take it. Himself wasn't pleased with any one of them."

Pat stopped to throw a few more marrows into one of the five baskets that lined the rows. A good frost would take care of any more preserving. Today, the cold seemed a long way off. Eleanor felt a companionship within the garden; she hated the thought of a good freeze. Mrs. McGlynn returned and picked up two baskets. Pat did as well. Eleanor took the last one.

"Why did you leave?"

"Tweedmouth?" said the mother. "Pat got headaches. The Reverend has a much calmer house. Now come in, come in. We'll have that tea." She opened the door of the cottage and seemed to inhale to get the bulk of her body and the baskets through the opening.

"I heard that he had become very religious after he became ill." That was an understatement, Eleanor thought.

"And what good did it do him? No amount of false praying would help with that desperate carry on." She dumped her load just inside the kitchen. "Ye'll have a little cake with your tea." She took Eleanor's basket.

"No, I couldn't bother you."

"Ah, ye will, so. Patricia put on the kettle for her Ladyship. I've a drop of whiskey?"

"No, no whiskey, thanks."

What Eleanor wanted to do was sit and eat hot brown bread with strong, black tea sweetened with sugar and milk. It was relaxing to listen to the lyrical tone of their brogue that reminded Eleanor of her grandfather. She missed him. She had written that she'd left her husband. As he hadn't written back, he must not approve of that either.

She had walked into the kitchen behind the women. The hall had been narrow, made more so by stairs that marched up to the Virgin's feet as she waited in front of a window—her arms wide. The plaster on the walls hadn't seen paint for years. She smelled cooking—fresh rosemary and garlic.

In the kitchen just above the fireplace, Mrs. McGlynn had hung a picture of a kindly Jesus with an open smiling face and his large heart worn outside his clothes. It was buckled and stained from years of boiling water and greasy vapors. At her grandfather's, it was crisp and well dusted, as it hung over the dining room table, or so she thought; she hadn't seen it for five years.

In the small kitchen, marrow was piled here and there, ready for winter preserving. A stew simmered on the Aga for the midday meal. The table was scrubbed and worn. Eleanor sat at it, nestling into its tucked-in comfort. The tea steam opened her senses. Fading blue paint on the walls wrapped her in a cheerful sky. She'd stay here forever if she could, in the stew of real emotions mixed with the pepper. As Mrs. McGlynn poured out the tea, Eleanor understood why her grandfather had visited here so often when he was around.

"Right, so, are you comfortable, then?" asked the mother. She opened a tin of homemade Christmas fruitcake. A strong smell of spirits came off it.

"Have you any brown bread?" asked Eleanor.

"Of course we have, you wouldn't be wanting that would ye?"

"I'd love some."

Out the back of the house, a feathery coop was empty of chickens. The birds scratched at the dirt in the yard, and with what seemed like impaired movement, they turned their heads in a jerking manner to look at the ground with either eye. A pig rolled in the muck. There wasn't a stitch of grass.

Eleanor needed to resuscitate the thread of conversation. "Any other sort of carrying on happening at the house between Lady Charlotte and Lord Tweedmouth? How did she react to all this criticism?"

"She wasn't going to take to the church no matter what he wanted," said Pat.

"Holy God, the thought of it," said Mrs. McGlynn.

Holy God is right, Eleanor thought. "Renard sat with her, calmed her?"

"They could knock down a very good time for themselves when the Baron was buried in his room or library reading scripture," said Pat, warming to the chat.

"When you were there, did anyone threaten Lord Tweedmouth?"

"No, I didn't hear anyone. Anyway, I've heard that the asthma took him," said Pat.

"Yes," said Eleanor. "I just feel that there's something more than the obvious in this death."

"Jaesus, would you look at that old rooster getting up the hens," said Pat. She tore out of the back door. "Shoo, Shoo, you beggar. Get away from the ladies." She waved her apron at the bird that shed feathers as it ran, flapping its wings.

Ignoring her daughter, the mother said, "He was an ol' bullock. I've seen them like that. My mother-in-law was like that. Do you remember Grandmother Aileen, Pat?" Mrs. McGlynn asked as her daughter returned. "Bred from the soil that woman was and wouldn't return to it. She buried four of her ten grown sons before she went. Will I put more water in the pot?"

"No, thank you, Mrs. McGlynn. This has been fine."

"Are ye off, then?"

"I think so. I do appreciate the tea and the company. You can't think of anything else about the family? No one ever threatened anyone?"

"No, no. Pat?"

"No, not that I heard. There were a few bits and pieces in his trouser pockets. The ones I got from Jack. I tossed them in the bin."

"Would ye be wanting something like that?" Mrs. McGlynn reached over and opened the lid of the tea pot. "Get them so, Pat, while I pour out more tea."

Eleanor was beginning to feel the effects of the strong drink crawl up her spine. Her hands had developed a shake as she reached for the papers that Pat was wiping at with her apron. They reeked of heat mixed with old meals —soon to have been hog fodder. She scanned a handful of Bible verses probably in the Baron's script.

"Lucky the pig didn't get it," Pat confirmed.

A picture of a child with a name or date washed away on the back. The edges of the paper were worn. They'd been in his pocket for some time, forgotten there in an old pair of breeches.

"Thanks so much for everything." Eleanor hated to leave the warmth of these women.

"Not at all, and have your cook ask for more marrow when yours are gone. We're knee deep in it."

They weren't the only ones.

As the McGlynns chatted Eleanor out the door, a rooster-startled hen flew at Eleanor's face and banged into her hat and tangled in its netting. Held in a death grip by a long pin, the hat listed to one side. Her hat slid over the side of her head and covered her ear. Feathers from the squawking, flapping bird stuck to her lips. Her own black feathers at the hatband were done for. She was down on one knee by the time the Mrs. McGlynn got to her.

After chasing the bird and clucking over the state of the hat, the older woman fussed over Eleanor's hair. "I should wring his neck and serve him for dinner."

"I'm fine, no really, fine."

She got into her carriage. Her favorite hat was done in. The feathers were nothing but broken cartilage. Damn it. She wasn't going home for a new one. Horses couldn't drag her back there, and no time to buy one. She tore the shredded decorations from it, straightened her hair, and pressed the hat onto it. She stuck it all on with a hatpin. If Faraday even chuckled, she'd box his ears, and then she thought of how agreeable that might be.

9

O let us love our occupations
Bless the squire and his relations
Live upon our daily rations
And always know our proper stations
—Charles Dickens

A t the train station, Faraday looked sideways at her hair. "Chicken fight," Eleanor said. She had hoped that by pushing hair upwards and then stabbing the hanging hairpins back into place, she had refreshed the original hairstyle. At the look of horror in Faraday's face, all hope fled. Damn it, she just had no patience with hair. When the pale Faraday fell asleep in his seat, she brooded and rubbed her knee, and stared out the window as the Whitney-to-London train belched, bumped and swayed down its narrow track.

Feeling narrow herself, she sat in the train noise, looking odd and feeling odd. Through the window, she saw now a forest, then a thicket of oak...white cottages...cows that never seemed to move. It was always the same on this train, on this route. He was sorry he'd kissed her. He was sorry that she had come to Tweedmouth's with him.

Oh, for God's sake listen to yourself.

His face was so quiet when he slept. She wasn't used to a quiet Faraday. He was pulling back, working on being more ordinary with her. That thought made her want a smoke, and a box of chocolate with no almonds.

"You know," he said with his eyes closed, "the biblical nature of this case reminds me of that Good Book and the Virgin Mary."

Eleanor smiled inside.

"She conceives, and an angel informs her of the name to be given to the Child—Immanuel, meaning God with us or something prophetic like that. Right from the angel's lips, a directive, what? Then, Mary has the child, and what does she name him?" He opened his eyes and fixed his gaze on Eleanor. "Jesus," he said with a flourish.

Eleanor laughed. "It was her favorite male name. The one she's always wanted to use for her firstborn son. The Lord could have left something up to her."

Laughing himself, Faraday pushed himself straighter in the seat. "Names are important."

"In the end, we are all in the end given the name that we deserve."

"Too true." Faraday stretched and flipped his head back and forth, testing, no doubt, to see if it still rattled. "Ah, my dear, I meant to apologize this morning for my behavior last night, but my mind wasn't up and running. I'm afraid the windblown strands of your lovely hair carried me away. I was a heel, and you should have slapped me. I promise to behave from now on."

The flutter in her chest was her heart falling into her stomach. "The name you deserve is cad then?" She hoped she didn't sound like an older woman jilted by her young lover. She couldn't bare him thinking she was being brave. She was getting foolish. To her relief Faraday kept talking.

"I wonder if money is a motive in this case or what money brings. I overheard Tweedmouth quote Saint Paul to the Duchess of Dover who, as you know, keeps rather loose marital vows. He said into her ear at a dinner party that she should walk by the spirit and not gratify the desires of the flesh."

"Imagine her shock at having to sit next to him in the first place and then that," said Eleanor.

"She boycotted that hostess's events for months after. His opinions didn't kill him, but they might have made the killing of him easier. He wanted to change people, not just complain about them. People are resistant to change, not only resistant, but also resentful and offended. He affected people that way." Faraday adjusted his jacket and smoothed back his hair. Hair was so easy for men.

"Enough to murder him?" she asked.

"Maybe not, but enough to encourage someone else to, or to hide that person. It will be hard to find anyone helpful. Finding that one person that knows something will be hard in this case. Tweedmouth's doctor, Brailford, doesn't like women by the way."

"What is it with men and women?" Eleanor's tone embarrassed her. It had been too harsh.

It's still Faraday, your friend. It wasn't much of a kiss. Hardly more than a peck on the cheek. Foolish girl.

"I'll go to Scotland Yard," he said. "Tweedmouth left gaping sores behind him that suggest all sorts of possible motives. It would be interesting to delve into his business dealings. He made money, almost overnight."

The offer to go to Scotland Yard startled Eleanor. "So you do think he might have been murdered?"

"Every possibility, what? I have a hunch that there are some great stories behind that man. I wonder if Louis is just too obvious."

Phew, there was at least that left. Eleanor could almost see Faraday rubbing his hands together.

He is here with you. That is enough. Eleanor tried to imagine this train ride on her own. The journey would be two hours of her mother's voice in her head. "Shall we meet for lunch at Le Meridian?"

"Great idea. I'll call and reserve," he said. "What are you going to ask Brailford?"

"Should the death warrant be signed? Asthma is a tricky disease. One might be at death's door for a month and then improve overnight. It's a simple question. It should only take a moment. I meant to show you this earlier. Pat McGlynn and her mother found it in some trousers they bought from the Jack's. The entire contents of the Baron's room are on the street."

Faraday raised his eyebrows as he took the photograph. "He didn't seem a photograph-saving type."

"It's not in very good shape. Saving seems a stretch. It was sandwiched between some verses and stuffed into a pocket."

"Do you have the scriptures?"

"Not in good shape either."

"If you give them to me, I know an expert."

Once in Paddington Station, Eleanor strolled on Faraday's arm to avoid porters, prostitutes, and pickpockets. She bought an orange from a little girl with dirty hands. If only she were younger, Eleanor kept thinking. If only he hadn't kissed her.

On Praed Street, men walked the sidewalk in sandwich boards that advertised Monkey Brand Soaps that promised to "scour the country as General French promises to scour South Africa." Eno's Fruit Salts claimed to be "the antiseptic of an Empire." Bovril promised to promote health and was given to wounded soldiers "upholding the British flag and contributing to the success of British valor."

"What do you think of the war?" she asked Faraday in their shared cab.

"We peers need full pockets. Africa is keeping most of us funded. You'll find a peer able to excuse most anything for a well lined purse."

"The flags suggest something more heroic...romantic."

"An inspiring flap. After all, we can't appear like robbers."

She had to admit that she thrived on her ostrich feathers from Africa and cheap tea, and gold, and all the luscious furs from Canada. Who didn't like the exotic? The South Africans wanted to control their own lives. She understood that too. Like the busy intersection in front of her, with carts, horses, autos, walkers, and carriages all heading somewhere and getting in each other's way, life was complicated.

She watched the cab take Faraday away. He was always so sure of himself. She was leaning on that. Too much she realized as she watched him being whisked away. Not but two minutes ago cold calling on Doctor Brailford had seemed the easiest thing in the world. Well, nothing for it now.

Eleanor could feel the tug of Bond Street and the fashion there. It was such a brief underground ride away and mere blocks from Harley Street. So much more enjoyable to shop than to confront the dismal doctor. Leave Tweedmouth to anyone who wanted him. She thought of the windows displaying bath powders, hosiery, and brooches, and moiré silks on the posed plastiques mannequins. They had to be ignored or her mother would never let her forget. Congratulating herself on her great self-discipline, she headed up the street toward doctor's row.

By the time she'd turned onto Braiford's stoop, she had the threads of a headache. The streets had been thick with carriages, animals, smells and standing tourists. Americans, Australians, and a large group of Japanese, standing their ground in front of a brick building, and she'd had to drunkenly wheel around their rooted bodies. Underground, the roar of electric trains pressed through the earth. A shroud of gray air made the noise feel less distinct which should have helped, but really made her more uneasy. Finally, she stared at a brass sign next to a Georgian door that simply said "Brailford."

"He is secure in his profession. I'm surprised the plate doesn't read, 'Brailford the best damn doctor in London—England—the world—ever.'"

She'd heard that Brailford treated the male sex, exclusively. Faraday had resisted offering his services in the visit. This was her idea.

Her boots sounded loud on the shiny, harlequin-tiled floor that led from the entrance to the waiting room. At the second door, her hat and her skirt hem introduced her, before the feminine line of her face and before the feminine sway of her hips. The stares of the men seated in leather chairs seemed a good grouping for a wax museum feature, "The Illnesses of Men."

The air was opaque from the endless cigars the patients smoked with a flourish. In this place, they didn't have to ask for permission. She figured she could detect which peer was in a room by the smell of his tobacco. Ill-humored and ill at ease, Eleanor walked across the room while delicately fanning away the fumy smells.

As if embarrassed about their ailments, the men's eyeballs rather than their heads followed her progress across the room. From the reception desk, the nurse, a big-sized man that taxed the legs of the chair in which he sat, called in a high voice, "Good afternoon."

Eleanor paused and tried not to stare. She could see she was having the same effect on him. She pushed back her hair again and remembered her card that she had ready. "Good afternoon, may I see Dr. Brailford? This is not a visit to seek his professional advice, as I am quite well. It is a murder investigation."

The nurse brazened through his shock like a man who had seen everything. He was smiling. There was an anticipatory glint in his eye, as Eleanor handed him her card. "It is a small matter. Lord Henry Faraday, the barrister"—she chickened out, used his name— "asked me to come by, not because the matter is unimportant, but because the matter just needs a moment."

Quiet lingered between them. She could hear her breath. Their eyes held and the nurse seemed to wait for her to flinch. He hadn't taken her card. It seemed to hover while being held between the finger and thumb of her glove.

"See here," a patient said. "You can't come in here no matter what the errand. Lord Faraday should know better."

Eleanor turned. She had recognized the speaker on her way in. She would have known him anyway by his voice. She knew he'd give her trouble. He hadn't changed. There was another man as well, both of them old brothel friends of her husband's. She noted the ashen pallor of the scoundrels. Whatever else happened today, it was worth the inconvenience to see those two simpletons suffering. Nightly, they had laughed their grotesque laughs in her home until she hated the sound of their voices, their footsteps. That they were watching made her desperate.

Eleanor turned back to the nurse and held her card closer to him. "It's just a very few questions."

You rogue, take the card.

The nurse finally reached for it with sausage-like, manicured fingers. He told her to wait a minute and heaved his weight from the chair. The imprint of his backside in the black leather was permanent. The nurse was not a fast walker. Father Time was a sprinter in comparison. With the men harrumphing behind her, she put a hand over her thumping heart and applied pressure.

"No," the nurse said as he collapsed into his brave seat. He watched her, a cat waiting for the mouse to move.

She felt the terror of the rodent. God, now what?

They were all watching her—her husband's old friends, the smirking nurse. She wanted to pull all their lower lips over their receding hairlines. The bulk of the nurse felt like a brick wall. She couldn't breathe. One patient, the dearest friend of her husband, had his eyes locked on her, and then he stood as if to manhandle her out the door, just let the ass touch her. She noted the empty chair beside him. Eleanor felt her mind tingle.

She swirled to face the nurse. "Well...then...I will sit and wait until the doctor is free. I will sit between these old friends of my husband's. It has been a long time since they have been guests in my home. I'm interested in what they have been doing this past year." She swept to an empty chair and sat as if she meant to sit there forever. The man on her left straightened, and the other man, on her right, seemed sunburned in the dark shade of the room. He began to sweat in its cool interior. She smelled his illness and his fear of it. Eleanor winked at the nurse. "I can think of a few reasons why these two aren't feeling too well." The damn nurse would have to lift her out.

"You poor thing, you look just awful," she said to her husband's old friend on her right.

The nurse, too big to be intimidated, stood. He was too smart to let the drama continue for a moment longer even if it might be for his own amusement. His shoulders quivered. The brute was laughing as he again walked away. After a time, the door opened. "He'll see you."

Inside the inner sanctum, Eleanor ran into yet another surprised, male patient. "Oh, close your mouth," she muttered. "I'm not the first female you've ever seen in your life."

Brailford didn't peer at her from behind his thick spectacles. He didn't even glance up. He continued writing.

I can wait.

The place was glisteningly bright. Electric lights. So Brailford accommodated invention. The medical tomes that stood at attention on a bookshelf, all with his name as author stamped in gold letters said as much. He didn't just cure people. He studied their diseases. A thesis lay on Brailford's desk, *Five Orders of Skin Diseases and Innumerable Subdivisions.*

The title was easy to read upside down and from a distance in the artificial light. The window was excessive. Through it though she appreciated the well-tended, prodigious red roses that preened in the natural sunlight. Love. Not Brailford, she thought as the man continued to put her in her place by ignoring her.

The sound of the pen nib on paper stopped. When he did lift his head, his eyes held no anger as she had expected. As he was inspecting her, she remembered her featherless hat. He didn't address her. He waited and scrutinized her without blinking. Her palms itched and she rubbed them along her dress.

"Baron Tweedmouth is dead," she blurted out.

"When?"

"Yesterday."

"Do you know how?"

"The doctor said asphyxiation, but he had also fallen from a balcony."

Brailford waited. She noticed that his beard was trimmed to the last hair, and that his face was shuttered with suggested boredom, but his eyes gleamed. The shine of his polished desk seemed muted against them.

Eleanor remained standing after the opening words, though none of the sentences had been spoken in her favor. Being in the room with this man was like being made to play cards with a balding uncle at Christmas, the uncle always had to win. In this light, she was sure that Brailford could see the heavy thump of her heart against her blouse. He had a way with women that made them want to jump out a window. "Was Tweedmouth close to death?" she asked after a moment.

"I have no idea."

"Sir?"

"I...have...no...idea. Tell Lord Faraday that, if you please."

"He was your patient." She felt she was hustling to return a serve in tennis.

"Why is it again that Faraday asked you to come?"

"It's just a small question, Dr. Brailford."

"It's an enormous question. I do not talk about my patients."

"So, he is your patient."

"Just tell Faraday that I don't know." He turned his chair to shelve a book. He shoved it into place with too much force.

Standing in her place by the door, she studied Brailford. She watched as he moved the sheet he had been writing on to the top of a very neat pile. He took a clean sheet and smoothed it. He peeked up at her and seemed surprised that she was still in the room.

It came to her, then. His curtness beyond impatience; his precise hair; his polished desk; and his smooth leather thesis, Tweedmouth wasn't his patient anymore. Tweedmouth had left this precise, vain man. He'd had the unmitigated gall to turn his back on this God-physician, but Brailford was still interested in Tweedmouth, and he wasn't going to let on.

"Why would Baron Tweedmouth leave such a skilled doctor as you?" She measured her voice for awe and humility. She absorbed his direct glance and kept her face polite, not haughty. She delighted under her hat that sat low on her forehead and shaded her eyes.

"Tell Lord Faraday that I have no immediate knowledge of why the Baron died. The man was a fool."

Nothing for The Times there. It was a good start, though. Eleanor tried not to smile one whit larger. "Yes, indeed he was a fool." She waited for the doctor to vent further.

"The man has been following the advice of quacks for months now. He's been trying all their trumped up, illogical, money-grubbing remedies. Who knows what he's been eating or drinking? He went to Bath against my advice. There, Lady, he bathed next to people with weeping sores. The waste there is full of the regurgitations of the sick. The place is toxic. Quite frankly, with all of that and with his wife up his nose smelling like a morgue full of decaying lavender, I'm surprised that he lived this long."

"Scent bothered him?"

"Harvey," Dr. Brailford bellowed like a bull in rut.

"So you thought he was dying? Was he going to die from his asthma? What about the twenty-four-hour rule? Will you sign the death certificate?" She tried all the questions at once, hoping he would answer, no, no, yes in a reflexive manner, but the office door opened within the breadth of her four sentences, as if the nurse had been there all the time.

"See the lady out. And Madame, next time, tell Lord Faraday that he must come himself."

"You ruined his day," the burly nurse said to her in the hallway.

She held back, as he called in a patient. "I don't suppose you would like to answer some questions about Baron Tweedmouth?" Eleanor asked when Harvey returned. Why he would, she couldn't imagine after the card incident. He motioned for her to follow him, and he took Eleanor to a closet-like room off the reception area. He gestured toward a small, rectangular table. She'd never seen a simple oak table shine so. Two immaculate teacups, England's own, perched on a shelf above the table—on doilies.

When he took two cups down, she understood that he was about to serve her tea. She noticed the scent of oranges and cloves haunted the room, and she searched for the source. She found the punctured fruit on another shelf in a Lenox bowl. With piqued interest, she watched the big man move about his tiny closet with slow grace.

On a wood stove that filled the end of the room and heated it, the nurse put on a black, iron kettle. She studied the man's back. "Nurse" was an amusing word for him. She realized that curiosity danced between them. He wanted to know about her and she, him. He hummed.

This is a man who likes drama and likes gossip.

"Be right back. Got to pull some papers. Here's the pot. It's been scalded, and tea's in it."

Eleanor rose. With oven mitts and the steaming kettle, she scalded the cups, and added water to the pot. She was sitting when the nurse returned with a jug of milk and a sugar pot. He took out some spoons, poured the tea into the cups, and sat down.

The nurse smiled. "Harvey Mitchell."

"Eleanor Albright."

"Not lady?"

"If you like, but not over tea in a man's back room. Why all this?"

He seemed to appreciate the answer and the question. Harvey filled the room. He must be brilliant when it came time for lifting patients.

"I didn't know you'd come about Tweedmouth," Harvey said after his first sip.

"You didn't like him?"

"God no. I'll have to come and go, mind you, when the bell chimes."

"Oh yes, of course. I imagine that Dr. Brailford never bellows."

"No. Today is an exception."

"I may have been talking to the wrong person altogether. You would know quite a bit about everything that goes on here."

Harvey preened in an Olivia-like manner. Eleanor had to admit, it looked better on Olivia.

"When the Baron first took ill, oh, years ago, he was in here every day," Harvey said.

Eleanor sat back into her seat. It had been padded with purple cotton, Egyptian, it felt like—three hundred count.

"He was doing well, then he was here ranting and demanding better care. 'I can't breathe man,' he'd say. 'Fix it.' Then, he'd fall quiet, wheezing like a fireplace bellows."

"Sounds like he was getting worse."

"Sudden like."

"When was that day?"

A bell chimed. "Excuse me, there's his chime. He wants the next patient."

What to ask...what to ask, she thought. This gossipy man was like a gift from heaven. She wondered how such a conversationalist as Harvey had remained in a job like this. The door opened, and Harvey was about to edge past her when he asked her to exchange seats with him, to get to the door easier, he explained.

They exchanged teacups. Harvey refilled his and offered Eleanor more. "How did you ever get into this?" he asked.

"I'm worried for Louis. Do you know him?"

"Influenza. Came here for influenza. I liked him."

"So, when did Tweedmouth leave Doctor Brailford?"

Harvey leaned back in his chair and studied Eleanor. "Very good. You think the Baron was murdered?"

"Would you be surprised if I told you that Tweedmouth died from his asthma?"

"The doctor has theories. He's a good doctor."

"Tweedmouth didn't think so," Eleanor answered.

"Dr. Brailford was upset to have him gone, especially with the Baron doing so well for so long."

"What was he taking...when he was doing well?"

"Diet management."

The bell chimed again. Harvey stood. "Don't worry about them cups— those cups. I'll rinse them. Here, I'll see you out and let in a patient. Why don't I get you something Doctor Brailford has written on the subject?"

"Why doesn't the good doctor like women?"

"A very bad marriage."

She gave him a wry smile. "We do have something in common."

"I can meet you at Berners at four-thirty...with a book."

As she left, she thought that asthma was a tricky disease. If the brute had died of his illness, she'd be fair game, and her mother would have to move to Canada. More bad news, Tweedmouth didn't seem to have an attending physician.

❧ 10 ❧

Marriage is the triumph of imagination over intelligence.
—Oscar Wilde

As she walked past Cavendish Square and then along Henrietta Place toward the top of Bond Street, Eleanor noticed that she still had some time before meeting Faraday. She had survived a meeting with the devil and two of the worst of her husband's reprobate friends. A reward was in order. There was enough time for a quick shop, at least for a new hat. She couldn't lunch at Le Meridian with this one. She'd have her hair done. That sounded marvelous. She could brave anything in a new hat. Dressing with style was part of a woman's prerogative.

The dining room was off-season, and cream Rococo chairs waited for occupants. Escorted to a table where Faraday waited, Eleanor sunk into the well-padded chair. The pink marble columns against gold walls calmed her after the morning's activities. Oriental carpets hushed the few waiters' footsteps—a relief from the outside. The small dining room was set in an alcove along the main wide hallway that was lined with tables only meant for tea.

76

She felt so much more whole with her hair in place and a new wide winter straw hat with blue ribbons and ostrich feathers. Ostrich feathers. Life was complicated.

"How did it go?" Faraday asked.

"I had to blackmail the nurse to let me in."

"Such a necessary skill."

Eleanor laughed. Comments like this were what she loved about Henry Faraday. "I threatened to renew my acquaintance with some of my husband's old friends who were in the waiting room."

"Instead of ushering you out of the building, he ushered you inside."

"The male nurse appreciated the gleam in my eye, and two of my husband's old friends were there waiting to be treated. I said that I'd keep them company."

Faraday choked on the drink of red wine he had drunk. "Without doubt," he said as he wiped his mouth with his napkin. "So, you did see Brailford."

"Yes, but nothing came of it. Afterwards, the nurse, Harvey Mitchell..."

"The one who appreciated the gleam in your eye?"

"The same, gave me tea, a session that was much more profitable."

A waiter came, gloved in cream to match the decor. He was all deference, as they ordered roast lamb.

"I've never been to Brailford," said Faraday.

"His nurse is a man who has a Lenox bowl full of clove scented oranges in his work room. He's a big man that you wouldn't want to meet in a boxing ring."

"I'm not sure I'd want to meet anyone in a boxing ring."

"I suppose not. He knows what is going on in that office. He's bringing me a treatise of Dr. Brailford's on allergies. Berners at four-thirty."

"So Brailford didn't tell you much, but Harvey did."

Eleanor leaned forward. "On the bad side, Harvey told me that the Baron couldn't walk from 'a' to 'b' his last day with Braiford. On the other hand, it does seem unlikely under such circumstances that he'd be strolling along the parapet."

"It's a short stroll."

"Hardly worth the effort if one can't get from 'a' to 'b.'"

"It does mean he had gotten quite ill." She'd been thinking about how Faraday would take that news, like he'd hired onto a sinking ship. The mushroom soup had just arrived. It smelled of pepper. She was ravenous, and as he didn't say something like what a fool's errand you've got me into, she enjoyed telling Faraday the rest of the story.

"He also said that Tweedmouth's condition worsened. Brailford had put Tweedmouth on diet therapy that seemed to be working. The doctor was using him as a case study because it was working."

"Maybe he was off his diet?"

"The thesis will be an interesting read. There is something that Brailford told me. The Scented Woman was up the Baron's nose, or her strong perfume was."

"Up his nose?"

"Yes, up his nose."

"As in part of his breathing apparatus?"

Eleanor tapped her nose. "Do you think her perfume has any significance? If so, why would she wear so much?"

"To kill him? So many ways to kill a man, so little time."

"Brailford told me that the Baron was drinking vomit-infested water at Bath. I shall never go again with the same relish." She put down her fork. She felt that she was done eating.

"Let's go to Scotland Yard when we are finished eating."

"You didn't go yet? What have you been doing?"

"Recovering at Whites. I had another little nap."

She studied him. "You do look better."

"You should go with me anyway. I'll introduce you around."

Eleanor was touched. He had been casual about the whole thing, but it didn't matter. He was going to introduce her to people at The Yard.

Eleanor ate pudding cake and had coffee. She sat saturated in the place, the conversation, and the company. There was no one around to begin an inquisition, to cluck a tongue, or to point a finger. The lack of society was blissful. She had two cups of coffee and enjoyed the sound of Faraday's voice. She remembered the kiss. *Stop it.* He'd be shocked to know her thoughts, and she'd be embarrassed. How that peck affected her so. She needed to get it into perspective. Albert would laugh. She didn't want Albert anywhere near her thoughts. Good riddance. Oh, for Gods' sake.

"He did suddenly get worse," she said again.

"So you said. Shall we be off, what? I told Inspector Young we'd be there by one."

. . .

The Thames was busy with barges. Watching them, Eleanor felt the upset of the Brailford-encounter lift. She was spending more time with Faraday since this case started. She needed to be wary about that, but not today. New Scotland Yard the sign said. She got to walk deep inside the building without question. This was a good day.

Faraday paused to knock once at the door of an inspector before opening it. Inside was a fit man who continued to have a waist in spite of his advancing years. Raised, thick eyebrows met her gaze. The man must have had Scottish ancestors.

He glanced at her and then to Henry. "Faraday! Aren't you out of town for the season?"

"I am. Bagged a thousand red grouse yesterday."

The Inspector rounded his desk to shake Lord Faraday's hand. "Good day. So what are you doing here?" He bowed toward Eleanor.

"The Baron of Tweedmouth died yesterday," Faraday said as they all settled into chairs. "He fell from a balcony in the middle of the night. Chief Constable Owens, in Whitney, has called it death by natural causes."

"But he fell off a balcony?"

"The coroner deduced that he quit breathing. Owens deduced that he then fell," said Faraday.

The Inspector leaned back in his chair. "You're thinking otherwise?"

"Let me introduce Lady Eleanor Albright. She's very good at chemistry. She noticed a strange constriction in the body's irises."

The Inspector took in Eleanor. She colored at Faraday's words and at the Scotland Yard man's frank appraisal. It warmed her that he would speak professionally about her. He had never used words like that before. Probably, he didn't want to encourage her, but here they were.

"We're starting with the doctor. It seems that Tweedmouth was ill—too ill to be strolling along a balcony railing. He might have gone over with someone's help."

"Did you tell Owens?"

"Not yet."

The Inspector pushed a cigarette case toward Faraday. "Can't trust his instincts?"

Faraday shook his head no. "Only in fishing. Unparalleled in coarse bass."

"I don't suppose that Tweedmouth will be missed by many," said the Inspector.

"There's a fortune in money at stake. What do you know about the duels Tweedmouth fought? You ever catch him? Did he ever kill anyone?"

"The duels...of course." Young reached forward to get a cigarette and then remembered Eleanor and glanced at her.

"No, please go ahead," she said. On second thought, Faraday perched himself on a corner of the desk, and then he too took a cigarette from the plain brown box. They lit up. The office had darkly stained molding framed white, plastered walls. The heavy furniture made it feel masculine. The inspector had a few papers on his desk and a folded newspaper. A finger-printing apparatus sat on a side table with smudged prints stacked beside it. He had been practicing.

"Tweedmouth did maim a number of them—enough so that they went away whining. He killed one, a Boston banker. I always wondered why this one? Tweedmouth was a dead-on shot. He could have bagged all of them. He claimed at his club, Bootles, that he never intended to kill the man. His opponent did get a shot off that hit Tweedmouth's shoulder. Either the Baron let him get off the first shot, or the banker got lucky and that made Tweedmouth mad. No one brought charges, the banker's wife included. I figured she'd been paid off."

"Children?"

"Just a young daughter. He was a small, fierce man—not more than five feet six inches, seven stone, not much of a target. What his aims were in bringing Tweedmouth to the field, no one knows," said the inspector. "The good thing about that duel is that it was Tweedmouth's last. The city's last as well. Whenever we heard of a duel, we thought of Tweedmouth first. He was a provocative kind of person–smug, self-made, and young blue-bloods loved to try to best him."

The Young's S.H. Couch Company telephone rang. The inspector jumped and recovered. "Yes," he answered holding the earpiece as if it might bite his ear. He spoke into the mouthpiece. He also spoke word by word and in a low tone as required by telephone courtesy. The telephone instructions that the inspector had on his desk, also said to treat the phone as you would treat someone's ear and to replace the earpiece without dropping it.

She wondered how the old guard handled technology. The inspector seemed to be moving with the times, cautiously. She swallowed a giggle.

After the phone call, Faraday said, "Do you think those old resentments may have been resurfacing with Tweedmouth in a weakened state?"

"Most families took their young lads to task as being stupid and reckless.

They were glad nothing more had happened. As I said, the banker was killed, and that was all hush, hush. The widow wouldn't speak to anyone."

"The wife and daughter American?"

"No, English."

"Who invested in Tweedmouth?"

"This banker. Albert Albright was the second man at the duel." The inspector startled and glanced at Eleanor. "Begging your pardon, Lady Albright, I'd say that it's a long shot being murdered over something that happened over twenty years ago."

E leanor walked beside Faraday along Queen's Park with her skirt brushing the colored leaves as they walked down Queen's Lane and passed Spencer House and then York House.

"Albert is sleazy enough to help Tweedmouth cheat the banker."

"It's becoming more personal," Faraday said.

The heat from Indian summer was easing into normal October chill, but there was still no rain. A few workers ate in the yellowing park under the linden trees. There were no flowers late or otherwise, something Eleanor always had wondered at. Still, the park was clean in its simple lines of trees and grass. The Mall along Saint James Park had nary a soul on it. The trees though were gay with active squirrels. She could smell the odoriferous Thames.

"Albert can take care of himself. If I were still living with him, I'd leave him. As I've already left him, I'm ahead of myself and that's unusual for me. I'm always the first to be the last in line."

She ambled along the path with Faraday. "Any of the Baron's goodwill contrasts with all the self-righteousness that glowed from the man's tarnished halo. He, as a candidate for a natural death, may be wrong," said Eleanor, "because his past is so—"

"Sinful, and his conversion superficial, his goodwill but a drop in an ocean?"

"People, like my mother, can't accept that an ill man would be murdered. Just wait, they think, and let nature take its course. Eleanor linked her arm through Faraday's bent elbow. She walked closer to him. "The alternative would be to strike and to let his illness take the blame."

"Irritating people seldom recover from serious illness."

"Save the tread on the doctor's shoe." She gazed at his profile. Her heart warmed. She sighed and looked forward again. "What if there's a time schedule? He's lingering and lingering—"

"And lingering."

"Or...what if realizing that he is even closer to death, he is reconsidering his life, once again? For instance, his will."

Faraday stopped short. He took Eleanor by the shoulders and kissed her forehead. "For instance, his will," he repeated. "You are brilliant."

Once they arrived at Berners, Faraday opened the door and escorted Eleanor to a table. Harvey arrived on time to the clock striking the half hour and had brought with him a somber thesis entitled: *A Treatise on Allergies; How to Control the Asthmatic Reaction*. He put it in front of her and then sat like the gilded chair across from her was a throne. He placed his two index fingers on the edge of the white linen tablecloth. He rubbed his fingertips along the fabric away from each other and back.

Eleanor signaled the waiter to bring tea. Harvey sat in his carved chair as if on the point of a silver needle. A waiter filled his floral cup with the holy water of high tea, and joy suffused the nurse. As Berners was feeding and watering Harvey on gateau, pudding cake and trifle, Eleanor thought about Albert. Whatever she'd said to Faraday or to herself, she couldn't stop thinking that she may be married to a murderer. Weren't his other vices enough for God's sake?

Poverty and oysters always seem to go together.
—Charles Dickens

After strutting back to the office from tea and cakes at Berners, Harvey asked Dr. Brailford for a day off. He planned to catch the evening train to Whitney, and he needed time to look up the gentleman. He had news for Louis.

By six o'clock he managed to be sitting on a slatted bench in the train station in his Windsor tie and white shirt with wing collar. He had dabbed on cologne, combed his whiskers, and added brilliantine to his hair until it was stiff. He hummed to himself under the noise of the crowd in the station. Between the knees of his lounge suit, he had his hands stacked on his lion-head walking stick. The thing had cost him a mint.

With the train called, he sauntered to third class, tapping the stick ahead of him and tipping a derby to the ladies. He stopped once to take out a golden pocket watch. Harvey didn't care about the time. He knew it from a clock on the wall. He just wanted it seen, and he wanted to feel the weight of it in his hand and to appreciate the curved numbers on its face. How long he'd saved for the instrument, gone without.

Tucked into third class, Harvey was dizzy with excitement. He would arrive just in time for a late dinner. Lord Louis would have to put him up for the night. Maybe his information would gain him a good room with morning chocolate on a tray carried by some sweet maid who curtsied. Louis had seemed a decent type, the times he'd been through Brailford's office.

As the train rumbled toward the Cotswold, Harvey played the fantasy through his mind. Third class carriages smelled of inadequate hygiene, but the strength of Harvey's imagination transformed his environment to a luxurious first-class passage. With his walking stick again propped between his legs, he sat with a straight back, and he never moved all the way to the Whitney. Passengers getting on and off had to step around the girth of his calves and the length of his patent leather shoes.

In Whitney, Harvey had to secure a lift to the castle. He couldn't afford a cab. He loitered near the Hound and Horse Pub, stopping young men coming out with a touch to their shoulder. Few people passed by the castle on a regular basis.

Begging outside the local pub for a ride to Abbey Leix didn't match the persona of the gentleman that Harvey had spent considerable time and money trying to cultivate, but he couldn't do anything about it. He prayed for good luck.

When he walked down the drive under the lime trees, the sun had dipped below the horizon.

He knocked on the door just under a black crape ribbon hanging at eye level. Waiting for the butler, Harvey used the moment to dream of the welcome he might expect if he had been higher born, or if he had been clever, as had been the Baron himself. He envisioned himself knocking as a peer with three smart raps, and then he pictured the butler taking his overcoat and bowing over his hat.

The great door opened, and he entered, feeling his significance. He had after all important news for Louis. Harvey lingered in the great hall, waiting with his hat in his hand.

T he new Baron had him sit in an over-stuffed chair by a large fire and had put a whiskey in his hand. Every, single impression of the room inebriated Harvey. Every moment had flavor. The heavy gold fabric of the curtains warmed him; the blue carpet on the floor cushioned his step; the branched chandelier lit his face. Louis sat opposite him, a study in stillness, and his eyes, behind spectacles unfocused. Harvey was forgotten. Louis stared at the fire—uncaring, it seemed, about anything. Louis slouched under the profound bags that drooped from his eyes. Harvey hadn't expected mourning. No sane person would mourn Tweedmouth.

"Lady Albright came by to see Doctor Brailford this morning." There was no reaction from Louis. Harvey shuffled in his chair to hone his voice louder. "I said that Lady Albright came by to see Doctor Brailford."

"She what?" Louis coughed as if a dose of Scotch had tickled his windpipe.

"She wanted to know if the Baron's illness was bad enough to kill him. I think she's trying to prove he was poisoned."

That was good. Louis would be glad he came to tell him that. Harvey thought that they'd talk about the Baron's health or about silly women. He had pictured an, if not happy, then content son, glad of his father's death, and then a heartfelt thanks about this woman nosing about. This was beastly. "I told her he was sick, very sick."

Louis stood and walked to a side table like the weight of his body was more than his spine could support. He pulled a stopper from the neck of a decanter. His hand shook as he poured. The dose of scotch was large, four fingers.

He's gone over the bend. Harvey sat with his own drink held mid-body. He watched the new Baron drown himself in two of the four fingers.

Louis stood hunched over, leaning on the table. The man shuddered, whether from an undying ghost of a memory or from the Scotch burning through him, Harvey couldn't decide.

The fire was high. Louis sat again next to it. His thoughts burned red hot on his face, or the crimson color was the drink, or the flames.

Harvey gulped at his own whiskey. He had come for sherry—certainly not for scotch. Still, the drink was quality. Harvey ogled the now smoldering man. Maybe he had done it. The nurse thought he must say something more, or the evening would be lost.

"Brailford asked her to leave. Nothing, of course, will come of it. We are, after all, in total agreement."

Harvey noticed that that had sounded like blackmail. He could feel the sweat under his arms. Gentlemen didn't perspire. He felt cooler when Louis didn't respond.

"He told me once that he'd had two girls," Louis said from his deep engagement with the golden flames.

The sentence amazed Harvey. "Who...who?"

"And then he laughed," Louis finished.

The man had lost his mind. Harvey felt a right flounder in saying, "I came to you straight away. I came myself. So much better than a wire for these delicate matters. Your father was our patient for many years. I just wanted you to know that we are steadfast. I am sorry about your father." The room was too hot. Harvey put down his drink. He was sweating. His hand dived for a handkerchief. He couldn't be sweating here.

"Please, don't say that he was a good man."

"No, I wouldn't say...I mean...."

"Yes, I know. You don't need to go on."

Dabbing at his forehead, Harvey contemplated the room, the portraits of Lord and Lady Tweedmouth staring at each other. He remembered the mural in the hallway. All the rumors were true, then. He felt sorry for the kind, small man in the soft chair.

"Why do you suppose he would say that to me?" Louis seemed to speak from a sad place and into the room rather than to anyone particular.

The boy was unhinged. Things were all wrong. Harvey wanted graciousness, food and drink, gratefulness at lease. He wasn't even getting awareness. He inspected Lord Louis's fragile jaw and tender eyes that were so distinct from his father's. Harvey had no idea what to say to that. The room was so hot. "Girls?" Harvey faltered.

Louis started laughing. He stood and slapped the nurse on the shoulder and picked up the decanter.

Harvey held his glass out in front of him and felt the weight of it increase with the pour. The camaraderie that had been missing in the room was easing itself into the evening. Relieved, Harvey drank even though he hated whiskey. Still, to make the best of the evening, he sat into his chair, as all men of wealth sat—fully, and he pondered with deep expression as all rich men ponder.

Louis walked back to his chair from replacing the decanter. Harvey noticed that Louis's glass had been refilled. The nurse relaxed further and let the horsehair stuffing cradle him. Louis sat forward on the edge of the settee and against its arm.

"The Baron," Harvey coughed, "your father was—"

"What?"

"Ignoble." He was proud of using that word.

"My dear father was much more than that," Louis said with a smirk.

"Then, Lord Tweedmouth, let the words die with him," said Harvey.

The thought seemed to make a difference to Louis who turned his head to study Harvey.

"You're so right." Louis laid his head back and closed his eyes.

Numb, Harvey sat back too, until the butler and the valet put them both to bed without dinner At dawn, Harvey lifted his throbbing head to the sound of a carriage. Alarmed about his continued care, he shifted the curtains and confirmed his dread. Louis, without his jacket or cravat, in the cold and half-light of the morning, was getting into an unmarked vehicle.

W hile passing through the village on his return from an early ride in the brilliant morning sun, Faraday saw Harvey walk into the train station. Faraday sat back and considered the implications. Taking his watch from his chest pocket, Faraday noted that it was ten minutes until the London train. He wondered whether it would be worth anything to hunt this game down. He'd already guessed why Harvey was here, maybe he'd just check out his theory.

Standing on the platform, Harvey had gravity that gave Faraday's intuition pause. Still, Faraday was overjoyed at his find. The nurse, caught with his hands in both pockets. Why not? There's a good meal to be had at both venues. Well, maybe not at Louis's. Harvey appeared flagged. Time to bulk him up. A good libation loosens a man's stiff tongue. He didn't think Eleanor would see it that way, though.

"Mr. Mitchell. How was your stay?"

"Lord Faraday!" Harvey's body twitched. His eyes darted.

Probably looking for a barrel to jump into.

"Did the new Baron serve you well?"

"The scotch was exquisite," Harvey said with some disappointment in his eyes, resignation in his voice.

He knows that his days at Berners are at an end. "The conversation?"

"Somewhat undirected."

"Well, they are in mourning."

"Quite," said Harvey glancing away.

The nurse appeared green. *He's feeling a similar color, I'll bet.* So, Louis was drinking again last night.

"Too late for a restorative tea? I'm just coming in from a hard ride, and Dunn will anticipate me with a great spread. Are you expected back at an exact time?"

"I did have something of a light breakfast, distracted as the household was...and no dinner," he muttered.

Faraday dropped down from his horse. "Let me get us a ride."

At home, Faraday left his horse at the stable and clapped his leather gloves against his palm as he walked across the yard. He whistled Bach—his mood was good. "Dunn, a Mr. Mitchell is arriving to feast. Can we accommodate him?"

"Of course, my Lord."

Moments later, Dunn had Harvey seated. The big nurse fixed his eyes upon the room. Faraday followed Harvey's glance to ancient curtains and to the silver plate at the sideboard.

"I suspect that if I lift a picture, there would be a perfect square of a darker orange," Faraday said.

"You rent, then?" Disappointment flowed from the big man.

"The chairs are comfortable. I can take just about anything but an uncomfortable chair. Here's the tea, what?"

Harvey perked up at seeing the creamy Lenox cups. "I may have a clue for you, your lordship. There was one thing," he said in a conspirator's tone. "Girls."

"Not following."

Harvey shrugged. "The Baron said to Louis that he, the Baron, had had two girls."

"Really? He'd had them, or he had them?"

The nurse's eyebrows went up. "God knows."

"Does Louis understand the reference?"

"It seems to burden him. The atmosphere of the whole place is burdened. Unnecessarily, of course, unless he did it. Not that I would blame him." Harvey picked up a brownie and bit into it. "Delicious."

"Something new Dunn's discovered. So Louis is in mourning?"

"For that blighter?" Harvey's eyes widened with his slip of tongue. He patted at his mustache with the linen from his knee.

"No, you are so right," said Faraday.

Harvey busied himself with his tea and with stacking his plate with a feast of cakes. Faraday reached forward to a cigarette box and took one out. As he smoked, he assessed Harvey Mitchell. Not a fool. Likes his creature comforts. Gossipy. Not bad but can't trust him any more than an untrained hound. Comes to the hand that feeds him.

Faraday picked up a plate of sandwiches that Harvey had missed. "You must try one of these. Dunn has a twist to the spread that makes them perfect."

Faraday glanced toward the window when he heard a carriage. He leaned forward and took a cucumber sandwich. He kept his eyes down and smiled a little. Another chance encounter. Life was about to get more interesting.

When Eleanor walked in, Harvey stood upsetting his plate, and then he fumbled on the floor picking up brownie and pie and sandwiches.

"Harvey?" Eleanor gazed at the man's bent back and then to Faraday.

The nurse straightened, his smile brave but wavering. He was going to give reconciliation a valiant try. He had nothing to lose, and he could no doubt still taste the clotted cream from Berners.

"It seems that my guest here has paid a quiet visit to stronghold Tweedmouth. Have you any questions for him?"

Faraday's interest moved from the fat, hovering nurse to the woman who was staring the poor man down to his grave. He had never in his life seen Eleanor speechless. It took some moments before she sank into a chair and spoke. "Indeed."

Faraday offered her a cigarette, and she took it. Her eyes narrowed as she inhaled. The poor man was in her sights.

"And the Baroness?" She continued as if she'd been there all along.

Magnificent woman. Faraday could sit back now. She wasn't going to spit in the nurse's eye. That's what he loved about her.

"I didn't see the Baroness. Closeted in her room I expect," Harvey purred.

"Could you tell if she was there at all? What about Renard?" she clipped. The big nurse was wilting. Still, Faraday had faith in his maneuverability. He was an agile man in spite of his weight. What she could bring to his life was dear to him. Faraday liked anyone who could sport a gold watch and a lion's head outside his station with dignity, not to mention the china.

"No, I didn't see anyone else beyond the butler and a valet. Very quiet, all that despair a little thick if you ask me." Harvey seemed to be getting a bit of his spirit back.

Faraday refilled his cup. The man needed sustenance. Eleanor's hard look hadn't abated. He was in for a difficult dig out from where he had buried himself. Harvey drank the tea in a gulp, and then he stacked cakes on a napkin. "God, you know as well as myself that the Baron was, well, twisted. There, I've said it. No one else will. Except for the man being important because of the Doctor's thesis, I think Doctor Brailford was glad to see the man's royal behind. Let me just say this one thing more. Doctor Brailford is a great doctor, and he had the Baron's illness under control."

Harvey's nose was high in the air by the end of the oration. He stood, but Eleanor blocked his first step with her foot.

"Any other tidbits? What did you talk about? Did he speak of any conversations with a Chief Constable Owens?"

"Not a bit of it. Conversation, as I said, was as meager as the meal. Tweedmouth was always saying things like my son's weak or stupid. I think he killed his father. Guilt all over him."

Eleanor smashed out her cigarette. "Any proof?"

Harvey inhaled. Some crumbs fell from his mouth to his to his shirt and then to the floor. "What I meant is that I'm surprised Louis shouldn't have killed him at any time. The Baron was awful to the boy."

"Yet he managed to slog on," Eleanor said.

Harvey gathered the ends of his napkin full of food and glanced toward the door.

"You're an intelligent man, intuitive," said Eleanor. "Anything happen at the castle that was out of the ordinary besides the general pallor?"

"Out of the ordinary? Have you seen the place? The whole place is out of the ordinary. It is a general pallor. It's like a blasted shrine to the God of religious excess. Gave me the willies. You couldn't be normal and live there."

Harvey clutched his sweets and added, "Maybe I do have proof." He eyeballed Faraday. "Lord Louis left early this morning. Early. Without his cravat." He paused like he was waiting for Faraday's brain to catch up. "Well, I did say that I'd be back for the afternoon appointments." He'd milked this cow.

Faraday stood and extended his hand. "Thank you, Mr. Mitchell. I'll ring for Dunn and have him bring the car around."

"Anytime you want my advice, absolutely anytime. At your service." Harvey pumped Faraday's arm.

"Thank you. I'll remember that. Goodbye."

Eleanor sat back. "Another party heard from. Louis will hang himself and end it all. I want to cry."

As he listened to his car leave, Faraday lit another cigarette. The engine sounded harmonious, all the cogs in unison. "My God, what a cast of characters," he said into the room. "Looking up at the lip of that balcony, I knew what Owens was thinking, that nobody is going to miss the old tick. Even in death, there was something horrifying about the Baron. Let it be, murmured the consensus of everyone's deep collective thought. Owens had been the most desperate of all to let dead dogs die. Louis had won, I thought." He took a drag on his cigarette. "Light conquering the darkness. The good Lord had answered his prayers, or maybe Louis had answered his own prayers. Either way, I say bless him. The Baron was a great Old Testament character. He would, could, and did sacrifice his son." Faraday's retriever walked into the room and dropped at his master's feet. He sat forward to stroke the dog.

The animal reminded him of Louis, fair, loyal, kind-hearted. "It's not going well for him."

"I said he couldn't keep it down."

"Superior judgment." Faraday liked Eleanor sitting across from him on his sofa. The deep blue of her eyes, the depth of her soul, and the impulsiveness of her nature that kept her thoughts fresh, made him tingle. He appreciated the way she smoked with her fine, tapered fingers cupping the cigarette in the curve just below the bed of her pink nail, and the way she blew smoke from her almost parted lips. Faraday didn't want her to change. This hunt would change her. It was already changing him. "Harvey was a bonus. Are you here for something?"

"The Will. I think that we should get a copy if possible. Is that possible, at all, through some line of action? I still think that Charlotte is involved. She is self-absorbed and has never shown a bit of conscience that I've ever seen. Louis could be protecting her. Renard would know something."

"Possibly, but her solicitor has the will, and we can't see it until the executor posts it after the reading and after the burial."

After a loud knocking at the door, Dunn entered the room. He handed a piece of paper to Faraday, who handed it to Eleanor.

She grunted. "Owens has solved the case."

❈ 12 ❈

We are all Adam's children, but silk makes the difference.
—Thomas Fuller

When Lady Darnley entered the drawing room of her house, she walked in with a certain fierceness that delighted Faraday. As usual, she had found him at a painting of hers that hung hidden on a narrow wall beside the door. She sat, her back stiff with her hands folded on her lap, and then she glanced at her daughter. After giving Alannah Darnley flowers, Faraday sat and crossed his legs. He saw that her principles continued to be as steadfast and upright as the white corrugated columns that segregated the walls of the room into panels.

"I didn't ask for you to come as a pair."

This was the only room for which Alannah had not painted the fullness of her natural landscapes. In between the columns, another artist had painted murals of the sea Battle of Copenhagen. An exception—Girl at the River—that's what Faraday called the-painting-by-the-door each time he asked to buy it. The small canvas was an antithesis to the buttoned up and tight collared men that dominated the room. By putting it there, she had made sure that they had not been allowed to take the room. Faraday knew it irritated Alannah that he had found it and had realized why it was here.

He knew that it irritated her further that he was forever standing in front of it.

"Five hundred," said Faraday.

"Not today," Alannah said.

"Trying times deserve flowers."

"Imperial lilies," Eleanor said to her mother. "Majesty."

She smiled a tight smile and put them on the table.

She's been ready for this for a while, Faraday thought.

"Since you're here Lord Faraday, I'm depending on your good sense in this matter. You must persuade her to stop this foolish thing."

"Eleanor thought murder from the beginning. She has your innate intelligence."

"You are well greased today."

She was very unyielding, unusually so. He realized that she was frightened by this case. His heart broke for her.

"She will stop if you go away," Alannah said.

"You know she won't."

"Without you, she will fail."

"I am in the room," Eleanor said.

"You want her to fail?"

He watched her face narrow as the ends of her mouth dropped. To Faraday, Lady Alannah was not made for silk. Silk was a fabric called upon for sitting. It was like a shroud to Alannah. It wrapped and bound her. Her natural gaiety had become too pronounced, too fake, probably from the first day she put on her wedding dress. He liked to imagine what she had been before, a real, feisty Irish lass.

"She doesn't need me for this."

"We will be destroyed," Alannah said.

"Have some faith in her."

At the window Eleanor smoothed her blouse over and over. "Enough," she said. Faraday watched Eleanor stand taller as she realized that she wouldn't be able leave her mother to him.

Alannah simpered as she sniffed the lilies. "Columbine would have been more marking."

"Folly?" Eleanor thundered. "What about barberry?"

"Without doubt. Just look at yourself...ill temper...tartness—"

Faraday spoke with a large voice. "We have yet to discover why Louis is acting like a man with a secret."

Eleanor and Alannah turned away from each other. The daughter seemed to watch a bird at play on a branch through the window. The mother lifted the lid of the teapot and peered inside.

"I've been thinking about that," Eleanor said still watching the bird. I think it's his mother. She—"

"Does he like his mother that well?" Alannah asked, putting the lid down with a clang.

"Damn. Oh, never mind."

"Your language is appalling. Some brandy, I think." Alannah stood and walked toward the servant bell. "You two don't have a fact between you." She yanked the cord. "What do you know about any of them? What do you know about Renard?"

"What do *you* know about Renard?" inquired Eleanor.

Alannah shrugged her shoulders. "In my position knowledge comes in handy."

"Renard then," Faraday said sitting back and crossing his legs.

"Was in his youth, a member of the Fourteenth Regiment of Line. In his first week of duty, he shot into hundreds of men, women, and children. The poor of France were protesting against the government. His regiment was in charge of containing it. His mistake ended two lives and the rule of Louis-Philippe and Guizot his minister."

Good Lord, the woman was a bloodhound. He wondered how often Alannah used her information.

"I've vaguely heard about this. It was the horse's fault," said Faraday. "It was a peaceful demonstration of lower-class men, women, and children who were marching through Paris. They were complaining about repressed workers, famine, and unemployment. Guizot's suggestion for them had been '*enrichessez-vous*.' A horse whinnied, at which time a nervous soldier fired into the crowd. That soldier was Renard?"

"Guizot had told them to become rich?" asked Eleanor.

"And why not." Alannah glared at her daughter.

"You don't mean that," Eleanor said.

Alannah waved her daughter's comment away. "The movement of a horse startled Renard, and he shot into the collection of people. He killed a woman and her child. Guizot, the minister, King Louis-Philippe, and Renard, the *tellum imbelle*, left for England within days of the collapse of the government."

"That king was Catholic. Renard was protecting a Catholic government. Charlotte is a stanch Huguenot. Why would she take Renard in?" asked Eleanor.

"What does she care about politics? He is French, and he pets her vanity."

"He can't go back?" asked Eleanor.

"The French have long memories."

"You would be good at detecting," Faraday said to Alannah. "You paint like that, exposing people's hopes, thoughts, and desires."

"Not people, Lord Faraday, cows. I sent a note to your house because there is a croquet party this afternoon, and Eleanor is expected to attend. She is expected."

He heard the finality of Alannah's tone, but didn't understand why Eleanor would give in. Maybe he didn't understand because he was the last of five brothers. Men tend to disregard female voices. Eleanor didn't give up. The skirmish raged for a while—shots and volleys—two women exploding from their chairs, and then recouping their positions.

"We should read Tweedmouth's will," Letty said as she breezed into the room.

Faraday stood and leaned over Letty's outstretched hand.

"You are such a dear boy—such manners. Tweedmouth's solicitor is Hartford of Hartford and Banes, and Hartford's sister is in my book club. Book clubs are so informing. You know, Alannah, I think I will skip the croquet party today...out of principle...well...protest and go to London instead. I think that things at the party will go so much more smoothly without my disapproving glare round every corner, don't you think? With the extra time, I could visit Caroline. I hear that she's very close to her brother. I might call on him. What do you all think?"

Alannah didn't answer. She mirrored the posture of the determined sailor behind her. She must have felt that somehow, in spite of Eleanor's retreat, she was losing the battle.

"May I help?" asked Letty. "I would love to help."

"What a good idea," said Faraday. "See if you can find out to whom the estate might have gone and any oddities."

"I will wear my topaz blouse. Eleanor, you should wear gray this afternoon."

"I look awful in—"

"Exactly," Letty said with a wink.

"You are all against me," Alannah moaned. She wended her way from the room. Her face was theatrically long. The hurt Faraday saw in her eyes was ancient; too long nurtured, he felt.

"I'll tend to her," Eleanor said with exasperation, concern, and tedium swirling about each other in the tone of her voice and in her slow step toward her mother.

Faraday watched them walk away—a wounded soldier leaving the field of battle on a fellow soldier's arm.

"Tut, tut, my boy," said Letty as she gathered the flowers to her lap and smelled them. "Don't give it a moment's thought. Keep doing what you're doing. Eleanor will promise her life away, and Alannah will recover."

"I like Lady Darnley."

"So do I. Now, is that all you need, oddities and inheritance?"

"Anything else you can throw in."

She clapped her hands together. "What fun. I will do what I can. You, young man, go to the party. Eleanor will need saving, and parties are fountains of information. Don't you agree?"

"Do you have a plan?"

"Oh yes. As you know, with his father out of the picture, the son controls the funds. Louis is about to become the object of a good number of mamas' eyes. Even more so with the Baron gone. That ups the pedigree. Lady Kessinger, Hartford's sister, married well. She'd like to keep that ascension rolling, but the daughters she has to marry off are horrible, and she has three of them. Louis would be a perfect match for one of them, you see. She would, of course, need to be sure. I'll suggest to her that you seem to think there might be some irregularities with the will. That will chill her soul. She'll find out because she'll want to stay ahead of the pack."

He was clearly impressed. "What a miracle worker."

"Don't let Peacock and his lectures on morals and patience dominate Eleanor the entire party. She may want to kill herself by the evening's end."

"Peacock is a decent chap."

"Unless you're after stimulating conversation. Alannah has ulterior motives."

Letty held Faraday in a steady gaze.

"Oh, no."

"Oh yes."

❧ 13 ❦

The man recovered of the bite,
The dog it was that died.
—Oliver Goldsmith

The families of all the large houses in Gloucestershire in the Cotswolds were at Cornbury Park, as was the clergy, and so was Eleanor. In back, the lawn had been groomed for croquet. Wickets marked the grass like thorns. A sturdy tap sounded when the players' mallets hit wooden balls that often rolled wide of their targets. The women laughed, a pretty sound, when they missed, while the men encouraged the ladies' next shot. The exercise was not strenuous. It was a pretty picture for some starving Monet.

Eleanor sipped punch at a table opposite her mother. Peacock sat between them. He wore a brown cutaway. Eleanor had on pink and her mother a light burgundy. She felt that they resembled two blushing cheeks separated by a nose. Peacock was leaning in to match Eleanor's tilt backwards. Lady Alannah sounded like a telegraph machine with an insistent message. Tap, tap, tap, taptaptaptaptap.

"She's a good girl. The first year he was so attentive. She loved him. He hid it from us...his preferences. Is that legal in the eyes of God? We have no idea where to go from here. We've come to you for guidance."

On and on. The quiet souring that was year two, and then year three when Albright had lost track of his stories, and then year four, the absolute silence; Albright had lost track of her presence. Alannah had the nodding reverend, the grip of her fist in his well-oiled hair.

After listening to mother's confession for her life and watching Peacock's reassuring smiles, and his eyes flickering to and from her face, she burst out, "Maybe I don't want to be a divorcee. I know I wasn't the cause of the marriage's failure, but I don't want to admit that it failed." No tears, not in front of the Peacock.

After her outburst, her mother and the reverend began talking as if behind their hands, more church-like.

Oh, for God's sake. She needed to walk, but then she heard Peacock say Tweedmouth's name. She had forgotten that the reverend knew Tweed-mouth. The Baron had come to the Peacock about his marriage: God to god.

"Baron Tweedmouth was having trouble as well?" Eleanor asked with a weepy, sweet voice.

Under the table, her mother kicked her.

"You'd be surprised how often I have this conversation," Peacock said. "The sanctity of marriage is a bond most couples strain against."

"Yes, yes." She had to stop and compose her tone. "I do hope that the Baron died without regret. How horrible it is to die while grasping to an unraveling moral thread. Tell me your skill helped his marriage remain intact."

Alannah was bruising Eleanor's ankle with the tip of her leather boot. She glanced at her mother with a hard look.

"I redoubled my prayers, and they continued in marital bliss until the end."

Damn it, Eleanor thought.

Alannah smirked.

Peacock pressed a dry hand on Eleanor's knuckles. "I'm here to help couples press through the doubt."

Eleanor moaned and glanced away. He reminded her of a lizard with a long, forked tongue. The appendage had flickered away the entire afternoon. She couldn't take anymore. The insensible sound of him, she had to get away.

"Even the best marriages wither," he droned on. "You did your best. With your inexperience no one could have done better."

She saw Albert. Perfect.

"There's my husband now. Would you excuse me?"

Peacock preened. Her mother's face wore suspicion. Equally perfect. They deserved it. She stood and left.

Albert's stomach was becoming more pronounced with age, and his hair thinner. Too bad. His hair was his best feature. She wondered how she had missed his character flaws years ago. She was young. They were obvious now, around his eyes, and his mouth. Caught unaware, his eyes were dull; his mouth was a tight stripe above his chin. The family had needed money. He had been young when he stood up with Tweedmouth, about Faraday's age, but already decaying.

He wouldn't tell her anything, unless she surprised him. He had always overawed her. She was glad to notice it was wearing thin.

"Albert." She waited for him to turn, which he did with an exaggerated slowness that was meant to mock her. *Ass.* "You owe me money."

"You missed lunch."

"Regardless. Tell me something and I'll skip this month and move on to the next." Albert liked to keep his money. "Tell me why Greenburg called out Tweedmouth, and why he killed him."

"No." He began walking again.

She dogged his steps. "A business deal? All three of you?"

"No." He walked faster.

"You cheated him?" she called when she couldn't keep up.

He turned so fast she collided with him. He smelled the same. Horses. His face looked down on her upturned one. He grasped her forearms. He was bruising her. Holding her, he ogled her chest, her neck, her face.

He could kill more than red grouse, she thought. She'd never seen so much hate in him. "Did you?" she brazened, knowing he couldn't hit her here. He was hurting her. She had second thoughts about him not striking her as well.

He dragged her into a garden labyrinth and pushed her against the shrubbery walls. "You are a fool."

"For marrying you?"

"Bitch," he spat, and pressed his lips to hers. She squirmed away.

He took her by the arm again and lead her deeper into the lanes. She yanked her arm away and he laughed.

"You have no right to treat me like this."

"Like what? A husband kissing his wife?"

Eleanor reviewed her tactics. She had come on too strong. Albert didn't like strong women. He liked girls. She did wonder at the strength of his reaction. He hated her for leaving him. She hadn't thought about it. He hadn't shown enough interest in their marriage for the thought to occur to her. Fear must be showing on her face. He stepped closer. She could smell the mingled scent of her cold sweat and his lust. He liked fear in women.

He laughed and then took a cigar out of his pocket. He patted himself down for a light. "Don't suppose you have one? Be useful for a change. You know you've squeezed every drop of...God...I don't know...softness out of yourself."

"Don't start. Your wonderful mother has said it all every month for eight months. What was the duel about?"

"I haven't the foggiest idea. My father said be the man's second, and I was. I was just glad Tweedmouth was a good shot. Even if I knew, I wouldn't tell you. You are a nosy, higher than thou, shrew."

He put his smoke back in his pocket. He grabbed at his wife and attacked her lips again. His arms were strong around her waist and behind her head, and his tongue the same. She gagged. He let her go and she almost fell. Opening his wallet, he pressed a wad of bills in her hand. "Here you go. Enjoy being a working girl? You're right about forbidden fruit. Come talk to me again anytime." He leered at her and sauntered away. "So sorry I can't help you out. What a maze." Passing Faraday, he said, "Have her."

Faraday turned to follow Albert. She grabbed his arm. "Forget it. He was just being an ass. Your socking him won't change that."

"I'll feel better, what?"

"I don't want to see you hurt. God, I wish Peacock had seen that," she said brushing herself off. "I didn't even get any worthwhile information."

"Are you all right?"

"Oh yes, yes. Bruised in mind, spirit and body, but I asked him about Tweedmouth, and he didn't like it."

"Damn it. You shouldn't take such risks."

"And he said that he seconded the duel because he was asked to. I doubt he was being truthful. I think I need to sit down for a moment. I wish Peacock had seen that," she repeated.

Faraday walked beside her along the leafy, green walls. Their bodies swayed into each other on the uneven ground. "I can smell the rain coming, can't you?"

She wanted to hold Faraday's hand as they meandered around corners of the maze. She needed his touch and his words that she was doing the right thing. After Albert, she wanted Faraday's validation. When all he did was take out his own cigar, she knew that she'd have to motor on alone. No not alone, he was here.

"My mother is digging in. Bringing her along is like making a donkey go uphill. I think that if I continue with this case my mother's heart will fail her," she said.

"Your mother is as strong as a young plow-horse."

Eleanor chortled. "Anything but that, a drudge animal with yellow teeth and poor posture. I think she'd truly faint. It's hard. I've been brought up to be her one adoring minion."

"We will both adore her. Now she has two."

Eleanor counted her footsteps as she walked the maze. A few people passed by. He left her to her thoughts. Thoughts that his legs were so long he had to slow down to match her gait. Every so often he put his hand at the curve of her back to guide her through the turns.

"The word according to Peacock is that Tweedmouth and Charlotte were not getting along. She was sticking it out."

"They'd both be out, the lap dog and Charlotte."

Eleanor dropped to a bench and took a drink of Faraday's whiskey from the flask he produced. She took two more before she handed it back.

"Who told you they weren't getting along?"

"Peacock."

She took the flask back and drank again. What a day. "Maybe he was about to cut her out of the Will?" The suggestion sounded tired, even to herself.

"You were right, as you are always right. The Baron was not destined to die, as Charlotte put it, in his bed with his devoted family around him."

Eleanor's mood evaporated.

"This is a mess, what? Have you any idea where we are in this maze?" asked Faraday.

"No. I thought you did."

"Not a clue."

The light in his eyes danced and leapt with good humor. He took the world at face value with a hint of humor. She laughed as she was meant to, as she always did with Faraday. She loved who she was when she was with him.

"Well, then we must do what I do in these cases...walk straight through the hedge. Let's not be discovered yet though." She walked beside Faraday's broad smile and let it envelope her. She leaned into him now and again, the contact cheering. The strain was to remain apart, but he made no move to put his arm around her. "Do we think Louis did it?" she asked.

"He did something."

"My grandfather used to say, 'Saints make terrible murderers unless their eyes are closed, and then, they're apt to miss.'"

"The boy isn't holding up well."

"He is, pardon the hunting pun, a sitting duck."

He gave her a warm smile. "Delectable to have you back."

She nudged his shoulder with her own. "Delectable to be back. You think maybe Tweedmouth, with the Peacock around so much, was building up to a deathbed confession?"

"It would be inadmissible."

She glanced around. "Oh well. I suppose we can't stay in here forever. Albert knows we're in here."

"Sod the man."

"Excellent thought." Eleanor felt the crushed edges of the money she still clutched in her hand. She smoothed the bills and tucked them into her corset. No lunch this month. What a blissful thought.

Without Faraday and picking leaves from herself (she seemed to be always picking leaves from herself these days) Eleanor wandered among the guests who were moving inside for the after-croquet luncheon. While she was looking for her mother, Lord Haversack caught up to her. He bowed in front of her and asked for a moment's privacy.

"You have gone too far!" he began without preamble in a low voice after guiding her to a private space by an oak tree. "If I had suspected, I would have held you to your chair at the shooting luncheon. You have destroyed him. Meddling woman. Yes, that's what you are. Louis has surrendered himself to Owens."

"What!" Eleanor clutched at her heart.

"A lady should never take advantage of a gentleman," he said anyway.

"What do you mean?"

"Lord Faraday. It is quite an interesting profession he has, and I'm sure that from the parlor a little dabbling must seem very attractive. I assure you that dabbling into something of which you have no skill, things of this importance, things that constitute life and death, is irresponsible." Haversack's voice wound higher.

"For the love of God, Lady, find another outlet for your boredom. You've done enough damage. He is like a corpse in that place. He has quit eating. Go back to your husband and stay there! He should have more control over your behavior!" The Lord turned then, a snappy about-face, and he was sucked into the ebb and flow of the crowd strolling in for food.

Eleanor rubbed her arms up and down from the cold of the bone-numbing blast of hard-packed words, the chill from thinking of Louis as her fault, and even from Albert. Her feet and hands were too heavy to move; her heart was too heavy to pound. Which pressed more on her breast, anger or embarrassment or sorrow, she did not investigate. She leaned on a tree trunk.

How dare he! She was the most sympathetic to Louis of all.

She stood upright and stretched a frozen smile across her face. It melted from the heat of anger. Forcing herself to walk back inside, she sat on the edge of a straight-back chair at the luncheon table. She couldn't leave her mother behind again. Peacock had plopped into a chair at her elbow. She would calm down within his single-minded conversation. She drank water from a crystal glass. She had suffered slights before, but never this potent, like he had shot her, his aim exact. He could kill. If she had been a man, her credibility would not be in question.

Eleanor changed her drink to the wine punch. She was relieved that it slid all the down to her stomach and stayed there. She took a deep breath, inhaling the lavender scent of the woman next to her. Charlotte had said it was finished. The Baroness wore lavender as a shield and as a sword. Scent can make asthmatics ill. Charlotte bathed in it. Eleanor needed to talk to Louis.

Across Peacock's plate, Eleanor watched Olivia bubble as her father leaned over her seat to talk into her ear. Resentment crawled inside Eleanor's thin skin. Maybe Louis did do it. Maybe he had felt as she did now. She could throw her wine into Olivia's happy face, and then Lord Peacock's pallid face crossed her line of vision. He seemed to want an answer to something.

"Are you feeling all right? You look a bit peaked."

If Peacock has noticed, she must look retched. Eleanor answered, "I'm fine. A little headache from the sun." Was the excuse weak? She couldn't tell. Escape, that's what pressed against her temples. Anyway, he'd believe it.

"I hear that you've been doing some detecting work of late."

Eleanor braced herself for his next words. She felt herself wince under the anticipation of more criticism.

"When you're handy that way, you need to speak out."

"What?" She had wanted to rip off his face and tramp on it under her boots.

"Careful, of course, not to overdo it. A good woman knows the difference."

The pudding was more interesting. "The difference is so very clear," said Eleanor.

"Salt is good; but if the salt becomes unsalty, with what will you make it salty again? Mark chapter nine, verse fifty," said Peacock.

Religion! Oh, how she was tiring of it!

❧ 14 ❧

A little alarm now and then-
Keeps life from stagnation
—Fanny Burney

Lady Caroline Hartford, now Knightly, lived along Hyde Park in a fashionable residence. Letty arrived a little earlier than was respectable. The park was quiet. With her news in hand, Letty knew that Caroline wouldn't mind an early arrival; her daughters had matured into homely butterballs for whom husbands could not be bought. Caroline was desperate. She had had the three in succession, forever spitting out the same baby in different colored hair, by a shade.

Letty still felt her card between her fingers, with a handwritten note on the back, when Caroline herself was on the doorstep. Caroline pushed at her colorless hair. Her smile was predatory and ugly, but she had very few options. That Letty was bringing Louis on a plate brought color to her well-formed cheeks.

I knew it.

"Caroline, how are you?"

"It is so good to see you," Caroline said. "Why are you in London?"

"I have some news for you and a favor to ask."

"Tea," Caroline said to her butler. She entwined her arm through Letty's.

"I know that you don't read the paper, so I thought you might have missed this. The Baron of Tweedmouth has died." A sparkle as bright as a newly minted gold sovereign appeared in Caroline's eye. Letty added sugar to her tea as she let Caroline plan in the silence of her mind forgetting her own beverage. To further embed the idea, Letty added, "Louis will now have one of the largest fortunes in England."

"Not much of a title though," said Caroline.

"No, not the best I suppose, but Louis is such a love."

"The old Baron dead." Caroline nearly rubbed her hands together and smacked her lips over the delicacy.

"You and your daughters must come to Whitney to add to the support from the community for the grieving son, being the sister to Tweedmouth's solicitor. It would be expected."

"Harold!" Caroline smiled.

"You may stay with me at Lady Darnley's residence. Before you come, you might want to clear up one thing." Letty took a sip and waited until she had Caroline's full attention. "It seems that there may be a problem with the will. Naturally, you'd want to find out if Louis has the title and the money. Let me give you any aid in this matter that I can."

"He might not inherit? That's absurd."

"Well, the Baron was an odd man. I've just heard rumors. It's safer to be certain." Letty loved feeding foolishness to foolish people.

Letty gazed across the lip of her china teacup. To Caroline's credit, she shrank from the thought.

"Are the police involved?" She was feeling her way forward.

"They have ruled the death an accident, so far. There are some irregularities. Should you clear things up, Louis will forever be indebted to you." Letty replaced her cup in its saucer.

One of the daughters walked into the room. She had most likely smelled the cakes. Letty appreciated the timing. The poor thing hadn't changed much, still a few spots on a face as round as a clock, and as pale. She'll never get them married, Letty thought.

Caroline may have had the same thought. "Come to Harold's office," she said, "just before one when he leaves for lunch. There's a place there we used to hide in as children when my father had the office. Mind you, my brother is something of a fanatic about work and only takes half an hour for lunch."

· · ·

At one, Caroline said hello to her brother on the pretext of returning a book. She introduced Letty. Caroline was stammering somewhat. She was going to give up the game. They left his office, and Caroline pushed Letty toward a small crypt-like closet at the bottom of some narrow stairs. She smelled mold. Their skirts had raised dust, and Letty held her handkerchief over her nose trying not to sneeze. The urge was so strong that it brought tears to her eyes.

She exploded.

"Quiet!"

As if anyone could hear her sneeze in this basement of death. She concentrated on the strip of light at the bottom of the door just at the toe of her boots.

They heard Mr. Hartford close the door as he left. Letty sneezed with relief. Caroline pushed at the door. They both ran into it in a rush to leave, but the door didn't open.

"I'd forgotten how the latch catches sometimes. It's an old building," said Caroline.

Letty sneezed again. It became a spasm of sneezes each deeper than the one before. "What if we push hard on it?" Letty managed to say.

"No, I'm afraid not."

"Well, we must do something." Letty sneezed again.

"Feel around for something to pick the lock."

"Like what?"

"Like a thin ice pick."

Letty wondered at the remark, as if most women knew about lock picks. Whenever the darkness of the tomb they were in lifted, Letty would be seeing Caroline in a whole new light.

Mime-like, she felt around the piles—and sneezed. Dust seemed to sprinkle everything like powdered sugar on teacake. Over and over, she bumped sides with Caroline. "There is nothing in here but bottles and boxes. How about a hat pin?" Letty asked.

"Great." Caroline didn't sound great.

It was hard to tell how much time had passed while Caroline scratched at the lock—too much anyway. Letty tried to think of the clever words would she say as Harold Hartford let them out of the closet. *Just getting a breath of fresh air*. She sneezed again. The close darkness was wearing on her nerves. She wasn't usually upset in tight spaces, but with Caroline muttering to herself in a hysterical tone, Letty felt the four walls. She closed her eyes to try and keep sane. She hummed until Caroline yelled at her to stop it.

The time! The hatpin didn't seem to be working, or Caroline had lost her skill.

Oh, for heaven's sake. Letty had to move. She reached down and between boxes searched for something more substantial. As Caroline knelt at the lock, Letty's face hit the other woman's pompadour. A hairpin scratched her nose. Was she bleeding? She touched the sore place for moisture.

Squatting this time rather than bending over, Letty began the hunt again. Everywhere she touched had either yards of fabric from their skirts or cleaning bottles or mops that smelled like day old urine.

In a minute, she'd pound her way out.

"I have something," Caroline screamed. Standing, she knocked Letty's jaw and pushed her back into a pile of rags.

"What?"

"A wire hanger.

"Get on with it."

Letty heard the scrapings of the wire against the lock. She leaned against the wall in between a broom and a duster with her handkerchief over her nose. In just two more minutes, she was going to get violent, and then Caroline broke wind. The closet fogged with the smell. "It's not truly locked..."

Au contraire. Letty fanned the fetid air around their box. After this, she was going to have an entire bottle of Moët et Chandon in an iced glass.

"So, it won't take much to get the bolt to release. There, I have it."

The rush of sweet air was never as welcomed. Letty dived into it. She saw from the clock that they had ten minutes.

"Stay in the anteroom and watch for Harold," said Caroline. "I'll go into his office."

"Do be quick. We have a very few minutes." Letty stood guard at the window all the while wondering what mischief this law firm had helped Tweedmouth create. How odd that such an insipid family as the Hartfords would produce a solicitor with the proper sensitivities for the Baron, and now Caroline is ransacking her brother's office. The woman had picked a lock to get them out of that infernal closet.

The assistant's appointment book and lying open on his desk, called to her. She flipped back a few pages to the day after the murder. "The Baron of Tweedmouth, in home, eleven o'clock." She ran her finger along the neat penmanship of the secretary. She flipped the pages back just as Caroline came to the door, five minutes left.

"I can't find anything."

Letty pushed by her.

"I searched through the files. It's not there under Tweedmouth or wills. Oh my God, the time. We have to leave." In a nervous gesture, Caroline pressed close to the window. She was breathing too rapidly.

"Breathe deeper! You'll pass out," Letty said. Everything is labeled, she thought. She pulled open a cabinet.

"I looked there," said Caroline.

Letty stooped to a lower drawer.

"There too," Caroline said in a voice heavy with panic.

Panic was beginning to shake Letty's bones as well. Letty perused the room.

"He's just appeared around the corner. We've got to go."

Letty noticed a filing box labeled with the date the day after Tweedmouth's death. Hartford missed his appointment with Tweedmouth. The box was full of documents. It had been a busy day for the solicitor. Letty picked up the whole pile and threw them one by one back into the box.

"Oh, my God," Caroline said following with unhappy eyes the path of each piece of paper. "You can't do that." She kneeled to straighten the pile.

"Keep your mind on the prize which is Louis!" Letty rifled through document after document. She looked for key names. Caroline watched out the window.

"We have to go, now! He's coming," said Caroline. She lunged for Letty, who twirled out of her grasp.

With the pile half gone, Letty's hands began to shake from raw nerves. "Burns, Bowman, Chapman," she read.

"He's to the first landing."

Letty threw the top documents back into the box. "What will he do if he finds us?" She asked as she was dropping some papers in trying to get to others.

"He...he's a pugilist. He's not good at managing his anger. Oh God, he's at the steps." Caroline rushed over to Letty and tried to tear the sheets from Letty's hands.

"Give them to me. Give them to me."

"He won't hit a woman or his sister. He won't miss them. They were at the bottom."

"What if he looks for them to file?"

"His secretary would do that," said Letty. "Anyway, we'll be gone."

"Put them back!" Caroline pulled away some top pages. A key turned in the lock. Taking Letty's arm, Caroline pulled her out of the room, back down the six stairs, and back to the closet. Letty tripped on her skirt. She heard lace rip.

Damn it. It was from Brussels.

Caroline strong-armed her upright and pushed her back into the dreadful, creeping space.

One door opened while the other shut.

"Until what hour does your brother work?" asked Letty while leaning on a small space of wall.

"Late," was Caroline's suffocating answer.

E leanor relaxed in her room. Her mother, downstairs, continued to act in a play of her own making. The winter sun had set. In spite of the warmth, she felt the dark pressing upon her. Lassitude was heavy on her limbs from the extreme emotions of the afternoon. She shouldn't have gone. She should have stood up to her mother, put her foot down. She'd put her foot into it with Louis. She felt beaten up and tender. Peacock had talked about her husband until horns had seemed to spring from the good reverend's temples. She rose to pour more tea for herself. She fortified it with sugar.

Letty had wired that she'd be back by the last train, an iota of cheer. There was a knock at the door. Eleanor's maid stepped inside.

"Are you in for the rest of the evening?" Her maid had brought cheese and crackers.

"I'm waiting for Letty. She wired that she'd be here about ten."

The maid put the tray on a table. "Tonight?"

"Tonight. Has mother been putting more almonds out this evening?"

"She's been changing out the old pomegranate, I think."

Eleanor picked up a cracker to nibble on. It seemed without flavor, but eating eased her nerves. "This case is something of a fine mess."

"From what I hear, you are just trying to find out what happened to that poor man."

"No one else happens to see it that way."

The maid turned down the bed. "Do you need anything else?"

"No, nothing, thank you."

"If Louis Montfire did it, it's his fault," the maid said as she shut the door behind her.

Her mother had retired before Letty came into Eleanor's room like an exaggerated kiss blown to the masses. She began peeling off her gloves. "I need a brandy." She unpinned her hat and pushed up her hair. "First, I'm getting out of this corset. I've been in a closet for three hours, and that's enough of tight places. Caroline and I came out looking like the dry mops around us. Caroline's pompadour hung to her eyebrows all the way back to her home." Letty sprang up laughing a little. "Would you ask for a brandy while I'm gone? Oh, I've got bad news."

"Not more," said Eleanor. Did she moan? She thought she heard herself moan. She must have because Letty laughed.

"Nothing like that. My husband is arriving. Fiennes has shot all the birds with Wales, and he's on his way. He's heard about all the fun we have been having up here." Letty hesitated at the door and turned. "You were in the gray, this afternoon?"

"Pink, but mostly seeing red."

Letty reentered a few minutes later. After her first sip of brandy and an appreciative sigh, she chose a soft chair. "I hope the husband's arrival won't cramp our investigating. Where's your mother?"

"In bed."

"Fabulous." Letty must have heard herself slur because she waved her hand. "I had to have a drink or five when I got out of the tomb in the basement of Hartford's office. That experience would make a criminal cry. I can't tell you what a pain in the ass Caroline was. The reason we are still speaking is that she is sending her well-fed daughters to you to help them meet Louis—"

"Letty—"

"I know, I know, but it's not their fault they're homely and didn't do well last season, or the season before, and you could be such a positive influence. Needless to say, as Louis is now one of the richest men in England. Caroline did get the message that we needed some information exchanged for a first crack at him."

"It's not that. Louis has confessed to the murder and is in jail. It's my fault."

"You can't be serious. That is...oh my God. Dear, don't cry. It's not your fault. It's not."

"Owens was right. I should have left it all alone."

"No, he wasn't. No. Dry your eyes and let me tell you why. Drink some of this. Caroline and I hid in a bloody broom closet until her brother left for lunch. Somehow, the bloody Caroline managed to lock us in. Can you believe that?" Letty took her glass back. "When we got out, Caroline dashed into her brother's office, like she could find anything, and she didn't, while I was left to sentry duty in the anteroom, no doubt her conscience perking up. Anyway, what do you imagine I find on the secretary's desk?"

"An appointment book."

"Right, then, too obvious. I thumbed back to the date in question. "You won't believe it! Hartford was meant to come to Abbey Leix Castle the next morning—the day after Tweedmouth's death. Of course the Baron was supposed to be alive then."

"You are a wonder."

"It's not over. Drum roll please." Letty took another drink—a long one. "That woman clawed my arm off. I tore the lace on my new dress."

"Not the new one."

"Yes, while Caroline was throwing me back into that closet. Oh, and between us, we couldn't find a thing. I left Caroline on her own too long. By the time I started helping her, her brother was at the outer door. But I," Letty said, preening, "hung on to a pile of papers. I waited for two hours in that dank space with Caroline moaning the whole time. I thought of stuffing the mop down her throat. I hid the papers in my dress in the dark. I had no idea if I had anything, but I wasn't going to leave that closet empty."

"You brought something!" Eleanor let the feet she had tucked under herself drop back to the floor.

"God, yes. By the time we got out, Caroline had forgotten that I had it. I tossed most of it. But here, take a gander at this." With a flourish and bow, Letty handed Eleanor a crumpled document.

"You do the honors," said Eleanor.

"Tweedmouth...da, da da, da, da, da...is seeking guardianship of one Daniel Miller aged five." Letty looked up. "Can you believe it?"

The room was quiet as a lull in a storm. Eleanor heart seemed to have stopped and only the grandfather clock in the corner of the room ticked. "Oh my God, another child. The photograph!"

"A nephew of some level?"

Eleanor opened a drawer. She handed a dog-eared picture to Letty.

"He doesn't resemble Tweedmouth at all."

"Regardless, the boy was destined to become another castle inmate."

"Maybe a bastard son taking over Tweedmouth's title—seems appropriate enough for the Baron," said Letty. "He was just that distasteful of a man."

"Have the boy's mother and father signed it? I know that I'd never let my son step over the castle's dark threshold," said Eleanor.

"The signature line says Mrs. John Miller. No father."

"An underage boy." Letty tapped her nose. "Money involved."

"Does Charlotte know?"

"Does Louis know, should be your next thought. That boy wouldn't give a fig if the whole thing went to his fifth cousin. He didn't do this, whatever is on his mind."

"She planted lime trees," Eleanor said. "No greater foe than a woman scorned. The new owners would toss her out. Renard must see his life as better without the Baron. Oh, we do need a more detailed autopsy. Owens will never give us one. Charlotte must be pressing to get the body released. So she and Renard smothered or poisoned him, but how did he fall over the wall and why? Why go to so much trouble and then draw so much attention to the thing."

"Maybe he threw himself over the wall to send a message," said Letty.

"Oh my God! That's so brilliant. Damn it though, that would rule out suffocation. He was dead before he hit the ground. When Charlotte gets her hands on the body, he'll be six feet under before the cockcrows, a merry morning to them all. We need to narrow our suspects. We need to branch out. What am I saying? I don't know what I'm saying. We need more time. If I go to Brailford again, maybe I can delay the handover of the body."

"The duel," said Letty.

"I'll write a note to Faraday. We need to find the man in the duel."

She had no idea if Albert had a motive or what it could be. How little she knew about her husband. On one side, Albert deserved it. On the other side of the dark coin, she'd be the wife of a murderer. Not to worry. She had a Peacock in her pocket.

❧ 15 ❧

There are no whole truths; all truths are half-truths.
It is trying to treat them as whole truths that plays the devil.
—*Edward North Whitehead*

The sun's heat beat on Faraday's shoulders as he drove. His driving gloves clung to the wheel as he wove the car in and out of London traffic. Beside him, Eleanor smelled the acidic air from the burning fields around London—a regular autumnal clearance that mingled with the city's fog and coal smoke. Her heavy wool coat weighed down her shoulders. The morning had been cool, finally, but now she wished he'd stop so she could shed the extra layer.

"Criminals," Faraday was saying, "consider laws man made. I've sat long hours in jail cells listening to clients' long stories meant to exonerate them of even their worst crimes. I present in court each one's point of view. There's always some kernel of truth in the heartbreak tales, some lesson to be learned. Those who present no excuses are a tale in themselves."

"What happens when the guy did it?"

"The defense for evil is it exists as a part of human weakness in all of us. We are all meant for so much better."

"Albert?"

114

He nodded. "Good example."

Faraday was also coated, and the heat of his garment must have been making him thirsty, because he pulled in to a wayside pub.

"I'm thinking she is resentful, Mrs. Absalom Greenberg, that's the wife of the man killed in the duel. She is possibly a woman who hasn't wound down or forgotten anything. She had probably prodded Mr. Greenburg, a small man by all accounts, until he had had no option but to call out Tweedmouth. She will have kissable lips and pushed-back shoulders. She'll wear a corset as a weapon and take romance to the bank. She is a woman men are excited by."

Eleanor raised an eyebrow.

"In my professional opinion." Faraday grinned.

"But why, why did she prod him into a duel? One thing is for sure, in this Tweedmouth wasn't a hero being served ale from the skull of his dead enemy." She liked the implications of Faraday's smile. He liked the good sides and the bad sides of people. Anything less would be dull.

According to the instructions from the Scotland Yard telegram, Faraday drove to Wigmore Street in Marylebone, to Mr. Greenburg's wife. He parked with a flourish and Eleanor lounged with him in his motorcar and stared at a detached home with a bright green, Georgian door.

"She was a determined one," said Faraday.

"Her daughter would be about two years older than Louis," said Faraday. "Good mother or bad, do you think?"

Couples strolled in the fine weather, the men's canes tapping rhythmically on the sidewalks. The women's parasols were fragrantly colored and added gaiety to the tinted, fall leaves of the park. Eleanor watched them as she considered her answer. "Always the center of attention. Is that a good mother or bad?" She opened the car door.

On the sidewalk, a butcher passed in front of Eleanor with a basket of entwined sausages that lay heavy and bloated.

Faraday opened and closed the gate in a black iron fence that pointed to heaven. The sound of metal hitting metal was mimicked at other gates in front of the other houses as tradesmen came and went. He knocked a gentleman's knock. A jack-of-all-trades maid opened the door.

"Mrs. Greenburg is not home presently."

"When may I return? My visit is important."

"Who is it, Ellen?"

In those few words Eleanor heard a sweet voice that had perfect pitch in its melody of words, like a series of crystal bells.

From them Faraday anticipated the woman. "She will be fine boned with full lips to form such perfect words. She will walk with the grace of angels. Her eyes will be clear and blue," he whispered to Eleanor's ear.

When a thin, sharp face entered the hall, Eleanor chuckled. Head to toe, her flesh-covered bones were being held together by joints, stays, and lace. She resembled a dressed up greyhound that hadn't been well fed. She was about the same height as Faraday. She was neither old enough nor provocative enough to be the mother. She'd never have started a duel.

"Lord Henry Faraday," the housekeeper read off Faraday's card. "Lady Eleanor Albright."

"Yes?" the thin woman said.

"We would like a moment of your time," said Faraday.

A morning fire in the receiving room smoked. There was the lightest smell of it. The chimney needed cleaning, something quite standard for this time of year. The lithe, Spanish figurines in a glassed case had escaped the dulling film of ash that covered Waterford crystal bowls on a mahogany side table. The long windows needed washing. Expensive things, but one servant and too much work.

"We're sorry to interrupt your day," Eleanor said.

"Would you like some tea?"

"Yes, thank you," they both responded.

"Mary. Tea please."

The woman who was probably Greenburg's daughter sat with her hands in her lap and disinterest in her face. When Faraday said, "We're looking into a death." She didn't blink.

Lord, she has the most consistent face, thought Eleanor.

"Of Lord Tweedmouth," Faraday finished.

There was a change in her face then. It was vague, but it gave Eleanor hope for their assumptions. She's worried about us being here now. She's sorry she ordered the tea. Nothing for her to do about it but to brave on.

The daughter pulled down on a cuff with a stiff motion. If possible, her cold expression had become colder. Frostbite could linger on her face and not do any damage. She swept back a strand of light brown hair that had loosened from her chignon. It had fallen forward like a persistent lock that refuses to stay in place during exertion. Eleanor noticed a stain of some sort on the edge of her fraying cuff.

"Tweedmouth?" she said like she'd pulled the name from a dim place. The young woman perked up, relieved, it seemed, to hear a voice in the hall.

Mrs. Greenburg walked in without hesitation, in fact, with great and practiced aplomb. This woman peeled her gloves off as she entered as if the entire world watched her. She had the daughter's eyes, but this woman had them to greater effect. This woman was stunning. The daughter was a shadow of the real thing and had lived in that place beside her mother all her life.

Faraday's nod to Eleanor said that, yes, things were falling into place.

"I noted your cards at the door," said Mrs. Greenburg. "Such notable visitors; haven't you rung for tea yet, Virginia?" the mother said. "Forgive us. We rarely have the opportunity to entertain."

"I did," the daughter's petulant eyes flashed. "She's late."

From all his gab in the motor, this woman was what Faraday had expected to see in the daughter. She had her daughter's lilting voice. She was shorter than her daughter who had hidden her long legs by tucking them back against the seat. Contrary to her statement, this woman had entertained.

It occurred to Eleanor that this woman was everything Charlotte Tweedmouth wanted to be and thought she was, without the strong scent of lavender. Charlotte had one thing that this woman didn't: sticky, back-room sensuality. Mrs. Greenburg was a translucent statue of a woman with heavy breasts, somewhat covered. She was made from hard but quality marble.

Faraday stood. "Mrs. Greenburg?"

"Yes, yes, you are so clever. A barrister with your credentials should be, shouldn't he? Can you believe the weather, Lord Faraday, for October? Oh, here the tea is. Please sit. I'll pour."

Eleanor hated women that only talked to men.

Now, what were you talking about?"

"I'm afraid that Lord Tweedmouth has died," said Faraday.

"He has died," said Mrs. Greenburg. The three words spoke of the past and of an end to the present. They were sad and not sad, more like the third curtain call of a play that had ended long before. It was a good performance if she already knew. She seemed to genuinely feel the loss, but she didn't let the moment linger. "Why are you here? Just to tell us that?"

"He was killed, mother. Isn't that what you meant when you said that you were looking into a murder?"

"And after all these years you're coming to us? How flattering."

She smoked cigars in her room alone and drank whiskey neat. Eleanor would bet money on it.

"How did he die?" she asked Faraday.

"He may have been poisoned."

"May? You're not sure? Certainly modern medicine could help you."

"In time, Mrs. Greenburg."

"Are you representing anyone in this matter? Is that why you are here? Are you accusing us? Tell us when he died, and I'll tell you where we were."

Faraday sat a little deeper in his seat. The mother would require handling.

"Have you heard from him in any way in all these years?" asked Eleanor.

"No." This was from the daughter. She seemed to be an abrupt person by nature.

"He has been a welcome absence from our life." The mother could be bitter and beautiful. If she had feelings about Tweedmouth, she didn't let them ruin her face.

"So you've lost touch?"

"The man did kill my husband."

"You loved your husband?" asked Eleanor.

There was a hiccup of a pause, like she had to think, either because she hadn't anticipated the question or because she hadn't loved her husband. Mrs. Greenburg smiled her first warm smile. It was focused on Eleanor. "Of course I did."

"The secrets of the duel have been kept very well," said Faraday.

"It's easy to keep a secret when there is no advantage to anyone in its telling," said Mrs. Greenburg.

"You haven't heard from him?" asked Eleanor.

"I had no reason to hear from him. Mr. Greenburg called him out. It was stupid, and he paid the ultimate price for doing something so reckless. It's not the way to solve problems. I blame Mr. Greenburg, not Lord Tweedmouth. If you're going to shoot at people with your life at stake, you'd better be good at it—don't you think?"

"We've never seen your husband," Eleanor said as she stood and walked to a side table. She picked up a gilt frame that decorated the picture of an upright man and a beautiful woman. "Is this he?"

"That picture was taken, on the continent. Paris." Mrs. Greenburg rescued it from Eleanor's grasp. She pressed it to her breast face down. "We'd had such a good time. The chocolate, the wine. Glorious, simply, simply glorious."

"You no longer harbor any anger?"

"I was never angry. My husband did a foolish thing. I was embarrassed."

"It wasn't about money? Tweedmouth didn't cheat your husband?"

"My husband never spoke to me about money. It could have been over money. I just don't know. How he thought that a duel would ever solve anything...he was foolish."

The daughter shifted. "Mother——"

Mrs. Greenburg raised a ringed hand. "If I may, let me get this straight. Lord Tweedmouth is dead in some unknown way, and you think we had a hand in it because Tweedmouth killed my husband twenty-five years ago?"

Mrs. Greenburg stood. "How dare you come here? Isn't it enough that the man did kill my husband? Should we have to continue to suffer under this man's influence? He was not a likeable person. If he was killed, look to his own family. I'm sure you'll find all you need there."

Fifteen minutes later, Eleanor slid into Faraday's car. "First, Mrs. Greenburg has never played a man straight in her life. Second, money or love, the duel involved that woman. I'd bet this car on it."

"We need to visit my aunt. She knows all the gossip. I have a Mrs. Jeffers who works for me. She's just the ticket to talk to the overworked maid. That woman will have a thing or two to say," said Faraday as he dropped in next to Eleanor.

❧ 16 ❧

To lose one parent, Mr. Worthing, may be regarded as a misfortune; to lose both looks like carelessness.
—Oscar Wilde

Eleanor had never sneaked out of the house and into the cold dawn. She was out the door before her mother ever had thought of getting up. On the way back to London—to Brailford, she thought how similar this death seemed to a gradual death by arsenic—the effects of a slow poison hidden by symptoms of a vague and general nature. By the time Eleanor stood before the doctor's house, she knew what she needed from him.

Brailford's home lacked femininity. The paintings were as dark as the wood paneling on which they hung. The sweet smell of pipe tobacco was his perfume. It clung to every curtain, book and wall. A herd of cowhides had been sewn into chairs.

Sitting, Eleanor didn't make a dent in the frame-stretched leather. She got comfortable. If he didn't want to see her, he'd have to throw her out. She adjusted her dress and prepared to wait. He'd make her wait like all the women everywhere had made him wait. The watch pinned to her chest read an hour since her arrival. Brailford didn't know women. She'd waited longer for her hair to dry. His man would walk by the open door every ten minutes and glare in. She lay in wait by the opening for the valet's third pass. She stood. "This is so important," she said close to his face, "that I may have to search room to room for him."

"Never mind, Pool," Braiford called to his butler, "I'm here." The doctor's voice was a monotone of yawning boredom. "What can I do for you, Lady Albright? You are definitely a woman in your persistence." He didn't invite her to sit. They stood in the hall. He tamped the tobacco in his pipe. She wasn't sure if she sensed a more positive mood. Now and again humans may feel benevolent to pesky spiders. After all, they catch flies.

His manner was no less dignified today, but somehow less grand. She had read what he had written; she knew his thoughts, his hopes, and his dreams. She handed him back his book.

"Faraday didn't send you last time."

So, he had done some inquiries of his own, Eleanor thought. "We are working together, but he didn't send me."

"You are interested in Lord Tweedmouth as a friend?"

"No, I am not," she said, perhaps a bit too quickly. "I am interested in finding out if he died a natural death. I ask that question, because it interests me, and because it is a question that in an honest society needs to be asked."

He smiled a weak smile.

"Harvey, no doubt, gave you tea and information."

"I like him," Eleanor said to her own surprise.

"He is soothing. Well, let us conclude this interview. You understand that even if you have the initiative, you have no authority." He raised an eyebrow.

Eleanor refused to be made small by this man. She tried not to shift from foot to foot. "I have what no one else seems to have, Doctor, the desire to make sure a disliked man was not killed by stranger, friend, or family. I also have the desire to see that the correct person is brought to justice."

Brailford had no retort for the moment. The sudden quiet in the room was heartening.

"Interesting isn't it that I have already given you the answer. Please listen this time. I can only surmise the cause of Baron Tweedmouth's death."

"The Baron was your case study?" He didn't answer, so she continued. "It seems to me that you would want to know the contents of his stomach in a detailed autopsy. In the first autopsy, the coroner tested for arsenic alone. I know that the Baroness will not allow for a second one unless she is ordered to do so. For the police to order one, they must have a reason." He wouldn't be forthright. She watched him, almost daring him to take the high road.

He opened a box on a table and took out a match. He didn't light his pipe but just held the stick. His eyes looked down as his mind swirled. Opening his mouth, his thoughts blew out like a razor-line wind. "Tweedmouth's life was not threatened under my care. I cannot say what made him so very ill. The prognosis was in his favor. Over the centuries, physicians of little diagnostic skill have pronounced with superficial evaluations humid or dry asthma or both when the cause was cardiac.

"These physicians forgot to set forth the onset, progress, and termination of the symptoms. In separating the heart from the lungs, I have further distinguished what Leonardo Botallo described as respiratory allergies. I have further delineated them into the odors, for instance, of lavender, of which, in part, we are all grateful to Botallo, and into the digestion of food as symptom inducing agents. Are you following me?"

Eleanor held her temper by picturing the pertinent pages of Brailford's book. The pages flew past each other in her mind as in a gale through an open window. In one speech, Brailford had raced through chapters, as he, no doubt, had intended to do. She was glad for the pause. She used the time to put on a scholarly face. To her delight she could say, "Yes I am. You are trying to prove that food produces allergies that trigger asthma."

Brailford frowned. He hadn't expected this answer. It deflated his robust lungs. He and Olivia had much in common. He was still within Eleanor's sights. "Wouldn't an autopsy find the forbidden fruit, or should I say egg?" Eleanor asked. "We must in essence prove that the Baron was poisoned."

Here, Brailford smiled again. Such a damn superior smile. "It's not that easy. What needs to be proven is that he ate enough to be a fatal dose. That seems, unlike poison, to vary by person. What is toxic to one patient might cause only sight breathlessness in another."

"Was any particular food toxic to Lord Tweedmouth?"

"Not in the doses he ate, and his level of toxicity is an unknown. Food made him sick, but it didn't seem lethal. If you've been following my logic, you'd see that what is not lethal today may be tomorrow."

"His asthma has never been..." Eleanor wanted to say, life threatening, but she felt that Brailford would smile his condescending smile at that. She reworded to: "...as severe under your care before?"

"No."

"Then, we might say that given usual circumstances, he should be alive and well."

"There is always the possibility of anything."

Eleanor's head hurt. They were going in circles. "You are saying that asthma is never predictable?"

"No, I'm not saying that either."

"His pupils were contracted when he died."

"I wouldn't know anything about that." Brailford scowled. After some moments of waiting and fingering his pipe he said, "I have not studied this particular fact, therefore I cannot give it any decisive weight, but the Baron almost died once in taking the dose of aspirin I had prescribed for his gout."

That was it! What she'd come for. He had decided to give it to her. The heaviness of the interview lifted. Don't smile, she told herself. Don't do it.

He worked on lighting his pipe—a consolation of sorts. He walked away from her. "My butler will see you out."

"Did you ever prescribe aspirin again?" Eleanor held her breath.

"No."

"Because you assumed he'd get very ill again?" In Brailford's silence, she assumed the positive. He loved to let her know when she was wrong. "Who knew this?"

"I have no idea."

"You need to tell the chief constable on the case."

"As I said, it is a theory. I have no research to back it. I will not support the idea until I do."

"He died too soon," Eleanor said.

"It's not provable."

"How much aspirin did he take?"

Brailford sighed. "A packet."

"Will you refute the coroner signing the death certificate?"

"What did they find as the cause of death? I'm sure you know."

"They are saying that he died from the asthma as proven by mucus and swelling of the lungs." The information sounded bad for her, was bad, but Eleanor decided not to lie.

"Well then, untreated, without a doctor's care, he may have slipped. I cannot argue with the coroner's findings. They are correct. I would, in fact, sign the certificate. Unless of course, the coroner also found aspirin in him." On the Doctor's face was a hint of a condescending smile.

"How did you learn about allergies to food?"

He shrugged. He'd had the last word, and he knew it. That was all she was going to get. She had no idea if it was going to be enough, but it was something, and anyway, she couldn't wait to leave. She stepped onto Harley Street and with blood again circulating to her feet. Still bitter, and not willing to testify; he'd sure as spit sign the dead certificate. Brilliant. We all live foolishly. Oh God. Tweedmouth might well have been killed by asthma after all.

She couldn't think of any way to slip anyone aspirin. It is a most foul tasting drug and would be impossible to give to a man who knows he's allergic to it. Very grim, she thought as the cabbie settled her in and was waiting for instructions. The birds were annoyingly bright sounding. Tweedmouth might have been desperate enough to try some medication of his own choosing. He stopped believing Brailford. If so, then the stupid man killed himself. Close enough to an accidental death.

"Where to madam?"

A flock of magpies flew over them, heavens the piercing sound. Eleanor then thought of the Chelsea Physic Garden, a cornucopia of medicinal herbs. Perfect. Thank God.

The cabbie helped her out at sixty-six Hospital Road. An apprentice with an exuberant nature and a young, bright face walked her down the rows between garden beds. She passed the pond rock garden that had stones in it from the Tower of London, also Icelandic lava. Often, while Eleanor, as a girl, picked daisies, her mother painted the lovely river that ran through the gardens. Here her mother taught her the textures of leaves. Eleanor felt her small hand in her mother's smooth, warm one as Alannah had pointed at blossoms. They'd sit by the river, and her mother would read to her. Her mother didn't come to the gardens anymore.

She passed the Maori, Aboriginal, and South African tribal herb beds. If the variety of herbs was anything to go on, the South Africans had been taking care of themselves very well. She had to quickstep to keep ahead of the student botanist. The perfumery and aromatherapy borders used to be her favorite place and her mother's. Attar of roses, lemon verbena and lavender, the plants made her cough today.

"Are you all right?" the apprentice asked close to her.

She noticed his moist skin. She rounded a flower bed and read: analgesia, anesthesia. "Would you tell me about these plants?" she asked with her elbow up between herself and the apprentice.

"That one with the crocus-like flowers, the Colchicum, is a lily. Its seeds and bulbs are used for rheumatism and gout. The Hyoscyamus is a genus of nightshade."

"Are any to do with aspirin?"

"Naw. There's an apothecary just down the road."

A bell rang when she opened the door. Behind the counter, stripped leaves that had been dried and jarred crowded ceiling-to-floor, mahogany shelves. Plain, white labels striped the upstanding soldiers. On the labels typed in all capitals were black words: foxglove, and belladonna, with the Latin names underneath. Next to the encased plants were smaller bottles of all sizes and colors—a happy rainbow of relief. These drug-company bottles had clever pitches on the labels with pictures and bold lettering. Eleanor read Batley's Drops, Sydenham's Laudanum, and Bayer's Aspirin.

The powder with the Bayer's label looked barren, like chalky soil. It seemed even more innocuous when she remembered that she had taken it herself with the best of results. The chemicals in many alkaloid plants were toxic in excess—that had to be kept in mind.

"May I help you?"

The proprietor was a very small, manicured man in need of the tall ladder behind him. He wore spectacles that magnified his eyes, and he still squinted. Deep lines creased his forehead above his nose from years of bad eyesight.

"I need some information," Eleanor began as she laid her clasp on the counter, "on the herbal forms of aspirin."

"Ah, you mean salicylic acid." The man pushed up his glasses. His nose was shiny with perspiration. The room was warm and had the balm of drying plants.

"Yes. Do any of them work?"

"I can recommend something that isn't as potent, of course, but it can produce similar results."

"What would that be?"

"Willow."

"Isn't that what Bayer makes its aspirin from?" she asked.

"Yes, but in its original plant form, is it not herbal? Willow and then all the birches—sweet birch, black birch, yellow birch. There's teaberry and Calycanthus from which wintergreen syrup is extracted for tobacco."

"In tobacco?" She examined his shelves looking for inspiration. "No, that won't do. That's all, then? Just those?"

"What more do you need?"

"I'm not sure. Is there anything else? The powder seems to upset my cousin's stomach and the willow, I suppose you make a tea from it. It must be unpalatable."

He straightened a row of jars on the counter. "There are lots of forms of salicylic acid, almonds, apples, blackberries, currants, oranges, peaches, birch beer, of course, and in wine."

"In large amounts?"

He shook his head. "No, no, traces. There's also marigold, and tulip if you want to know the lot. The highest concentration is in the willow or birch. You'd get nearly the same benefit from that as from Bayer's. They make the powder from willows."

"Bayer has done all the work," said Eleanor.

"They buffer it. If you find the taste of willow disagreeable. I find the powder worse."

"Yes, it's very recognizable."

"Not so much in its natural form." He pushed up his glasses.

Damn it, she hadn't asked Brailford about Tweedmouth's level of toxicity to aspirin. How much powder must make a difference in flavor? "Do you have willow?"

"We suggest the teaberry seeped in hot water."

"Some teaberry then. Oh...is there much in almonds?"

"More than in the others except willow and the birches."

The next time her mother brought them, she'd eat the morning almonds in her saucer.

Eleanor accepted some teaberry in a brown paper package. The bell jangled as she left. Her mother hated apothecaries. The mingled bouquet of so many leaves and blossoms would arrest Alannah's forward motion at the doorstep. She considered the combining of cut flowers extremely unwholesome. The mixture of scent in a floral bouquet in a patient's room was thought of as unhealthy—a possible cause of death.

Alannah met her daughter at the door of their house. "Where have you been? Where did you go this morning? Charlotte arrived an hour ago and has refused conversation and refreshments. She walked into the room like she'd blend into the generals behind her. What is she doing out of her house? She's in mourning."

Seeing the Scented Woman sitting in front of the Admiral Lord Nelson with the same aura of divine arrogance, Eleanor moaned. Thunderclouds were gathering over the bright sea. Charlotte had been waiting for her enemy...without tea.

"We are sorry for your loss, Charlotte," Alannah began.

"Really."

"Yes," Eleanor said.

"I'm here to see your daughter if you please, Lady Darnley."

"Have a walk in the garden. The air may freshen your spirit."

"What I have to say will not take long."

"The weather continues to hold. I'm sure that you haven't been out much these last few days."

Charlotte exploded to her feet. "Fine," she said. "Eleanor?"

Eleanor opened the French door, took up a sun umbrella, and waited for the Baroness to precede her. They walked as far as the fountain in silence. It sounded playful, lilting—not like Charlotte at all.

"You are the most rude of women, Lady Albright. Stay out of my private affairs, or I will have to address the matter with my solicitor."

"The facts surrounding this death are not in order."

"Oh really! What right do you have to increase our suffering? You must be mad. You are drying up into the withered thinking of a spinster."

"If by a spinster you mean a person of independent thought, I welcome it." Eleanor would fight this time. Let being the good girl boil away.

"You are a pest of the highest order."

"Lady Charlotte, any person has a moral obligation in suspicious circumstances to seek the truth."

"My husband was not killed. Louis did not kill him whatever he says. Louis takes on guilt like an overzealous martyr. The asthma killed my husband. Even the coroner says so. This is all preposterous. He was a very ill man. I will not have your meddling malign my good name. You will cease and desist. That I've had to come here at all, and in mourning, tells just how unmannered you are."

"Your husband's health inexplicably worsened. He couldn't tolerate certain foods—foods that can be ground into pastes or powders. Plant alkaloids like opium, and foxglove in the right dosage are poison. Aspirin to him was a poison."

"You have no idea. Well then, fear for yourself. You are a fool, and you're making Faraday look a fool."

"Lord Faraday makes his own decisions."

Charlotte glared at her. "That's not what people are saying."

"People are wrong. Trust me on that, Lady Tweedmouth. How did

Renard and your husband get along? Renard saw your misery. He's killed before. It would be an end to everyone's misery."

"My husband died from his illness, that's all."

"How easy it would have been to hurry that along."

"Yes, and then have Louis throw Tweedmouth off the balcony. Louis has turned himself in to the police from all your nonsense. He thinks that he killed his father. See what you have done. You will stop. Do you hear me? If you don't, I will have you stopped." Lady Charlotte walked away toward her chaise.

Women's voices could bend iron wills as well as break glass. Charlotte's words, their sounds so shrill and chilling. Arrggg...Eleanor wanted to smash the cylinder that played round and round in her head. She stayed in the garden fighting memory of Charlotte's lips moving and spitting out agony. She picked the flowers, pulling hard on the stems.

Her hem dirty, her feet without shoes, Eleanor put the flowers on a table at her mother's side and then flopped down on a chair in Alannah's dressing room. Her mother was listening, her head back, to the Bach's pastoral. Her eyes were shut to the world. A compress covered them. She was like this on the days when her father would go to the Irish National Club on Henrietta Street in London.

"I've ordered tea," said Alannah. She lay unstrung on the lounge. Alannah had two moods in a panic, shear momentum or *mettre de l'eau dans son vin*—feminine fragility. "The nerve of that woman to come here. It's her family that's odd. The reason she's even marginally devoted to Louis is because she read somewhere that the French family bond is close."

"She could be the killer."

Not an involuntary flicker moved Alannah's body. Her mother hummed along with the music but then said, "It must have been quite a shock to Charlotte's affections when Tweedmouth turned religious. One day, she's not married to Lothario any longer but to Saint Paul. The day before, her "Frenchness" is appreciated, sought after. The next she is a harlot. One day, she is the vessel of his love. The next she is Eve enticing Adam."

While her mother recovered, Eleanor walked to a front window and drew back the lace privacy curtain. She could hear the soft whir of a push mower. The grass was getting its final, winter cut. "Mother?" Eleanor said over her shoulder. "Did he love her?"

"They appeared to have a deep connection in the beginning."

"I suggest that her heart was cut open. What would you have done?"

"I wouldn't have killed him if that's what you're after."

"You'd have thought about it."

"No."

Eleanor watched some birds peck at one another. "Well, I might have."

"You wouldn't."

"The way you talk about Charlotte, she might." Suddenly the music and her mother's room overwhelmed Eleanor. "We should walk, Mama, the weather is fine."

"Where, pray tell? We are lepers."

"Oh, for God's sake. To the village. We have to go anyway. Where are your walking shoes?"

࿓

"The chiffchaff have gone, but the tomtits are back." Alannah pointed with her handkerchief at the trees along the road. She paused to watch starlings in the stubble on the fields, eat blackberries, and smell a Guelder rose.

On the return trip, Eleanor knew she would be gathering slips of dogwood berries and crimson toadstools to paint. Normally she liked to amble the roadside with her mother, but the aggression in her blood needed more action. Like stampeding the photogenic cows. Breathe. She inhaled the perfume of autumn. She tried harder to enjoy the red leaves of the sycamore and maple.

"I haven't seen Letty all day."

"Her husband insisted that they go to London. You should at least have the grace to look embarrassed."

Crestfallen, more like, she thought as she matched her mother's pace. "They will be back?"

"Maybe he feels that things are getting out of hand."

Letty will get him back Eleanor hoped, prayed.

The church steeple was the first sign of the village and then the Bull's End Pub. The proprietor was throwing slop onto a pile in the alley as they came around the corner. The rest of the village tilted down the wide street to the Windrush where a small bridge took walkers to the Angler's Rest Pub.

The small village mirrored the quiet babble of the sweet Windrush over its pebbles, except for the train station. The station had been built at the top of the town and faced the downward slant of shops. The building had just digested a trainload of passengers, and they streamed out its doors. She noticed a figure in black with swaths of netting covering her face trying to enter the station. She recognized the dress and its numerous faceted-jet beads that reflected light. The dress had been draped across the chair under Nelson.

With a blast, the train soon moved forward. Eleanor watched until the last car rounded a bend. If the Scented Woman was off to her solicitor, so be it, she thought. Eleanor rubbed her eyes and thought how easy it would be not to care and to sit with her mother and drink tea and rest with her eyes shut. To not care like Owens did was a gift. Especially now when he finds out that Brailford is going to agree with him. Eleanor had given the man a gift, all wrapped in a pretty bow.

It's naïve domestic Burgundy without any breeding, but I think you'll be amused by its presumption.
—James Thurber

Milliner's shops often lifted a woman's sorry soul. It was easy to forget the world when choosing head decor. Eleanor wandered from hat to hat. She should go see Louis, maybe leave her mother with a cup of tea. She picked up a black hat that was banded with imitation dahlias and striped bows. A thought pushed to the front of her mind. The castle is unwatched.

"Holy mother of God," she said to her reflection in a mirror. Eleanor's heart beat faster. Louis is in the police station, and Charlotte is on a train. Eleanor fingered the edge of the black felt. Maybe Tweedmouth's valet was still in residence. She had been wondering, dreaming even, of seeing the balcony. Faraday hadn't seen it. Owens had, and he had seen nothing. Renard was at home, no doubt. If Charlotte was already talking to her solicitor, there was no loss in trying. His mother was right—Louis had always suffered from the weight of excessive guilt.

Eleanor made her mother angry on the walk home, hurrying her so. Finally, she had John drive her to the castle. She refused to glance at the angels while she waited for John to ask for the valet at the servant's entrance.

"The butler won't ask for him," said John.

She'd get around that, first to get inside. The butler would have to let her in to speak to Renard, and Renard wouldn't turn her away. He would be bored. He would think her harmless.

The house was very quiet. The holy figures on the walls seemed hushed. The air was alive with dust, not specters. She was shown into the library. A Bible, leather bound and large, lay open on an ornate pedestal by the window. Here was the oratory. Light glowed upon it. It was opened to Thessalonians. How appropriate. She felt the need to move far from the Holy Book. A gout stool had been shoved into a corner. The Baron must have been in pain. The blotting pad on the desk was clean, but a newspaper, today's, was beside a chair. It had been read. Bifocals rested on a simple mahogany table under a lamp that dripped crystals. Tweedmouth was being displaced from his sanctuary.

The Baron had left the décor of this room alone. It reflected the castle's original, Tudor design and screamed Henry VIII, which is probably why it had been restored rather than changed. So the Baron had taste. It was a simple room of elegant cherry paneling done in patterns of squares. With a fire burning in the stone fireplace, it would be a snug place against the elements.

A good glass of hot whiskey and sugar would be the thing here, especially if one were in the grip of a cold. She thumbed through the smaller desk-sized Bible near the inkstand. It was worn and had scraps of paper jutting out here and there. Eleanor matched the sprawling notes to their insert pages—to-do messages based on holy passages. Cleanse Lady Marie Marcotte from the ways of the flesh, she read.

"Lady Albright."

She spun as Renard joined her with two glasses of claret in his hand. He had once been a tall man, but time had shortened him. He was still thin, the French never tended toward fat. His silver hair was thin as well and combed and lacquered to the side. That suggested vanity. The lack of cravat suggested confidence. His face had no fear, passion, or even warmth. The worst of his life had been lived. He spoke in simple French. "Would you like a glass?"

Prohibition gone, everyone was drinking at Abbey Leix. A pearly glass of claret sounded wonderful to her. "How are you, Monsieur Renard?"

"I am remarkably well, Lady Albright."

"You have lived here a long time. I have never asked you how you like England."

"It is cold."

"So the current weather agrees with you? France is so beautiful. Why do you stay here?"

Renard's shrug conveyed a lack of commitment, a quick disregard. "It seems that I am a religious man."

Eleanor watched his body language for a clue to the meaning of that. His body was still, his mouth relaxed. "You and the Baron had things in common then?"

The Frenchman was being a cat at play. Not a poodle at all, she thought as she could see that he was enjoying his private joke. He gave her one of the glasses of wine. She wondered what Renard thought of the Tweedmouths, the family he had lived with as a visitor for so long. "You will be staying on, I suppose, now that the Baron is gone, in spite of the weather?"

"The weather has been fine. The place is finally palpable, don't you agree —the air clear and breathable. How is your claret?"

She had taken a sip. "Very good."

"A merchant friend of mine sends it from France. I hope it is not wasted on you."

"No, it is not. You say that you are religious?"

"God is a heavy concept, either playing Him or on your knees praying to Him."

"You appear very well, Monsieur Renard. Do you ever take aspirin?"

"This," he replied, toasting her with his glass, "is what I take for my many ailments."

"Did you notice anything suspicious on the day the Baron died?"

"He was quieter than usual which was a blessing."

Renard wore as many rings as Charlotte. They were large stones, but just under gaudy. He was a man who appeared comfortable in his clothes. His blue eyes were always shuttered. She imagined it was an expression he had adopted after the accident in France. Even as an old man, he didn't sit in chairs. He lounged in them. She imagined that he saw himself as Charlotte saw herself, as a victim.

"You will never do this," he said without rancor, without emphasis.

"Do what?"

"Prove the man murdered. Even with that poor boy Louis...with a good barrister, the punch will become inconsequential. We both know that science is limited in these things, do we not?"

"So he was killed."

He shrugged his French shrug. "My religion says, in the end, no one will ever think murder, will want to think it; therefore, it does not exist. We can only prove what we believe."

"Do you know that he wasn't?"

"His illness killed him. Our illnesses will kill each of us. Do you understand?"

She was quiet for moment.

"What is your illness?"

Renard smiled at that and bowed his head.

"I think you are capable of killing Baron Tweedmouth," she said. "Expediency is everything to you. You have nowhere to go, or you would have gone there by now."

"It is a big world. There are many places to go."

"Where would you go to be so adored, so watched over, so taken care of? Where else would your existence be so cherished? We all need to be cherished."

"Tweedmouth cherished no one, except himself."

"And he is gone now, and you are in his library."

"His Bible is in his library. I would love to read to you his favorite verse. Would you allow me? The Book is still open to it."

Renard strolled to the bookstand. "Ah," he said as he glanced up at Eleanor when he got there. He used his finger as a guide and read in English. His command of the language was impressive. Trying to sound like Tweedmouth, he scoured his diction of French vowels.

He read: "'Let no one in any way deceive you, for it will not come unless the apostasy comes first and the man of lawlessness is revealed, the son of destruction, who opposes and exalts himself above every so-called god or object of worship.'" Renard closed the Book, letting the pages flip down in sections. He returned to his seat and his wine, and then he watched her.

"Maybe you played God and killed him to save yourself and your grand life here," she said.

"I would have liked to."

"He was about to demand that you leave."

Renard finished his drink. "You must see that this is pointless. If you cannot see that, then you must excuse me, Lady Albright. In any case, I have an appointment."

He left her to finish her wine in the quiet. It was too good to not finish. Her grandfather used to say, "Don't trust any man who can quote the Bible well." *Quite a performance*, she thought. She should stand and applaud. There were so many actors in this play. Tweedmouth had met his match in this man, that's why Charlotte loved her lap dog. He had sharp teeth, and he'd had enough of Baron Tweedmouth. His life was better, port in the Baron's library. Renard could finish out his days here now.

The old Baron's valet walked into the room as Renard left. "Excuse me, but you shouldn't be in here. You've got to leave."

"Here, the room, or the castle?"

The man clucked at the closed Bible. "Now he's done it," he said to the room. He opened the Good Book and flipped through the pages. He seemed to know where he was going.

"Done what?" asked Eleanor.

"Gone and upset things even more. He's always doing it with that slick smile of his. The master won't allow it, and to whom else will he be coming but to me to get his say. Do you see what I mean? There's a ghost here. I can't leave, anyway. I'm missing pay."

"Hamlet?"

The valet looked at her.

"Most ghosts come...for retribution, isn't it?"

"Ellen swore she's seen him. She's gone. She left the day after his lord-ship, Louis, had us empty...well anyway, she said to me, 'That'll stir him up. I'm not staying around here now.'" Gillette snatched the newspaper and closed the eyeglasses. "I'm sorry," he said. He walked toward the door.

Eleanor stood. "Maybe I can help. I suppose that I might be on the Baron's side." At her words, she felt queasy. Still, it was a good argument. "I'm trying to find out what happened. Who killed him? Isn't that what the Baron would come back for?"

The valet stopped, his back to her.

"I suppose, Lady Albright."

When he turned, she noticed his pale face and the bags under his eyes. He hadn't been sleeping. The distrust in his eyes belittled her. He must have been loyal to the Baron, galling as that might be, or maybe he was protecting someone else. Not Renard, obviously.

"I'm trying to help Louis. I am." If the valet were sizing her up, maybe that would help. "I'd like to see the balcony. Just the balcony," she said. "Has anyone cleaned it?"

"No one's been there. No one would go there. There have been terrible things in this house. A woman who used to work here had her throat close up. She had to stop eating for thirty days."

"Forty nights in the desert without manna?"

"I've never liked this house."

"Mr. Gillette, isn't it. Did you know that Lord Tweedmouth was to meet his solicitor the morning of his death?"

"He expected a visitor."

"He didn't tell you whom? Do you know what Lord Tweedmouth wanted with his solicitor?"

"I didn't know he expected his solicitor."

"He didn't tell you or the family?"

"No."

"Any changes in his routine, diet?"

"No, he was careful as always."

"A change of medication? What doctor was he seeing?"

Gillette shook his head. "He'd didn't see anyone. Called them all quacks."

Brailford must have loved that. "No doctor then. He was suffering from asthma and gout. I mean his ankles looked like tree trunks, and he wasn't taking anything, even laudanum?"

"It's an opiate, he'd say. There were some days. 'Gillette, where's my package.' I heard that from the Thursday until it came on the Friday."

"Who delivered it? What did the man look like?"

"Never said anything to me. He always had a cap tight on his head down low, close to his eyes. Clean hands though, except that last time he had a bruise, here just under the nail. I think the nail will come off."

"How did Monsieur Renard and the Baron get along?"

"Called him a French bloodsucker. 'I'll pull that French bloodsucker out of my vein,' he used to say."

"And Charlotte?"

Gillette shrugged.

He won't comment on the family, she thought. The valet was a hairy man, which made his name, Gillette, quite funny. He didn't keep a beard, but one was already sprouting. His eyes were widely spaced and had the look of a man about to jump out of his skin, like a man under pressure. This wasn't a man who enjoyed puzzles. He took life at face value.

"The balcony may have some answers, if you'd allow me to have a gander. I'm sure the Baron would approve. He'll not bother us."

Eleanor followed Gillette back out into the hall and up a staircase and then down a narrow hallway to Tweedmouth's bedroom. It was as barren as Gillette had described, as barren as an abandoned outpost after the plague had swept through. The scene only lacked the inevitable dust, cobwebs, fallen chair, and abandoned doll. She entered and seemed to feel a breeze that came from nowhere. No wonder the servants wouldn't come here.

The heavy velvet curtains that hung over the balcony door were closed. Gillette parted them. The light stabbed at her eyes, and she walked out with the glare burning her retinas. Relief eased through her as she moved onto the balcony where a sweet sun livened the mood. She gazed at the vista for a moment to let her eyes adjust. She breathed in the warm air and let the eerie, vacant room ease from her thoughts.

Eleanor began a search at the farthest point of the balcony. She worked around the area and found nothing but a light layer of dirt and bird droppings. She put her hands on her hips and surveyed the couch, and a blanket...most of it on the floor.

She started, "What have we here? Has anything been moved?"

Gillette walked to her side. "A constable did lift the blanket corner, just here, to look under the couch."

"Did he find anything?"

"No."

"The table legs are on the blanket." Eleanor crouched and glanced up at Gillette who was looking over her shoulder. "Did the constable knock the table over and then replace it?"

"No. The constable picked up a glass that was on it."

"I've been told that nothing was in the glass. Was it here to take some medication? Did he drink water to take his medications?"

"No, never, he thought it unhealthy. He'd drink it for the cure, at Bath. That's all."

Regurgitation cocktail. "You've never brought him water?"

"I'd never bring him water. Anyway, I didn't bring him that. There was no silver server. I'd have brought it on a silver server."

"Who brought it then?"

"I couldn't say."

"What did he take medicine with?"

"Tea."

"Did you bring any medications?"

"He didn't take any medications. I brought him his tea, and I took it away." She sifted through the invalid's blanket. When she found nothing there or on the sofa, Eleanor searched under the high-legged couch on her hands and knees.

"There's something here," she said. "Let's move this. It's dried to the floor. The wood is not sticky here. What can we scrape this up with?"

"I've got a sixpence."

"I suppose my nail will do as well."

With the bit of paper in her hand, Eleanor sat on the edge of the sofa. She inspected it, holding it up to the light, a bit of medicinal paper maybe and under the sofa of a sick man that took no medications.

She took in the hypnotic wave of the green hills and felt that if she were very ill, she would like to sit here too. "What happened that evening, Gillette?"

"I just gave him his package and his tea. I came back for the pot and the cup. In the morning, I came back with his tea again. He wasn't there. I waited, and then heard a scream from below."

"Louis stayed the night at Haversack's?"

"He...he had forgotten his gun, he said."

"Thank you, Gillette. I'm forever indebted to you. Shall we tell the Baron to let you be? You've done your duty to him." She gave the balcony one last turn and noticed a smeared line of dirt, faint and in between the sofa and the railing. "Let's gird ourselves to go back through that room," she said to Gillette.

She laughed to herself later as she rode in her carriage through the village. It would be etched in her memory forever—the two of them running through Tweedmouth's bedroom, her skirt well up her ankle.

❧ 18 ❧

It is only shallow people who do not judge by appearances. The true mystery of the
world is the visible, not the invisible.
—Oscar Wilde

A jangle at the door announced Eleanor's entry. The village chemist popped up from behind his counter and smiled. This was the man she'd sat with many afternoons. As a child full of awe, she had laughed at poufs of smoke or at color-changing liquids. He was a modern man who could have been an employee of Bayer or its ilk except that he loved to help cure the ailments of the people he had grown up with in the village. He was a smiling favorite of all the spinsters at the village dances. Eleanor put the fragile square of paper on the counter in front of him. She had decided that a witness was important.

"Mr. Smyth, I'd like to test this piece of medicinal paper for salicylic acid."

"Knowing what to test for is most of the job." He crossed his hands together in a scissor motion three times, like a magician performing an act, and then opened his hands as a magician might in showing the trick done and the item reappeared. "Come into the back."

She walked around the counter and followed the graceful man through a narrow aisle between the tall shelves. Before he opened the door, she could smell the laboratory. The rotten smell of acid and alkaline diffused from the room. The odor made her feel childlike again. Oh, the days here watching him concoct his patent medicines, on the sly with her mother in bed with the vapors. He sold his own tinctures from five-gallon demijohns and his own remedies for burns, colic, poisoning and constipation. Mothers loved him. He made his own confections as well, and Eleanor popped one in her mouth.

While she chewed, the chemist handed Eleanor a glass tube held by a clamp. He told her that her paste for making hands white was selling well as he pushed various chemicals in narrow jars toward her. "Aspirin is a member of a hydroxy group."

"We use ferric chloride. The chemical reaction with the salicylic acid should turn it deep purple."

"Excellent."

With tweezers, she dropped a piece of the paper into a test tube. She added water and then some chloride solution. The solution turned light purple. There wasn't much aspirin on the paper, but it was aspirin. The real thing.

Eleanor swirled the liquid around in the glass. "He'd never take a dose of aspirin unless he was in great pain. Say he hurt enough to try again. That's a possibility that has to be considered. Thinking Brailford a quack and himself superior, he'd try it one time. So this may be the one time. The problem is aspirin doesn't constrict the pupils."

Smyth eyed his former pupil. "That's what this is about—the Baron of Tweedmouth?"

"What would a person with severe gout who couldn't take aspirin take instead that constricts the pupils?"

"Laudanum, but I wasn't sending him any. I can't decide if I'm happy you've taken an interest in this." He took the test tube she handed him.

"I've been told that he wouldn't take laudanum, and anyway, laudanum is a liquid. Oh, I don't know. There *must* be something else on this paper. Something that constricts pupils. The powdered form for laudanum is—"

"Opium, just pure opium."

The shock of the word had Eleanor staring at her mentor. "Close your mouth," he said to her.

"Opium!" She paced the floor. "The unmitigated gall of the ass. Hypocrite of the first water. Won't take laudanum, but he's stuffing his gob with opium. It does makes sense, and it would hide the taste of aspirin and constrict the pupils."

As Smyth set test fresh tubes on the table and took down more jars, he said, "Was this an accidental death or murder then?"

"If we have both aspirin *and* opium on this paper, it has to be murder. No one would take both, especially Tweedmouth. It's not trace amounts of aspirin either, like a slow poisoning. Somebody wanted him dead."

"Opium is an alkaloid like aspirin—a phenanthrene—two percent formaldehyde and sulfuric acid. Light this up." Smyth pushed back his glasses again as he waited for the end result. He held the glass tube up to the light.

Her eyes met Smyth's. "That is definitively opium." Eleanor dropped into a chair. A slow smile spread across her face. "I have him," she said.

"Have who?" Smyth sat down next to her, his face a mixture of pride and worry.

"The killer. Tweedmouth was in pain, and he couldn't take aspirin. Opium's a drug he probably knew well from his wild youth. So much for accidentally falling off the balcony; the man couldn't breathe well enough to walk from the aspirin, and he must have been comatose from the opium."

"Or maybe deeply disoriented."

"Or disoriented? Disoriented! No, I still have him. Disoriented or not, he wouldn't have taken both. The question is how was he getting his opium? What with the Christian Union for the Severance of the British Empire with the Opium Traffic of which he was a card-carrying member, it had to be kept secret, and he was house bound. Someone knew his secret."

Smyth patted her hand. "I'm not sure I want to encourage you in this. The opium trade is—

"Not a place for a woman?"

"Not a place for anybody, male or female."

"Nor is murder, I've been told."

E leanor stepped from the shop back into the sunshine, knowing she needed either Faraday or Owens again. The problem of tracing the deliveryman to an opium den seemed insurmountable. Not much to go on either—a bruised fingernail. She had no desire to rush over and tell Owens. *Oh yes, I'll help you with that, Lady Albright.* In a pig's eye. While she thought on it all, she decided that a celebration was called for anyway. The new information was vital. She had found out one of the Baron's little secrets.

She walked into a pastry shop two doors down and eased into a yellow patterned chair. She hadn't realized how tense she'd been. She dropped her shoulders as she sat in the pleasant, low-ceilinged room. It smelled of sugar. She ordered a sticky bun and wished she could remain here for a long time, as home had become difficult. Over time, the tea ritual made her almost somnolent and the cake boosted her feeling of wellbeing. She was getting closer. She had created doubt for Louis.

A woman just entering the shop caught her attention. Olivia! Oh God no! Eleanor tipped her head down to hide behind the broad brim of her hat. Of all people. She tried to hunch down further. Oh rot! Not now.

Someone called out to Olivia, and the girl searched the room. Olivia smiled when she caught sight of Eleanor. It was not a pleasant smile.

The girl made Eleanor think of her father. Lord Haversack who had been forced to live next to Tweedmouth for ten years. They had hated each other from day one. As Olivia Haversack was engaged to Lord Charles, Louis' best friend, that was going to be an awkward, impossible wedding. With Tweedmouth there, it was not destined to be the perfect occasion Olivia would expect and demand. With all this hoopla for the wedding, all the prominent guests that would be coming, The Haversacks had a reason to keep the man sick. Maybe they had wanted him sick, but not dead. Well, death would work too, especially a natural demise. *Tidy and dead, and I am fouling the mixture.*

Olivia had Eleanor in her sights. "All alone?" Olivia said as she sat. She turned to a server. "Tea, scones, three bags in the pot to that table." As if to confirm Eleanor's thought, Olivia said, "You are a pest. My family is beside themselves over Louis."

"He is the household saint of choice," Eleanor snapped, then regretted it.

"Oh please, do be serious for a moment. Can you? Louis has all but stopped eating. Charles feels guilty. I said to him yesterday, what could you have done? What could you have said? Eleanor's impossible. It's all upsetting the wedding plans, but I must think of what's best for Charles and Louis. How it got to this point, I don't know." Olivia looked at Eleanor like she was a slug to throw salt on.

Eleanor decided to continue with the hand at play. She had questions for Olivia. No better time than the present. "If it's any consolation to your family, I don't believe Louis did it. I am working for him."

"What a good friend you are. Is that how it goes? You work on his behalf, and he ends up in jail? You have made quite a mess of things." Olivia preened her feathers. Eleanor didn't know if it was Olivia's statement to her or as a response to the compliments from a passing man that had made the feathers shine more.

"The arrest is all on Owens' shoulders," said Eleanor.

Olivia rolled her eyes. "Do you know anything about anything? Tweedmouth was awful. The Baron ruined people lives. He's ruined Daddy's, and he's ruining my wedding, Charles is so worried."

"How has he ruined your father?"

Olivia stared at Eleanor for a moment, and then she smiled. She wagged her finger in front of Eleanor's face. "My reason for coming over was to have you stop detecting. You see, you're so bad at it anyway."

She'd get nothing from Olivia. Watching the girl fish into her bag and pull out a tissue, Eleanor wondered if the Haversacks could feel that entitled, to try and get rid of Tweedmouth for their land and for the precious wedding. She decided yes.

Olivia brought the tissue to her lips and then squeezed the middle together. She must have noted that she was being watched. "It's sort of sweet that you don't swallow," she said while placing the tissue on Eleanor's empty sticky bun plate. "It's supposed to be good for teeth. Charles swears by it."

Charles would know. His teeth could light up a dark room. Every woman in England had fallen for his wide, bright smile and his perfect teeth. He had always been a top choice in the marriage market. "I read about you and Charles, every day in the society section. He is quite a catch," Eleanor said letting some of her thoughts spill out.

"We are in it so often these days."

"You're keeping a scrapbook?" Eleanor watched Olivia soften.

"Oh, of course."

"Who's who, wedding in just a month. Your dress is—"

"From Paris. It's to be pearled along the bottom of the skirt and on the sleeves. I would not have the first twenty designs—too ordinary. It had to be original. I want to set a new style for the year." Olivia stopped. Her eyes darkened. She considered and then said, "Why don't you go to Owens and say that you did it? You owe Louis that much."

"I will get him out of jail."

"You are so dreary. Tweedmouth died just in time," Olivia said.

"What does that mean?"

"You're the detective, read darling. I do. She searched her bag and brought out something in a wrapper. "Here. You're going to need to smile more to get out of this mess." Olivia laughed. She stood to go.

"Won't your father gain back the parcel of land that was in dispute with the old Baron of Tweedmouth? Won't Louis just hand it to him? Charles, your fiancé, is his best friend. Not to mention the problems with your wedding guests should Tweedmouth have to be included."

"As if I'm not having wedding problems now, thanks to you? Tweedmouth dying was a boon to one and a favor to all. No one likes you for interfering. Not even Louis. He dislikes you most of all." Olivia stood, picked up her skirts and joined her large table of friends.

*E*leanor *walked home by herself. Olivia was right, her mother was right. Like the dust on the road that was over-powdering her face and dress, her social life was a parched thing and was sticking to the roof of her mouth. If Olivia was right, and she probably was, she'd lost Louis too. Eleanor wiped the corners of her eyes, over and over all the way home. When she met Letty in the hallway of the house, Eleanor just stopped herself from flying into the woman's arms.*

"Darling, you look as if you've been rolling on the road."

"It's all quite hopeless," Eleanor blurted out. "Everyone wanted the man dead. It's impossible. So many motives so little time. The man will be forgotten and buried before I get to him."

"Come, come, tea first and then a bath."

"No, something Olivia said. First I need the newspaper."

"Fiennes read it in the library." The windows were large in her father's favorite room. He had loved light and his wife's garden. On the other walls were Alannah's paintings. Whenever Eleanor was in this room, she wondered why her father had left her mother so alone. Habits, maybe, he wasn't one to break any.

Eleanor found the London Times by the windows. "Read, darling,' she remembered Olivia saying, and this is what Olivia read, the social columns. Eleanor sat with the paper just as Letty carried in the tray. "The Bouffant Bride—"

"Who?"

"Olivia. I had the misfortune of seeing her today."

"Good name."

"No one wanted Tweedmouth dead more than the Haversacks. The man being sick and close to death was a golden opportunity for them. One that they might not have been able to pass by. Look, she's in the paper again today." Eleanor handed the newsprint to Letty.

"A good three paragraphs," said Letty. "Oh look, The King is off to France again, a French shoot of some kind. I must tell the husband. He doesn't read the social section. Knudson and wife are just back from America. Lord and Lady Reasoner entertained Lord Gampper and his awful wife at an elaborate dinner with grand decorations yesterday. The centerpiece was built of 'fruit with smilax entwined around a crystal basket. Fruit imitations of silk were mixed with tulle were draped on the chairs.' She always was one to overdo it.

"Olivia is mentioned four times. Their social standing will be impressive after the wedding. I don't know who is a better catch, the bride or the groom. Oh no, The Morrills declared bankruptcy. No wonder they've been so very—"

"Strained," finished Eleanor.

"Do be mother and pour the tea," said Letty. "I'm always interested in the pending divorces, such a brave thing to do." Letty glanced pointedly at Eleanor and then back to the paper. "The Horns, the Warners...now that's a blessing...Tweedmouths...good God."

Eleanor's head jerked up. "Tweedmouth. Letty—"

"Tweedmouth!" Letty crushed the paper onto her lap.

Eleanor leaned forward. She took the paper from Letty and read the announcement. "How could this happen? He's dead."

Letty leaned into the back of the chair and dropped her hands to her lap. "Well, divorce is a man's game. Maybe that's why he let Renard stay. He needed grounds for divorce."

"He had enough money to pay the divorce court for an annulment," Eleanor said as she folded the paper. Anyway, it's the timing. It's so timely."

Letty stood and pulled the cord for the butler. "We need a drink. He could have wanted to save the money, or nobody on the court likes him, and he couldn't pay his way out. All men have to prove is simple adultery as opposed to women who have to prove adultery and cruelty."

"Why did Charlotte have Renard in then? I mean his being there helped Tweedmouth divorce her."

"Brandies please," Letty said to the butler. "She must have been very unhappy."

"Think of it, Letty, the waiting period ended. The final decree issued on, probably, the day he died. She didn't know."

Letty sat again. "Personally, I think she could have proven collusion. I mean was she really having sex with Renard in that house with Tweedmouth there? The Baron must have paid off a maid or something to swear before the court that she was an adulteress. A day late and a shilling short. If she killed him, it was all for nothing. Poor darling."

"Poor darling, good God. I wonder if that's why she went to London. You know what else I found out, Letty? Tweedmouth was taking opium. Yes, mixed with aspirin, a drug that gives him severe asthma."

"What an amazing day you've had. Bravo to you."

Eleanor absorbed some brandy. "There are three problems. One is that without isolating the mixture in the Baron's system through a new autopsy, we can't prove he was taking it. Two, the cadaveric alkaloid defense. Even if we had access to the body, isolating plant alkaloids like opium and aspirin is unreliable. Substances named cadaveric alkaloids form in bodies after death. They're carbon based. These alkaloids mimic the reactions of qualitative color tests for vegetable alkaloids like opium and aspirin. There is the possibility that if I am allowed to run a test for either aspirin or opium on the Baron, the test will be positive not because of the presence of the drugs, but because of the presence of cadaveric alkaloids that are mimicking the drugs. Three, a jury might not convict a case of poisoning by aspirin."

"One or the other would have been sufficient."

"Someone was poisoning his opium."

"And thinking how well it was working," said Letty. "Or actually, not working fast enough. He did end up over the balcony."

🎖 19 🎖

Some circumstantial evidence is very strong, as when you find a trout in the milk.
—Henry David Thoreau

Eleanor studied the Whitney Police Station. It had been built in blocks of yellow limestone and was indistinguishable in character and form from the buildings next to it with their shingle roofs and Tudor style windows. The station was situated on a small green, a bit of park in the village, where lime trees shaded the park and decorated it in greenish columns. "Love?" she said to herself. "They should be stunted growing so close to Owens."

Opposite the station was a Norman church. From atop its doorway two rows of demons with large eyes and with something like fishing hats on their heads stared at the station's entrance. She understood the demons constant watch over the police station, but how could the lime trees grow so well next to such harsh conditions as in the constant cold blast of Owens' verbal blasts.

Mature red roses grew over an arch of steel mesh in front of the station door, love abounds. It was a door that didn't suggest warmth—attached as it was to Owens' place of ego augmentation. Eleanor hesitated to touch the doorknob, but it was important to keep Owens abreast of events and to try, hopefully, to win his cooperation. She felt better after Letty and that cup of tea, and she still felt good about her discoveries, but defending them to the obtuse Owens was similar to being on the marriage market again. Both needed a large, fake smile.

The door seemed impenetrable. She was tired of defending good ideas to men who subjected those thoughts to scrutiny, not on their merit, but because the ideas came from a woman's mouth. A little anger heated her. It did at these moments. From the heat, she always moved forward. She reached for the doorknob and pushed hard. Her entrance was one that a woman can make with wall-to-wall hat and six petticoats manufactured to rustle. Everyone knew she had arrived, and all heads turned to her. Perfect! Eleanor's walking stick thumped on the floor, and then she leaned forward on it. Constable Whitman sat at his desk. She greeted him by saying that she had important news. He nodded for her to pass.

Eleanor walked into Owens' office. The Chief Constable looked up and groaned.

"Yes, I'm here. I have news that you will want to hear."

"Lady Albright, you know that this is not acceptable for a woman of your stature. Why do you want to get involved in this? A real investigation isn't like in a book. Women shouldn't read. It puts such nonsense in their heads. Your father liked you to read, no doubt?"

"I can't think of a novelist who writes books just for men."

Owens appeared headachy. The proof lay on his desk in the medicinal paper, and in the glass of water beside it that distorted the packet's curves. The Chief Constable was hungover. The smell of his breath and skin and the bloodshot eyes confirmed that. The line of his muttonchops was less distinct today. The edges blurred into the growth on his unshaven face.

"It is important."

Owens groaned again and opened the medicinal paper. The powder melted in the water. His face warped from the taste as he drank the liquid down.

"It does have quite a distinctive flavor, doesn't it?"

"What?"

"Aspirin."

"What are you here for, Lady Albright?"

"Aspirin."

Owens shoved a packet toward her.

"I have some already, thank you. Mine is on this." Eleanor produced a fingertip-sized square of paper.

Owens looked at it in her palm. He didn't look long. "What is that?"

"A bit of medicinal paper."

Owens sighed, or maybe the sound was one, long, profound profanity. "Lady Albright, I don't need any more evidence for my case. Louis has said that he hit his father and threw him off the balcony. I have him in custody."

"Yes, Yes. The table on the balcony was up-righted onto the blanket, the smears of dirt from the sofa to the railing where he dragged his father, the spilled water. This case always seemed to have two unrelated parts. We could never put them together, and when I saw the table on the balcony up righted onto the blanket, I knew someone had knocked it over and then righted it again. If the Baron had knocked it over in a fit or in panic, he would never have put the table back on its legs and placed the glass on top. The water spilled. It stuck this paper onto the floor of the balcony. There were dirt streaks on Tweedmouth's nightdress. He'd been dragged. Lines of dirt on the balcony, made more definite by the water, prove it. Louis did hit the Baron in the face. In panic, he dragged him to the edge and threw him off."

Owens had been pulling at his sideburns and staring at his hand, stretching and flexing it. With her last two sentences, he glanced up with a hunter's pre-kill, satisfied smile.

"The Baron wasn't alive when his nose was broken or when he hit bottom. His heart wasn't pumping blood. No bleeding," she said leaning toward him and with her eyes glittering with challenge.

"Prove it."

The bruising you idiot! Could the man be any more obtuse? "According to the Times, the Baron was divorcing his wife. He was dead from what's on this piece of paper. Louis was just acting out deserved retribution. You can't condemn a man for killing a corpse."

"That's a good story. Take up writing."

As if it had palsy, her hand stiffened into a fist. "The Baron was to sign a new will and guardian papers and probably divorce papers. His solicitor was coming in the morning."

"Disinherited, the boy as the killer makes even more sense."

"My grandfather used to say, 'Secrets are like a sick stomach. You can't, for love, life or money, keep them down.' Yes, Louis had a secret. So did Charlotte. Divorce is a good motive too. Aren't you even the least bit curious about this bit of paper?" Eleanor put the paper on the desk between them.

Owens leaned back against his chair and folded his hands over his chest. "Aspirin?" Owens rolled his eyes.

"Exactly!" She stared at him, and she'd had some practice lately keeping a smile on her face, sometimes until her jaw muscles ached. "There is something else." She waited, feeling for her timing. She wanted his undivided attention. He would not take her for granted again. "Opium."

"Opium!" Owens lost his hard look.

That's better.

"Yes, Chief Constable, opium on medicinal paper found dried, by the water from the glass, to the stone floor of the balcony. Thank God it's been so hot and dry, or the proof would have been washed away. I analyzed it with Smyth. He'll testify to both. The opium drugged Tweedmouth, a dose of aspirin mixed in with it killed him and, I suspect, very small amounts of it had been in the process of killing him over the month of his illness."

"People don't die from aspirin." Owens face though was scrunched in worry.

Eleanor warmed to the change. The worry on Owens' face was delicious. "Most people don't. Tweedmouth's valet said that six months ago just the time Baron's asthma got worse the deliveryman of the Baron's opium changed to a short man with a bruise on his little finger.

"Of course you're realizing that the flavor of aspirin is so distinctive that it would take a blending of medications to get a man who is allergic to it to take it. Since opium is just as bitter as aspirin, it became the perfect vehicle."

"This is a string of fantasy that I'm not stupid enough to buy into."

She leaned toward him. "I've come straight from the Baron's doctor, Doctor Brailford of Harley Street, cross my heart. The renowned doctor said that he once prescribed aspirin for the Baron's gout. The dose nearly killed Tweedmouth. He's allergic to it, along with possibly eggs and milk and nuts. Ask the cook at Tweedmouth's club about how so picky the man is about eating.

"The killer must have been measuring out the grains of aspirin a few at a time. But it was dicey. Too large an amount could kill Tweedmouth. Do you suppose that the murderer's intention was to kill Tweedmouth or to just keep him very ill? Of course, he or she could suffocate him later—you know, just in case the aspirin didn't work—with one finger on the pillow."

"Whitman!" Owens bellowed. He leaned forward both hands gripping the desk's edge. A rush of air stirred her hair. Eleanor snapped open her fan to disperse the odor of his breath.

"Yes, sir."

"Take the lady's statement."

Eleanor stood.

Owens stood with her. His face looked like an inflated red balloon. He knocked over the glass on his desk. Water flooded the scrap of paper there.

"I believe that you have reenacted the evening of the murder, Chief Constable Owens. How clever of you." As he sputtered about, her smile felt more genuine and less painful.

She rescued her paper, and Whitman mopped up the water.

From a corner of the room Owens said, "Brailford or no, I never heard of anyone dying from aspirin, and a jury won't buy it. It's one doctor from many. Even if aspirin did kill him, Louis could have given it to him, and punched his face in."

"As Lady Tweedmouth might say, and toss him over the wall? Why bring attention to a natural death? I'm just bringing you up to date, Chief Constable. I think that we are working with two different people here. Tweedmouth had already divorced Charlotte. I saw it in the paper. Have another autopsy ordered. One that checks for aspirin." She knew what Owens would say.

"She had to kill him before he signed the will. He was dying too slowly. She had to give him an extra-large dose. I suspect she would have used the pillow next."

Owens gave her a terse nod. "Ditto for Louis then, and I've got a confession."

"I'd scan the bushes for a man with a bruised finger who has opium contacts anyway—just in case."

His smile was not warm. "Seems like a good job for you."

"Poisoning is for ladies and for very old men. Just now, when you took your aspirin, you took it with water. Most of us would bring water with a medicine packet to a patient, be that opium or aspirin. The valet wouldn't though, not to Tweedmouth. The man didn't drink water under any circumstances, according to Gillette. You have the water glass that was on the balcony with no silver server under it. Why was it there? Who brought it?"

"Not his wife," said Owens. "She must also know that he doesn't drink water. Aspirin doesn't poison people, or opium."

"Along that line of reasoning, Louis must have known his father didn't drink water. What about Renard? Renard was going to be thrown out faster than moldy rubbish."

"You've no proof," he said.

She wanted to say neither do you, but she stopped. She realized, maybe too late, that she needed this man's help. Owens was quiet for a long time. Eleanor bit the inside of her lip. She could taste the blood. She needed some doubt from him, a little doubt. He walked the constable to the door, talking to him on the way, and then he returned and sat down.

Eleanor waited. It was a long drop off a high horse. She noticed the fishing gear propped in the corner. A small mirror hung tilted on the wall with a dry shaving brush and a safety razor on a shelf beside it. On the opposite wall, all the taxidermy stared at her. She stared the weasel in the eye. The poor weasel, he never stood that dull in life.

In a way, she felt sorry for Owens. He was a superstitious, bully of a man, who had learned the first behavior from his mother and the second from his wife. Women could be powerful beings. Harassment came in handy for the small job of policing a village, but he'd never had to deal with a murder. She wondered how he'd ever made chief constable. Fishing with his boss, maybe.

From back behind his desk, Owens controlled himself. His eye twitched from the effort. "Thank you, Lady Albright. "The constable will take your report. The boy says that he did it. Who am I to call him a liar? Whatever you say, and I'm sure you think you're very smart, I just took a packet of the stuff, and I'm alive. **Aspirin don't poison a person**. The boy couldn't wait any longer for his money, or his anger got to him, or both."

"I would like to talk to Louis."

"Certainly, madam. Don't think I run a jail here." He laughed at his joke, and then paused. "Maybe you'll do the boy some good. Get him to eat. It can't look like I'm starving him."

Eleanor hesitated when she first saw Louis's gaunt face. He was a suffering saint, throwing ashes in his breakfast, without a God. Hopelessness caved his shoulders, fouled his body, and dulled his eyes. Louis looked like he should never have been born. He didn't or wouldn't turn his head to take comfort in her visit. She wished she had thought to bring him something. Her anger at Owens rose. Such a fool for bringing Louis here!

His hand shook as he brushed a fly from his face. "Martin! Tea!" She called out. "And a razor!"

Eleanor took Louis's cheeks in her hands. She tried to infuse him with her fury.

"Who is caring for you?" she asked. She yelled for tea again. "Fortified," she added.

"What in God's name are you doing to yourself?"

"In God's name?" Louis said. "I'm doing what's always done in God's name."

"I knew you'd do this to yourself. I knew there was something. Were you lacing your father's opium with aspirin?"

"What are you talking about?" She appreciated the exasperation in his voice. He backed away from her grasp.

"Your father was poisoned by aspirin in his opium. Did you put it there?"

"I hit him. I killed him."

"I told you he did it," Owens said from the door.

Eleanor ignored him. "Yes, *Ignis fatuus*, I know that you hit him and tossed the body over the railing." She took his hand, warmed it. "But he was already dead. He was already dead from the aspirin."

He blinked at her.

"Did you know that your father was taking opium?"

"My father! Taking opium! That's absurd!"

He'd never believe her. Tweedmouth in life had been too convincing. It was pointless. Louis had never lied in his life. After his singular try at it, he had turned himself in. She had always wondered how he could be Tweedmouth's son.

"Why did you hit him?"

"I couldn't...resist. He...he wouldn't respond. I couldn't take any more of his contempt.

"He never defended himself."

"It was the effects of the opium. Didn't you think he might already be dead?" she asked.

The tea came. Eleanor lifted the lid on the tin pot. A thin layer of leaves floated there. "Bring in the canister please, Martin. This needs to be fortified."

"Do you take sugar?"

Louis was now staring at her with his bleak eyes. At least she had his attention. "You thought he was alive?"

He took the cup she handed him.

"He wasn't. There is someone out there who is guiltier than you. It wasn't a secret in your family that aspirin aggravated your father's health, was it? You didn't know that your father had been taking opium, regularly. You were hitting a dead man, and he deserved it. He was a sick man. Afterwards, you threw him over the balcony hoping the fall would cover the fist-to-his-face, didn't you?" She wasn't getting the hope-filled reaction from Louis she was reaching for, and Owens stood in the corner, gloating.

"Can't have sons roughing up their sick fathers," Owens said.

She turned to the chief. "You're going to disregard the nose not bleeding just because it doesn't fit into your idea of the crime. He's an easy solution to your problem, and you're taking advantage because you won't go out and do your work." Now she'd done it.

Fed up to her teeth, she turned to Louis again. "Did you bring your father water?"

"My father doesn't drink water," he said in a tired voice.

"You straightened the downed table and replaced the spilled glass of water?"

"I dried my shoes. Footprints you know in the dust. I read Holmes." His face opened and then closed again like the joke had been on him.

Owens snorted. It sounded just like her husband.

"I'm not, in the end, as good as you think," Louis said.

Deflated, she leaned against the wall. Being good—it's all Louis had had, and now, in his mind, that was gone.

"If you can't convince the accused, how can you convince a judge at an inquest?" asked Owens. "It's time to bury the body."

Stupid cop.

E leanor arrived home to find her mother and the cook head-to-head over a menu for a tea party.

"Oh, there you are," said Alannah. "Is Faraday still in London?"

Eleanor was in no mood. Like the strike of a hammer on an anvil, she said, "Yes."

"For a day or so?"

"He's returning sometime tomorrow evening."

"I'm having a small impromptu garden party tomorrow. You will play for us?"

"I'm busy."

"It's just a small affair," said Alannah.

"Give it up, Mother."

"What are you talking about? Oh, I don't have time for this. Just be there."

"I'm so lucky to have so many with my best interests in mind," Eleanor mumbled as she walked away from the battlefield. She had to locate that deliveryman before the funeral and before Louis hung himself.

❦ 20 ❦

If you can keep your head when all about you
Are losing theirs and blaming it on you,
If you can trust yourself when all men doubt you,
But make allowance for their doubting too;
—Rudyard Kipling

leanor woke up in a terrible mood. She crashed around her room like a child with a temper. She'd tried the rest of the afternoon and evening yesterday to find out something about the deliveryman. Nothing. She needed to do more, and she didn't know what to do next, and Faraday was at his father's birthday until tomorrow. She couldn't go door to door to places that provided opium and ask about a man with a bruised fingernail. She didn't even know where such places were. Her green, brushed velveteen skirt with the creamy Brussels lace blouse hung on the corner of her wardrobe. Oh, she didn't have time to primp for Peacock!

"Your hair, milady."

Her maid tucked and pushed the thick hair into place with pins sticking out of her mouth like a cactus. Eleanor ignored her reflection. She thought instead of ways to find out how much of all this Charlotte knew. Eleanor laughed at herself. Detecting did lend itself to a woman's natural talent for gathering gossip. The way women handled it gossip was rough-edged and ugly.

Alannah appeared in her mirror. "I came in to make you change. I thought that you might be in that awful pink thing again." Alannah placed herself in a large chair beside the fire. "You will be in your best today. Not like at the croquet party, your pink against the green lawn was ghastly. The clergy have a certain influence. He is still single himself."

"Deliver me."

"I see that you're in a mood. I'm going. I'll see you at breakfast."

The maid poked Eleanor with a pin.

"Ouch. Right, but I'm tired of hearing how difficult it's been for her. It's not difficult now. I should be finding a husband for her, so I can live my life." Eleanor poked a finger into the pot of hand-cream and then rubbed in into her hands.

What foolishness. It's all foolishness. Ignis fatuus. Louis got it correct. It's the fire that burns in us all.

Too soon, Reverend Edmund Peacock, dressed exceptionally dapper for the afternoon, waited at the bottom of the stairs for Eleanor's cascade down. He smelled sweet from his toilet. He must have been here for some minutes as his perfume had diffused deep into the hall. Her mother was there already, and she led him into the military room—the duty room that was getting so much use these days. She and her mother had never used it pre-Tweedmouth. The room felt more like a wake instead of a party. Even Alannah struggled to find words. Eleanor had words if she were allowed to say them.

Alannah suggested fresh air. "Reverend Peacock, you are early for the party. Shall we walk in the garden for a moment?"

"How delightful," the Peacock purred. "The weather is perfect."

"This way then, Reverend Peacock," said Alannah, grabbing her daughter. "Do you enjoy gardening?"

"I enjoy beautiful flowers. I do not dig." He was brushing lint from his lapel, and almost walking into a potted fern.

Eleanor shoved laughter behind her cheeks and said instead, "My mother is quite skilled at flowers. Even at this time of the year, she has something blooming."

In the garden, she listened to Peacock with the external part of her ear and let her mother suffer. Alannah had brought this down on herself. Eleanor strayed a little apart and watched a goldfinch feed on thistle-seed; the trees were dropping leaves; the purple juniper berries were resplendent.

As they walked, Peacock rarely needed responses to his monologue. Eleanor noticed that the blackberry bush needed picking. She thought about the deliveryman. He had been in the process of murdering Tweed-mouth. What motive? Maybe Haversack hired him. He stayed as a beater, and then Haversack shot him. She laughed. Eleanor found herself back at the garden chairs before she remembered that her mother and Peacock walked with her.

"What is so funny, Lady Albright?"

"Oh good, Letty's here," Eleanor said and then watched her mother perk up as did Peacock, surprisingly as he didn't approve the woman's bohemian lifestyle. She was that charismatic, and Eleanor wished sometimes that rooms brightened when she walked in.

"Smell that luscious air. I do love garden parties," said Letty. "Reverend Peacock, you're early."

"Lady Fiennes."

"Have you been traveling much this year?" Letty asked.

"No, my fish wouldn't allow it."

"Fish did you say?"

"Koi, to be precise. It's a good-sized carp bred by the Japanese. They're bred for their color and size, you see. It's a hobby of mine. First the ponds had to be dug. I personally do most of the management."

"That is fascinating," said Letty. "I suppose you sit out on a fine afternoon like this and enjoy their flash?"

"Oh no, the bugs around the pond are quite thick this time of year."

Letty glanced at Eleanor and shrugged her shoulders.

"I should go in and wait for the other guests," Eleanor said. "Letty would you join me?"

"I'm sure that the Reverend would prefer to go inside as well," Alannah added.

"Oh no, oh." He laughed in a coughing sort of way. "No, no this is lovely. I didn't mean that I never sit out."

At an hour, then two, past the time set for the party, the rest of the guests had not arrived.

"Alannah!" Letty sat instantly and put her arm over her friend's shoulders. She squeezed saying, "Surely, they're all just late."

"All of them?"

"I thought that this might happen," said Reverend Peacock with a sad shake to his head.

For only the second time that afternoon, Eleanor looked at him.

"I was at a tea yesterday with the Haversacks, a small intimate party. There was some talk."

"What happened?" Eleanor's hard voice grabbed at her throat.

"Seeing how you've been somewhat irresponsible, investigating the death of Baron Tweedmouth and all. Olivia and Charles were encouraging everyone not to come. They're both so worried about Louis."

"What fools." Eleanor turned her eyes from Peacock's pious face. Here was a man of God, a supposed man of God, with no sense of compassion. This is where Tweedmouth had found himself, full of God, but not God filled. If Peacock said another word–

"From what I see, you have strayed. You are causing much suffering."

If she'd had feathers, they'd be ruffled. If she'd had eggs in her hand, she'd throw them. Instead she said, "Save yourself, Reverend Peacock, save yourself."

"Eleanor!" said Alannah.

"For heaven's sake, Mother, he pities us. Us, for God's sake. We don't need your charity here. Go back to those wonderful, generous people you were with yesterday and preach to them. A lesson on being asses, oh, but they know that one."

"Eleanor!"

"Bravo," said Letty.

Peacock stood to take his neck out the door. As he went, he said to Alannah, "Your daughter is out of control. She should go back to her husband. With a divorce and all this, not even a bankrupt title would consider her as marriageable. There is too much to disregard." Peacock bowed and left.

Eleanor expected a fight and angry words. Instead, her mother sat into chair as an erased woman. She had no expression, no vigor or life. She had never been so mute. She was going to have to be by her mother's side from now until eternity to bring even the slightest bit of pink back into Alannah's gray face. The room seemed to sigh along with the world, and then Fiennes walked in. His balding head turned as he took in each of the ladies.

"So, you've heard."

"You knew and didn't tell us?" Letty used the voice she reserved for idiots and miscreants.

"It's just come down the line. Intolerable."

"See," Eleanor said to her mother. "Thank you, Fiennes."

"For what?"

"Well, for your understanding."

Letty was watching her husband. Eleanor glanced at him. His face had wrinkled into a scrunched, puzzled look.

"What have you been talking about, dear?" Letty asked

"Another accident on the field. Damn intolerable. If you can't shoot, you should retire. Same beater as the last time too. God, the man seems to have a bull's eye on his head."

"Oh, Fiennes," said Letty.

"Was it fatal?" said Eleanor.

"Square through the forehead."

"Ghastly, darling. It is truly awful."

"Yes, and it's a fine mess. We had to disband. Cancel out. Two bad shots in a row, incredible incompetence." He gazed around. "Wasn't there supposed to be a party here?"

"Yes," said Letty, "but no one has come."

"Can't understand all the goings on. What is the world coming to? Never seen so many accidents."

"Mother, let's get you some soothing chamomile tea on a tray in bed." Eleanor had Alannah lean on her the whole way up the stairs and into the bedroom.

Eleanor backed out of the room and met Letty on the landing. She whispered, "I'm going to the mortuary."

"I'm going too. Why are we going?"

"Didn't you hear Fiennes? The same beater, this time the shooter killed him. Fiennes and Faraday say that these things almost never happen. I think I should check his fingernails."

"The mortuary is closed."

"If it were open would they let me waltz in and ask to see the body's fingernails?"

"Ah, yes." Letty shrugged her shoulders. "Dead bodies at midnight. Oh, a chill just went through me. Dear God, let's go if we're going, before I give this much more thought."

By the time a dark carriage pulled up in front of Mr. Grimm's, home of Grimm's Mortuary, a moon was rising. Eleanor walked up the stairs to the door of the residence. Without any innate curiosity and already finished for the day, the housekeeper opened and then closed the door. Mr. Grimm and his wife were out.

Sitting in the carriage again, Eleanor said, "The housekeeper sleeps at the house. The mortuary is next door. The place is unattended. I think we should try to get in," said Eleanor.

"You're not thinking of breaking in?" asked Letty.

"We might find an open window. That's not breaking in."

Eleanor walked with Letty behind the building. Cats ran from them and dogs growled. The days had gotten shorter and most of the light of the day was gone.

The back of the mortuary smelled from the refuse of the work done there. The sounds of active feet on the street in front of the building made Eleanor nervous. "There's the open window." She stretched onto her toes but was not tall enough to see inside. "There's a body in there. I can smell it."

"That's why the window is open."

Letty and Eleanor piled boxes that had the names of familiar chemicals stamped on their sides. Tonight was warm and the poor had not taken them away for firewood. Once the crates had been placed under the window, one on top of the other, she climbed. Straddling the opening, she tried to ease herself down the other side. Her skirt snagged. She hung half over the window, with the stench of rotting flesh on one side and Letty laughing on the other.

"Lift up a little," Letty choked out.

"I can't lift myself up."

"I'll have to rip it."

"For God's sake then rip it."

More laughing from Letty. "I can't...I haven't the strength."

The smell, Eleanor thought. "If you'd stop laughing—"

"I know, I'm sorry. Here, wait. I've got a finger-hold where it's snagged on a nail. "Rusty thing. Good that's your cleaning dress."

Suddenly, the fabric was free, and Eleanor fell into the room.

"Are you all right?"

"I'm brilliant."

"I'm coming."

"Maybe you should stay there."

"No, no. Wait for me."

Eleanor glanced at the sheeted body. "Yes, I'll wait," she mumbled, then coughed and pinched her nose shut. She watched a leg flip over the sill.

"I bunched my skirts," said Letty when she straddled the wall.

Half in the room, Letty moaned and commented on the rotting male smell.

"Let's get on with it," Eleanor said.

A stripe of light fell across the sheeting. It was hard to tell where the head lay. She knew she had to look at his head, the one with a hole ripped through it. She didn't know if the eyes would be open or closed. She had to try and figure out who he was.

Eleanor helped her slide down. "Hurry. This is awful," said Letty.

Letty picked up the sheet. Eleanor shuffled forward and gagged, and then clamped a hand over her mouth. She turned her head.

"What?" Letty adjusted the sheet to peek in.

"He hasn't been cleaned up."

"God." Letty dropped the sheet and said, "Do you know who he is?"

"Yes, his hair. It's matted… but it's distinctive."

"You want to take a moment?"

"God, no. We still have to look at his hands, for that bruise."

"It reeks in here." Letty stepped down the side of the gurney and lifted the sheet again.

"The hand is too shadowed," Eleanor whispered.

"What do you want to do?"

"Oh damn, I think I need to lift it into the moonlight." Eleanor stared at Letty staring at her.

In her squeamish, two-fingered grip, the dead man's hand rose as if seeking something itself. Eleanor singled out the fingers. She lifted the middle finger into the strip of moonlight. Letty nudged the gurney. The finger fell from Eleanor's grip along with the attached arm and hung from the narrow table. She moaned. She picked up the hand to return all the parts to the table. Letty dropped the sheet.

"It wasn't there. I have to look at the other one."

Like a general, Letty took a new position. She was getting less delicate with the sheet.

With her hand to her mouth, after a second, Eleanor followed. Her armpits felt moist, but she was direct, this time. She grasped the hand, singled out the finger, held the finger up into the shaft of light. Her head moved closer to get a better view until she bumped heads with Letty.

"Do you see it?"

"I think so. Do you?"

"Yes."

With the hand back in place, Eleanor smoothed the sheet. She looked long at the shroud-covered body. She remembered meeting the beater for the first time the day of the shoot just before sunrise. His informality had brightened the dawn and a nip of his special sauce had gotten her eyes to peel open. With a conspiring wink, he'd handed her his flask, saying, "It warms the mud."

That there wasn't any didn't seem to make any difference. His breath had smelled fresh and minty and whiskey laced. He'd helped her over the first ditch and then Louis had come back to stay with her. She'd been so happy that he'd only been grazed that first time, that Louis had been able to revive him. That the beater hadn't made it after all seemed more than just sad. He and Louis had been the only bright moments of that morning. He hadn't been nice after all. He'd been trying to kill Tweedmouth. "We need fresh air, Letty."

"There are no boxes on this side. We should have dropped some over,"

"You are not serious?"

"Look around. There's nothing. How could there be nothing? With a corpse in the middle of the room, we didn't think to check."

"If we walk out the door, we will have to leave it unlocked."

"Maybe they will think they forgot." Letty walked toward it.

"It probably leads to a hallway. We would also have to leave a back door unlocked. Two unlocked doors, Letty. Owens will think of me."

"Who breaks into mortuaries? They'll think it a coincidence. Even if he thinks of you, he won't have any proof." Letty turned the doorknob and pulled. She pulled again and again. "Damn, it must be locked from the other side. I was really hoping that we wouldn't have to use the alley window again. My leg is scratched. God, why does this room have to be so...lacking in viable exits? Like another door."

"No doubt also locked."

"Or a bloody bigger window."

"You'll just have to stand on me." Eleanor cupped her hands at the base of the window.

"Then what will you do?" asked Letty.

"You'll pass me some boxes."

"Won't they then *know* that someone has broken in? I say this door will open." Letty launched herself at it. All she achieved was noise. She rubbed her shoulder.

"Stop...stop, stop, stop. Oh my God, how will we explain a damaged shoulder? Just hand me some boxes. Yes, they will know someone was here, but I know that I don't care to stay here all night with him."

Letty was not a light woman. She liked her wine-soaked dinners too much. Eleanor sucked in her stomach to strengthen her back. When the last of Letty's leg slipped through the window, Eleanor waited, again alone with the body, in the dark moonlight with the smell of fresh corpse. Soon there was a wooden box pressing against the opening, turning and pressing again.

"It won't fit," Letty said. She pushed at a new box. "Oh my God, the box is stuck. Can you...shove it from your side?"

"I can't reach it."

Eleanor heard Letty grunt, and then the box was gone. "There aren't any smal—

"Shhhhh!" I hear something."

"It's a cat," Letty whispered. "I can see it on the window in the room next to yours. I must have disturbed it."

"I have to get out." Stepping to the gurney, Eleanor gently pushed the squeaky, metal, body-filled table under the window.

She climbed up near one side of the body and then pushed off the cart to get a leg up onto the sill. The motion against the table-on-wheels sent it across the room. It spun and a corner hit the wall. The body slid and then the whole cart upended. With a ripe melon thud, the dead beater's head hit the floor first.

"Oh, for the love of God, Letty—" Eleanor finished squeezing through the window opening and felt a rip as she left a wad of hair on a loose screw. She landed on the ground. She inhaled fresh air with a velocity that played her voice box as it rushed by. "The bed is on its side. The beater's spilled. He's on the floor."

Letty horse laughed.

The giggles bubbled up in Eleanor. "Abuse of a corpse."

Letty gulped back tears. "But we have the deliveryman, I think."

A dog barked at them. They sprang out of the alley and then slowed the pace to something more sober on the main street.

"And someone's shot him. Twice."

❦ 21 ❦

Bombazine would have shown, a deeper sense of her loss.
—Elizabeth Gaskill

Her bedroom fire warm, Eleanor watched the low flames. She felt the wing chair support her weight. The coal burned without noise until the faint whisper as it shifted. She had hot cocoa in her hand. From memory, she pictured Olivia's smug, condescending face from the teahouse. If she stopped, if she failed, Eleanor knew how Olivia would greet her at all gatherings from today to eternity. She felt herself sinking in high water, with Olivia laughing from the shore, with them all laughing, bloody bouffant bride. Eleanor knew who the deliveryman was, a beater, but not his name. The discovery may get Louis out of hot water, or her into it, or neither or both. If she stopped, it would be them both in the soup.

In the morning, they will find a corpse on the floor.

She laughed a tired laugh. She was losing hope, maybe even sanity in the late night. How to proceed? With her tired thoughts nothing but fragments, she had no idea. Sure she knew who the delivery man was and what he was bringing. She had no proof that the opium was ingested, and Owens was releasing the body. The beater was dead. The day still seemed ten million Olivia, one Eleanor.

What an evening!

Eleanor needed sleep, but her mind wouldn't rest. By the twilight hour, her wide-eyed wakefulness, and the absolute quiet increased her feeling of disconnectedness. She moved to the window. Away from the fire, she felt the coolness of the fall night. The glass felt cold.

"Always feeling an outsider." Vapor from her words misted the pane.

She watched the fog lift. She breathed on the window again and watched it clear. Her thoughts were as foggy. *When Alannah hears I have broken into a mortuary*— Don't think about it. How would she find out? Owens will suspect, but she won't.

Eleanor always thought of her husband after a day like this; exhausted thoughts were rarely happy ones. Her anger centered on his face—his dispassionate gaze and his dour mouth. Maybe she would divorce Lord Albright. She didn't want to be a divorcee. It sounded like failure. The marriage had been a failure.

At first, she would confront him late in the evening, night after night, when he came home from one of his various brothels drunk as a lord. Eventually, she just locked her bedroom door.

She wanted Faraday here. That was wrong too. She cried from fatigue, and stress, and unhappiness, and because, one way or the other, she was going to have to tell Owens about the beater in the morgue. Then he would know, and he would be the back end of a donkey about it. So tired of him... maybe she could just write it in a letter, dear Chief Constable Razzle-dazzle...

In the morning, the clip of heels moving back and forth outside Eleanor's door annoyed her. She got up to peer out, her face puffy from lack of sleep. With their arms full, servants bustled up and down the hallway. She stopped one. "What's going on?"

Alannah was packing for the Continent.

"I sent for tickets," Alannah told her at breakfast.

Eleanor served herself food from the sideboard. If she began talking, she would never stop. She sat and shoved a piece of toast into her mouth and then chewed it. She recognized the threadlike narrowness of her mother lips, like a hard crayon line drawn as an angry slash.

Alannah's words sounded crisp. "Letty and Fiennes think it for the best as well. They're packing."

Letty must have told Fiennes what they had done. It would do no good to argue, unless Eleanor wanted to sit over her eggs for the next half hour and listen to an endless list of her transgressions.

"Then I need to go into the village to send a wire."

"John can do it."

"I'd rather do it myself."

"Let's go to the village together then."

She isn't going to let me escape, Eleanor thought.

"Baron Tweedmouth's funeral is tomorrow," Alannah added. "Not a moment too soon if you ask me. Considering all, I can't decide if we should go or not."

Alannah insisted on taking the carriage to the village, as though they already needed to be invisible.

"I also have to talk to Owens, just for a minute. I will be back. I'll meet you at the dressmakers."

She walked away, not waiting for an answer, knowing her mother wouldn't follow. He mother didn't make scenes in public. She looked at the ground and watched her boots kick out an organza hemline. The skirt was tight, and she walked inside its narrow width. It was impossible to kick at pebbles—or anything fun and childish in such confinement. She needed some quiet time. She needed to think of a way to light a fire under Owens. Sitting under a lime tree on a bench near the police station, she watched a mouse run from root to root in the dust. "We are two cowering animals, side by side."

A carriage passed by the park, the horses driven hard. It stopped at the train station. A woman in black with a veil so thick that Eleanor wondered how she breathed walked into the building. She wore Charlotte's dress.

Dashing into London for a last minute, off-the-rack black for the burial, Charlotte? A voice in Eleanor's head screamed, follow her.

She shouldered a few pedestrians on her way up the hill. As in a dance, each person twirled, stopped and complained. At the crest of the hill, panting, and favoring a stitch in her side, she walked into the station and onto the platform. She hadn't missed her; Charlotte slipped into the number eight first class train carriage. She had the most to gain and tomorrow was her husband's burial. Not even a day between release and funeral. Tweedmouth would be appalled at the lack of advance warning for his person lying in state. Charlotte must hate him. She must. Eleanor felt it in her rejected bones.

The train whistled, galvanizing Eleanor into a fit of spontaneity. She swept back into the station and went straight to the ticket booth.

"You're buying a ticket for yourself?"

"Sort of a last minute trip."

"Any baggage?"

"Baggage? No."

"Return?"

"I need to get on this train." She peered through a distant smudged window. Charlotte had drawn her curtains. A whistle blew.

"Next train is in just fifteen minutes."

"No, I need this one."

"There'll be another one quick as a lick."

She hovered over every letter he printed on the paper.

He scowled and shoved the ticket at her. "Here, Lady Eleanor, pay me when you return. And don't you forget."

"No, I won't. Thank you, Mr. Edison. You just don't know. Thank you."

Mr. Edison motioned with his hand for her to scamper off.

From the train, there was a long gasp of released steam. Lifting her skirts high, Eleanor sprinted the distance. Thank the Lord for Charlotte's shut curtains. She opened the door of a carriage close to Charlotte's. Eleanor stepped up just as the train pulled forward. A man, his face an imprint of surprise, grabbed her arm and pulled her inside. The train rolled, and then it stopped. With the man still holding her arm, she crashed to the floor. The train pulled away from the station with the two trying to get her into a seat.

Eleanor laughed. What a graceless duck. She adjusted the tip to her hat and then sat under it for a moment until her hands steadied. She wanted to rub her knees, but grace and dignity were already glaring at her. Come to think of it, grace and dignity had never been close friends of hers.

The man's exclamations had been in French, so she addressed him in that language. "I apologize, monsieur. Thank you for your help and for sharing the carriage."

Indignity oozed from the Frenchman as he murmured offhand replies. He picked up his newspaper from the floor and snapped it into place. The sound was earsplitting—so much for a riveting conversation on the weather. She thought of Renard who slept through both the beginning and end of a conversation. The French didn't prefer to live in England. With Renard in her home, Charlotte had found acceptance, and bound to Charlotte, he had his vanity stroked by her absolute regard.

Faraday had said that after the Second French Revolution, when Louis-Philippe abdicated, his Premier, Guizot, fled to England. Renard had come too. He had written to Guizot early on when they had both lived in London, but the letters had stopped. The ex-prime minister must have thought the soldier a liability. Renard owed Charlotte his dignity. She wondered how either of them, Charlotte or Renard, could be attached to the beater.

Brick buildings that were bearded with soot replaced the rolling green hills of the countryside. The train slowed with a wretched, headachy squeak to the brakes, Oxford Station. A platform conductor called the name long and loud. The Frenchman decanted himself with a quick tip to his hat. She nodded back as a reflex. Colorless man, she thought while she watched for Charlotte. There was a woman in black, who had the Scented Woman's build, but the wrong hat. It wasn't the hat with the trio of black feathers bouncing on either side like the wings at Hermes' heels, an ugly hat not to be forgotten.

Oxford to Paddington would take about fifty-five minutes. Alone, and once again with the train noise all around her, Eleanor wondered where this trip would take her.

At Paddington Station, Eleanor scanned the crowd. The black feathers were on the move.

She could lose Charlotte in the soldiers that mobbed the platform. Eleanor felt like her heart was imprinted on her ribs. While trying to keep sight of the woman, she tripped over cases and cartons that littered the floor. What appeared to be a battalion of men, all sunburned, plodded in front of her toward the doors of the station. Kitchener had been calling for more troops to replace the volunteers, yeomanry, and militia that had put in their time in South Africa. These men's concave chests and rounded shoulders suggested that they had been living in Boer War blockhouses—single rooms that were thirteen feet in diameter and six feet high. With annealed wire entanglements all around, they had been their own prisoners.

She remembered the returning City Imperial Volunteers here just a year ago. They had appeared just as despondent as they marched from Paddington to St Paul's. People, hundreds thick in some areas had cheered them along the route. Not many noticed that the men hadn't seemed to want a parade.

Eleanor said "excuse me" as a mantra in trying to follow the sparkling jet on Charlotte's dress. Eleanor's height gave her some advantage when peering between the couples and families embracing each other on every square inch of cement and tile. Charlotte was pushing through the bodies with determination.

Eventually Eleanor could only see Charlotte's hat, and then not even that. She had lost Charlotte to imperialism and its horde, how appropriate. The cabs would be swamped as well. With lessening enthusiasm, Eleanor battled to the road where she walked up and down as she could while gazing between heads and hats for Charlotte. At this point, the crowd seemed to keep her standing still.

What awful rotten luck. Eleanor decided to search the cab line. At the corner, she broke free of the throng. There it was, the hat ducking into a hansom. What luck! She stole another from a young couple who had paused to kiss. The next thing she knew, she was on Henrietta Street. Her mother would cringe at the sight of the Irish National Club. Eleanor knew that Charlotte was not sympathetic to the Celtic cause either. Charlotte slipped into a building just three doors down.

Eleanor sat in the cab and stared at the shop front. Big Ben chimed twelve. She felt sticky in the increasing damp. There was a smell of rain in the air, the mingling of dirt and water, as the drops grew heavy enough to fall. With humidity beading at her temple, Eleanor despised the Scented Woman for a moment. Vengeance licked at the edges of her mind. She wanted Charlotte to have killed her husband.

The shop was plain, unadorned, ignored. The building had a simple cornice under an imperial roof. There were four steps up to the door with display windows on either side. The eye might skip over it like a plain woman between two beauties. In between two gilded feats of architecture, this place was ugly, had no personality, and seemed spiteful. In the windows stood a naked, dusty sewing form, and some hats. The place explained Charlotte's taste in clothes. She seemed to like out-of-the-way shops.

"I don't suppose that I'll be leaving you here, madam?"

"Wait for just a moment."

Eleanor walked inside. No one stood at the counter. She called out. A woman in a flamboyant dress came through a narrow archway sizing Eleanor up as she walked forward.

"Is there a Lady Tweedmouth here?"

"I'm sorry; I don't know a Lady Tweedmouth."

Eleanor walked back to her cab and got inside. She felt poised on the lip of her own grave. To keep from falling, she had to get inside that building anyway she could. There would be no backpedaling.

Thinking the proprietor might be watching, she had the cabbie drive forward. A few blocks down and out of the cab, she fished in her bag for coins, and handed them to the driver. "I need to get inside that place undetected. Can you help me?"

Being a businessman, he eyed the change in his hand and waited. Her hand dived into her bag several times more before the cabbie took off his topcoat and tie and laid them over his seat. "Down here, then."

He stepped off the curb with energy. Her coins jingled in his pocket. She followed the sound across the street and down the narrow alley that was not wide enough for spread arms. Keeping her elbows in, she avoided the over-flowing refuse bins with lids that sat like a drunken man's hat. The bins stank of old milk and gray beef. Empty bottles of bubbly were everywhere in heaps. Black cats licked empty cans of Beluga caviar. This was the rubbish that came out of the building Charlotte had entered. It was hardly a place for a woman in mourning the day before her husband's funeral.

The side door was dirty. She tried the knob and found it locked.

The cabbie brushed by her and rang the trade-man's bell. She stood by the hinges of the door and wedged next to a stack of boxes filled with open bottles that seemed to smell of stale urine. "What are you going to do?"

"Going to see if they need any work done, aren't I?"

"What then?"

"Don't worry, I'll get you in."

The cabbie rang twice more.

A very cranky voice on the other side of the door asked, "What?"

"I'm wondering if you're hiring. I have a nephew. He's got a good face. How about I take away all this rubbish then."

The cabbie disappeared inside, to get the job, it seemed. Eleanor waited so long that she had to put a handkerchief over her nose and mouth. She wondered if she should slip in. A rat ran over her toe. She whimpered and sprang inside and ran into the cabbie coming out. They bumped noses. Hers stung and her eyes watered.

"It's clear." He said rubbing his nose with his free hand. The other had coins in it.

"What did you see?"

"Boxes in a dark hall."

"Nothing else?"

"Nothing else to see."

"Thanks, and would you stop by White's to deliver a personal message for me? It's for Lord Henry Faraday. It's very important. Just say Lady Albright is waiting for him at 56 Henrietta Street."

"I don't figure you the type," the cabbie said before he cut away leaving the garbage as it stood.

She stared after him. What type, she thought. She watched him go. With the additional coins she had had to pay for the message, his pocket sounded loud. For a split second, she felt abandoned; he probably wouldn't deliver the message either.

She turned to the dark hallway. It smelled better inside that out, thank God. She left the door ajar. Her movement forward was like walking in a cave, feeling around and looking for light.

"I'm off, home. I'll bet he's a crook," a woman at the end of the hall said.

"Rob ya blind," another answered.

Panic had Eleanor groping around pillars of boxes looking for a hiding place. With desperate strength, she pushed a stack of boxes away from the wall, far enough that she could slip in behind it. Her hat wouldn't fit. She took it off, and turned and twisted searching for a place to put it.

"What did I say to her? I told her not to trust that one."

The voice was closer. Eleanor threw her hat on top of another high stack. She hurried behind her boxes while reminding herself that she was just around the corner from Cavendish Square and its rows of lovely houses.

"This place is on its last legs anyway, without her giving it away," said another voice.

"Will you tell her if he skipped out?"

"Couldn't be bothered. What has she ever done for me?"

The other woman laughed. "There are more rats than customers."

"I'm putting in at one of them posh 'otels. They pay better anyway, for making beds and dusting furniture."

The two voices passed by. "Lookie 'ere not a bit of it gone and he didn't even shut the door. Was I right?"

The alley door closed behind the two, cutting off light. Eleanor realized she could have stood smack in front of the two, and they would have waved her by. Silence and dust again reigned. She eased herself out from behind the boxes. The rough brick of the wall caught her hair and pulled it from her chignon. She eased her hat back onto her head.

The well-fed rats squeaked. At least there weren't any dead bodies.

Further down the space, a hopeful strip of yellow light along the floor indicated a door.

She made her way carefully toward it, placed her ear against the wood and listened. Hearing nothing, she eased the door open a crack. The bottom strip of light raced up the side and along the top of the opening. With one eye, she spied another hallway, this one larger with gas lamps and multiple doors in a line along one side.

She cranked the door wider and was about to step into the hallway, when another door opened and a woman's face appeared. Eleanor gasped and narrowed the gap of her own door until a distant door shut. The hall was so much brighter than her dark cave that she was loath to step into the light. She counted ten doors. A person could jump out of anyone of them, but then the women had said that the place lacked customers.

She stepped forward onto carpeting that was thick as an Eskimo's coat. Grass paper on the walls was peeling away in places. The doors appeared to be gold filigree. An aging spa, she thought, and then she remembered seeing a dress form at the window. It wasn't like any dress shop she'd ever been in.

Charlotte must be behind one of these doors drinking champagne and eating caviar. She'd plant lime trees over the Baron. Eleanor stooped to sniff for the Baroness's perfume at the bottom of each golden door. By now, Charlotte's room should be a flowerless lavender garden. By the sixth door, and just as she thought herself mad sniffing at doors like a spaniel, she caught the scent, heavenly lavender. Distrust. Eleanor heard the faint sound of a tango on a phonograph.

Curiouser and curiouser, Eleanor thought, coming out of the rabbit hole. Champagne...caviar...doors of a palace...this place has the feel of a celebration. Charlotte's husband is to be buried. The end is near. She is celebrating —with more than a new dress.

"Ahem?"

Eleanor stepped back from the door as if it had shocked her and faced a woman in a showy dress. Darned padded carpet.

"I'm sure that Lady Tweedmouth suggested this establishment to me saying that she'd be here today."

The woman appeared dubious. "How did you come in?"

Eleanor tried to lie, lies clung to her brain like a babe to its mother's leg, refusing to budge. "How many ways do you have for a lady to come in?" Damn, her mother could do better.

The woman stood firm until Eleanor scooted past her. She followed pointing out the correct direction when Eleanor had made a wrong turn. The sewing form seemed to laugh as Eleanor was shooed out the door, with the French-sounding woman saying that she would bring the police if she saw Eleanor again.

Eleanor stood on the curb, blinking. Damn, the turnaround from inside to outside was fast. Now...how to get back inside.

22

The composition of a tragedy requires testicles.
—Voltaire

Faraday watched Mrs. Jeffers limp across the street to the first house on the corner of Cavendish Square, the Greenburgs. Before beginning the stairs down to the servant's entrance, she paused to heft the load of eggs she carried. "The heavier the better," she had said. "Got to be heavy enough that they will ask me inside to put my pins up."

Faraday smoked on a bench and waited for the Scotland Yard lady. The woman breathed competence through an encouraging smile. Men and women wept on her shoulder. The housekeeper in the Greenburg household will have a thing to say to her, no doubt.

Probably could nip off for a cup of tea, what? Leave her to it, fake limp and all.

By the time he had taken the eggs from Mrs. Jeffers and had helped her back into the motorcar, Faraday had drunk three pots of tea and had strolled the green a number of times. "You're a peach. Two hours, what? I've had a glance at your ears, and they're still there."

"It wasn't all that bad."

"Grueling for you. You are a trooper. Foreign Legion material."

"Thank you. Really, though, it was one of my easier chats. The poor girl is completely out of her depth and without a bit of help. You know how it's getting. So many can't afford to staff a house. That girl is cook, butler, and lady's maid—well the list goes on."

"Would you like a cup of tea?"

"Oh no, I'm brimming over, thank you. I'll fill you in as you drive. This is a wonderful car."

"As it happens, I am brimming over as well. Let's take the long way back."

"I'll say first that I'm glad you filled me in on the case, or I wouldn't have gotten a useful thing out of her. I did drop the name Tweedmouth. She had seen it and had thought it peculiar. She told me that the name had made her think of the moving pictures. I'm sure you know, the ones, Lord Faraday, where the villains are forever putting cloth in the damsels' mouths to keep them quiet? I told her that I was old enough to remember that a man named Tweedmouth had killed Mrs. Greenburg's husband."

"What did she say to that?"

Faraday suddenly braked. "Damn donkeys. Why can't they look first?" He jammed the stick into first gear and trod on the gas. "I'm so sorry Mrs. Jeffers, continue."

"'Didn't a letter come from him,'" the maid said to me. "'Saw the crest, didn't I?'"

"You do a very credible maid."

"Thank you. I have drawn on it from time to time. Anyway, that's when the maid decided that the name was a funny one, and it stuck with her. After Mrs. Lawrence read the letter, she made off like a hen seeing a fox. She ran up the stairs calling to her mother. The carry on after that between the mother and daughter was—Tweedmouth this—Tweedmouth that."

"Lawrence is Mrs. Greenburg's daughter?"

"Yes, Mrs. Lawrence is her daughter and Mrs. Lawrence has a boy. The maid said that she's always babysitting him and no extra pay either. The upstairs conversation about Tweedmouth had something to do with Mrs. Lawrence's son. I asked her if the child was much trouble, you know, adding onto her list of duties. She said that he was. She called him—"

Faraday swerved to miss a brougham that had stopped in front of him. Traffic was becoming thicker with buses both horse drawn and motorized and with electric trams, carts, and carriages. Faraday sat up straight and goggled out, trying to pierce the curtain of rain. On his right, the Theatre Royal inched along as he drove down Haymarket.

"Sink the city," he said.

"It has become dreadful, so many accidents. It's very bad here. I'd try Cockspur Street. It's a less popular street this time of day."

"You're so right." Faraday turned. Drops of rain skated across his windscreen. "Sorry, what were you saying about a child?"

"Mrs. Lawrence's child, and Mrs. Greenburg's grandson is named Daniel Miller after Mrs. Lawrence's first husband."

"Hallelujah!" He smacked his steering wheel. "Now, a good gander at some certificates is the next thing."

"I did ask the housekeeper if the boy was toddling about still. She told me that he is ten and spoiled rotten."

"Louis would have been about twenty when the grandchild was born. When did the Baron marry Charlotte, I wonder? For that matter, when did Mrs. Greenburg marry Mr. Greenburg? When was this illegal duel that is a matter of folklore but nothing else but a dead Mr. Greenburg.? Oh, the tangled web."

Faraday shoved the Panhard into a lower gear and turned onto the Strand. He increased speed. Just short of the building that held the Law Courts, a brittle part under the bonnet gave way and the engine quit. Like a woman in full tiff, the shining motorcar rolled, haughtily to a stop.

Like it had been saving up, the sky pelted rain down. Pedestrians, caught without umbrellas in the pouring rain, hired the few passing cabs. The road was being abandoned. The rain sounded loud on the car's roof.

"We're going to have to walk a bit," Faraday said. "I have some umbrellas in the boot."

He ran around to the back of the car like a mad rabbit. He ran back the same way and dropped into the seat. Water filled the floor. "The eggs are fine, but I've just got one umbrella. Where did this squall come from after such a fine morning, what? Stay here. I'll find a cab."

Rain sluiced off the edges of his black umbrella. After hitting the warm pavement, the water rose again, finer than before as a dense mist. Fertilized by warm bricks, the fog grew up the side of the buildings.

His thoughts a blue streak, he kept his head down while trying to sharp eye his surroundings, but with a wind driving the rain, and uncertain footing, he had to stare at the walkway. He plowed through the murkiness like a diver through a deep ocean.

Damn weather won't give a man a sporting chance—qualified dead-end.

If he had to walk all the way to the Courts, he'd sell the damn flighty car for coins. Faraday could smell the rank Thames, just a block away. In the shifting black air, he heard the detached sounds of invisible men's voices. He peered through the cement colored air for a cab.

Overhead, Big Ben chimed three times. He'd been walking too long. He'd missed the Courts. "Bloody fog," he said as he about faced. If he heard that clock chime again before he reached the building, he'd have to go back. The umbrella was soaked through when Faraday walked onto the cobble-stones and then into the iron fence surrounding the Law Courts.

He walked straight into the building and into an office that smelled leathery from the furniture—not from the thick-skinned man sitting behind the desk. "Uncle Cornelius."

"My boy, you're soaking wet."

"The car."

"Stupid things, cars. You deserve it, then. Unreliable. Whittlebey and his wife were stuck for eight hours on a country road. Never happen with a horse. Outlaw the machines I say."

"Uncle. I've got a Scotland Yard woman waiting in it, only I can't find a cab."

"There you see. Well, I'm about to leave. We'll both deliver her. This should be a lesson to you. Can you believe the weather?"

His old uncle moved like an upriver barge. Faraday hopped back into the outer office to ask his uncle's secretary to have the carriage brought round, and then he lunged for his uncle's hat and stick.

Walking at Uncle Cornelius's side, Faraday put a hand at the aging man's elbow and kept the broad beam of the man on a steady forward course. Faraday felt better once in the carriage, even though the horse plodded through a gritty, black fog that hid large animals and nurtured criminals.

Big Ben had struck another hour when Faraday said, "We must have passed it." Another moment of searching was intolerable. He'd kick the damn car into the next world.

"You said you were near the Waterloo Bridge turnoff?"

"Yes, but it's past time."

"Maybe we should go just a bit further."

"No, let's turn around and stay next to the curb. We might run into the damn thing. Hang it, I should have thought of that before."

The horse stopped on its own with its head over the bumper of the car. Faraday dashed toward the Panhard while peering inside. Mrs. Jeffers was gone. She mustn't have walked. Thinking of her drenched without an umbrella, he stood upright trying to pierce through the fog in all directions, and then he opened the passenger's door. A white sheet of paper embossed with Mrs. Jeffers initials lay against the red upholstery. I have found a ride. Sorry not to have waited. Faraday breathed easier.

"She found a ride," Faraday said to his uncle.

"You are even wetter. What about the car?"

"I'll send Dunn for it. You wouldn't mind dropping me at White's and then taking me to vital records?"

"My boy, it's like pea soup out there. Why didn't you use your umbrella? Dash it, the seat is drenched."

"Sorry about the intrusion and the wet carriage. It's all to a good cause."

"You and your cases, confounded public defender. Your mother has always been too liberal with you, like the time you put the fish head in her soup bowl, and it was still breathing."

"It had been freshly beheaded."

"Shocking was what it was. You shouldn't have been out of the nursery. What did your mother do? She laughed."

"Last of a long line of incompetent males," Faraday said.

"Enter the clergy, boy."

"Religion seems to be sticking in my throat, lately."

"I have no idea what you're talking about. Seems blasphemous. Is this what you young people are on about all day? Waste of education. When I was on the board at Oxford, there was no room for sacrilege. Nothing but liberal fiddle-faddle, nowadays."

Faraday stared forward. He was dying to feed the fire but thought better of it seeing his uncle's red complexion.

"Absolutely, Uncle. You are a gem for helping me out."

"Boy, I know when I'm being patronized. Are you going to tell me what this case is about?"

"Tweedmouth's death."

Uncle sat like a brick until he said, "Here's your place."

Faraday moved to step out of the opened door when his uncle stopped him with the end of his cane on his nephew's shoulder. "Don't be long. I'm expected."

Faraday, dry now and sitting next to his grumbling uncle, noticed that Saint James Palace was a pale and shrouded version of itself in the gray, drifting air, as were the other structures down the short street. London hid behind the sinuous vapor. Faraday listened to the rain beat on the top of the chaise as it headed toward Kensington Park.

"Don't bury the man before you know." His uncle jabbed at his ribs. "Did you hear me?"

"I shall introduce you to Lady Albright. She agrees with you."

"You don't?"

"Initially, I felt it best that tons of dirt should separate the world and Tweedmouth."

Uncle took out his handkerchief and blew his nose. He folded it and stuffed it back into a pocket. "No, my boy, that much animosity must be sorted out. Society is changing. The resentments of new money and old must be sorted out."

"Nothing to do with old money, new money. He was just not a nice guy. Uncle, when you get in would you send a man for the motorcar? I just remembered Dunn is still in Whitney."

"Most of us are not nice guys."

Uncle liked the last word, and Faraday let him have it. He ticked off the records he meant to inspect: Daniel Miller's birth certificate, and the marriage certificate of Julia Greenburg—also Julia's birth certificate. The date of Mrs. Greenburg's marriage had become important. "What's Auntie's schedule today?"

"I have no idea."

"Uncle, twenty years ago, did you pay any attention to the Tweedmouth-Greenburg duel? Did you know a man named Absalom Greenburg?"

"Is that what you want to come over for? The man was Tweedmouth's partner."

"Was he swindled?"

Uncle tapped his cane on the floor. "He was given what was due according to the contract. Tweedmouth took all the risk." Uncle sighed and said, "He was just smarter."

"Was the duel over money?"

"The duel was within an inch of costing Tweedmouth his seat in the House of Lords. There were objections. Greenburg wouldn't back down over the thing. He was like a rabid dog. Americans," Uncle muttered.

"So it was over money and probably over the woman."

Uncle stared out the carriage window. "Isn't it always?"

Faraday decided to ask Auntie the same question. She soaked up gossip like a camel at an oasis soaked up water. She was never dry. Faraday liked her. He went home with his uncle. The records could wait.

In a gushing welcome, Auntie placed Faraday in the green room in the best chair.

"I heard you were as soggy as a cat left in the rain."

"I was left in the rain."

"I do like your motor car. Do come by and take me for a spin once it's running again, or I may never get the chance to ride in one."

Faraday chose a velvet green chair and sat down. Auntie perched across from him on a floral sofa. "I hope Uncle's carriage seat isn't ruined," he said.

"Don't worry a moment about it." She ignored her husband's mutterings across the room and poured herself tea. "It's been toweled off. I daresay it will survive. You're peaked. You won't be catching cold from this adventure. I've order coffee with a bit of brandy in it to fortify you. What are you up to anyway?"

"I need some very old gossip."

She clapped her hands together. "Oh good." Auntie Lizzy put the cup she had lifted toward her mouth back in its saucer. "I think I'll have a sniff of brandy myself."

"Do you remember anything about the love life of Baron Samuel Mont-fire, Baron of Tweedmouth before, during, and after his marriage to Charlotte, and anything about Margaret Brockway, who married Mr. Absalom Greenburg?"

Auntie's whole person snuggled into the depression she made in the padded seat cushion. She inhaled and with the air, planned. This sort of thing was her refuge and her strength. He observed her savoring the lovely thoughts that were being sorted in her mind. He knew she was deciding where to begin. Auntie knew the power of a well-told story. Faraday inhaled the scent of the robust coffee in its floral cup, its heat a cure to the wet and the gloom. A lacing of Auntie's brandy didn't hurt either. The gaslight she had flickering in the afternoon storm perfected the backdrop for good drama.

Auntie began. "Tweedmouth was on his way to becoming a baron from amassing a fortune in concrete. During his rise, so to speak, he was with Margaret Brockway, who was an acquaintance of De Crespsy's, Tweedmouth's friend from Eton. Her father worked the racing circuit in which De Crespsy heavily bet. Tweedmouth's father was an outspoken Calvinist minister. So you see, he is a chip off the block.

"The father had a decent income, and he was angry at the match." Auntie stopped for emphasis. "She was a heathen to Tweedmouth's father's conservative, clerical mind." She eyed Faraday in a knowing way. "She wasn't a heathen so much as she was imprudent and enterprising. She had a face, and I might add, a body that Helen of Troy would envy, and she used it. She had aspirations. I think she knew that Tweedmouth would make something of himself, even with Tweedmouth annoying the people closest to him right and left," she said.

"No different then and now," said Faraday.

"He was considered a bit of a lad then. Now, he's got the unique position of being considered the most annoying man in the peerage. Well, some don't consider him a member, but they do consider him annoying." Auntie waited and took a drink.

"When Tweedmouth got the title, Margaret thought that she had made it. She spoke to us all as if she'd been socializing with us for years. He could afford to take her to the theater, you see. The next thing we knew, Tweedmouth was engaged to the fore mentioned, best friend's sister, and Margaret was engaged to Greenburg, in that order, I believe."

"Margaret Greenburg is still a beautiful woman."

"Oh, you've met her, have you? Don't tell me that you are as enticed as the rest of them. That would disappoint me."

Auntie poured a little more brandy in her coffee and added more sugar. She was plumping out, but she'd always claimed that at her age there was nothing to do but eat.

"I wasn't."

Auntie laughed and wagged her jeweled finger at him saying, "Good boy. There's been blood in her eye for decades. She thinks well of herself."

"She slipped going up the ladder."

"Very well put, I must remember that." She leaned forward for a cake.

"I'm wondering if Julia Greenburg is Lord Tweedmouth's daughter."

"Oh, we all did." She waved around her cake. "Do you have proof? And the girl—she never resembled anyone. She could have come from the orphanage down the street. Society has always assumed that duel was over concrete."

"Not Uncle." Faraday often wondered if he had become a barrister because he liked gossip too. "I imagine Margaret wanted to make herself felt, having been shuffled about. A child sired by Tweedmouth could be used to get a stake in the fortune she'd missed. She'd consider such a baby her good fortune, blackmail bait." Faraday picked up a cake. Auntie was making them look tasty.

Auntie snort-laughed. "Not much. She had a daughter. Tweedmouth wouldn't think at all about a daughter, anyway there was no proof that it was his. It was born nine months after her marriage. Margaret just wasn't up to snuff compared to Tweedmouth's own ambitions. She got dumped."

"She was 'Eve' the woman with the bad apple, and he was done with her."

"Oh yes, well put. It would have been an uphill climb for him with Margaret in tow." Faraday watched her chew another bite. "Mind you, that girl was resourceful. What's this all about anyway?"

He poured them both more drink. "Baron Tweedmouth is dead. He may have been murdered."

"Amazing—or not considering the man. There must be a whole circus of suspects."

Faraday laughed. "Under the big top, the man was a ringmaster. If Julia Greenburg is his daughter, then her son, Daniel Miller, was possibly to be his favored grandson." It was Faraday who waited this time to let the story sink in.

Auntie's head flicked up. All the frivolous light had gone from her face, as if any sane and sober thought in life had fled the room. "Oh, my lord, he wouldn't bypass that tender young man? Disenfranchise Louis. The fool, the absolute fool."

It delighted Faraday to find his aunt and uncle of one mind for a change. "In spite of the birth, Margaret has never come up trumps. Her house is falling down around her ears."

"The girl wasn't as clever as we all thought."

"And there is the dead man and a solicitor's appointment for the day after the death."

She eyed him. "Do you have any proof or are you just here to eat my cakes and to taunt me?"

"So far, I have Mrs. Jeffers."

"Go away now, Henry. One must be first with the news. I do wish your uncle would put in a telephone line."

Faraday kissed his distracted aunt on her cheek.

The records office was a hive, loud with typewriters. Faraday bee-lined to a woman who knew him well enough to stare up at him with an encouraging smile.

"Been enjoying the sun?" she asked.

"Who hasn't? 'Fraid the sun is at an end, what?"

"I could find a towel for your shoes?"

"Thanks, but I'm right back into it. If you would, I just need two certificates of birth."

"Of course, Lord Faraday."

"Here, I'll write the names down for you. Oh, and a marriage cert...Mrs. Margaret Greenburg, her husband's name was Absalom. This name, Julia Lawrence, is her daughter. She may have been married twice, first being a Miller. I need a birth cert. for her and for a Daniel Harry Miller."

With the two certificates in his hand, Faraday thought of Mrs. Lawrence —he'd placed her face—Tweedmouth. According to Auntie, she hadn't looked like him at birth, but she'd grown into his profile. The boy's certificate was straight forward, born to Julia Miller. Had to be the same Julia. He was ten. Julia Greenburg's birth certificate, born January 7, 1871, was well within the nine-month time limit of the marriage certificate. Auntie had been right. Faraday speeded to the named father on Julia's certificate. Tweedmouth. Jesus, there it was in indelible ink. Margaret had written him in. He bet that no one had checked, that she hid it in her corset next to her heart. She was a personality that made trouble. She'd written it as insurance. She wasn't going to go away, not without money.

Faraday fanned himself with the paper. "I'll be whipped."

"Something wrong, sir?" asked the secretary.

"What? Ah, no." He gathered the documents thinking that Greenburg, smitten, had felt himself lucky to get her, or he had been given an incentive to marry her...money and the girl, his cup overflowed. Had the marriage been with music and flowers, or a visit to the court? He tapped his index finger on Tweedmouth's name. What a little man like Greenburg would do for a crème de la femme like her—anything. Die, perhaps. Faraday wondered if Margaret had instigated the duel, told her husband Tweedmouth had taken advantage. Maybe she wanted to get rid of Greenburg, or if he died instead, punish Tweedmouth. Who had first suggested Daniel as the inheritor, Tweedmouth or Margaret Greenburg? Either was capable of it. After all, Tweedmouth often called Louis a "British Queen" after a category of potato.

Time to take on Owens again. He almost felt sorry for the Chief Constable. With a man like Tweedmouth, it was either simple—the asthma—or so complex that a stack of documents wouldn't bring any light to the problem. Faraday knew which way Owens leaned, and he leaned there with the stubbornness of any bobby hot on his theories of a case. The information was circumstantial at best.

🖏 23 🖏

The ladies of St James's!
They're painted to the eyes;
Their white it stays forever,
Their red it never dies.
—Henry Austin Dobson

The headless sewing form in the shop's rain-streaked window seemed to laugh at Eleanor from its cozy nook. A good dusting would sort it. Fat raindrops wet the woven straw of her misaligned hat. Rain and locks be damned, she would crack this egg. At worst, egg on the face was pore tightening. She wondered about getting in. Without her cabbie, there remained two choices: the front door or another dreaded window. With the dusty feminine form at guard, the front door seemed barred. Well, nothing for it.

Eleanor hung her head and pretended to walk away beaten. At the mouth of the same alley, she darted down the length of the building. Rain began to pour down now. The orange ribbon, which had once burst jauntily from her hat, now bathed in the puddle gathering in its rim. She tried the door first and then threw her hat down, another hat gone. With the inner zeal of a saint, she climbed onto a bin to reach a high window. It wouldn't open, though the lock appeared broken.

"Of course not," she mumbled. "Why would one single moment of any of this be easy? Why doesn't the world just kick me, tie me to the stake, and boil me in oil? No, too good for her you say? Let's feed her to the cannibals." She jerked the window up multiple times, giving the pulls all her passion. The pane rattled in its frame. She ripped off her blackened gloves, and with one last heave, Eleanor managed to break the seal. Success thrilled her.

Now, the window wouldn't stay open. Holding the pane up with her shoulder, Eleanor gathered her skirts up to her thigh. She straddled the window. The curve of her neck and back kept the pane from closing. Thank God, no one had shrieked "thief" yet. She wasn't limber enough to make it an easy birth, and it was hard to breathe with her head pressed so close to her chest. She started laughing. The windowpane bounced on her back, which made her chuckle more.

"Keep moving, Eleanor," she mumbled. "I'm going to take to the drink after this."

Head inside, she realized that she didn't have a way down. In a split-legged slide, she tried to ease herself to the floor. Corseted and not being as agile as last time, she fell the last bit and landed sideways on her ankle and then thrashed about trying to gain her feet, tangling herself in dark curtains.

Hobbling like a three-legged dog, Eleanor tried not to cry out from the pain. She beat the fabric from her and made a vow—no more windows. Eleanor rubbed at her ankle thinking that sightseeing in Europe was now as dead as Tweedmouth. Her mother will be liverish.

She hopped into the hallway. The novelty of intrigue beginning to wear thin, Eleanor walked to Charlotte's door was as much purpose as she could with a gimp leg.

She slid inside. In front of her, through a glowing pane of glass, very wide and very clear, were cavorting males, naked cavorting males. These well-built men, gods with tight muscles, wrestled, bathed, and lounged beside potted palms. A playful waterfall ended in a glistening pool. Dripping a ring of water on the plush carpet, she stared with every eyeball she possessed. All the men seemed more naked than the day they were born.

Eleanor's modesty screamed at her to quit gawking, but the scene—so staged—drew her. The words "dangling participles" came to mind. Squeaking like a toy, she tried not to giggle. She couldn't help comparing the men to what she had seen of her estranged husband. She'd been cheated. No wonder he preferred girls.

"Lady Albright!"

Eleanor jumped. Charlotte reclined on a sofa, draped in satin. For a pretty woman, she was ugly.

"What do you do, just lie here and choose the best male specimen?" Eleanor pointed toward the window. She noted the draped bed. "The Baron was thinking of divorcing you, but then he found out about this. No, this, would never, never do. He must have accused you of all sorts of things."

"I will have your head."

"Said the Red Queen. You knew that everyone in society would agree with Tweedmouth. He had solid grounds for divorce."

"I have never been unfaithful to my husband. This is a business. I pay to be here. I am a patron."

"Oh, for pity's sake, where have I heard that before? We should all be held to a higher standard than this, don't you think? Did Renard protect you from your husband? You needed someone when this hobby of yours surfaced? Did Renard kill Tweedmouth, or did you do it? Did you kill your husband?"

"What?"

"With aspirin mixed with opium? I found the medicinal paper on the balcony. You knew he was taking opium?"

"Opium!" The Baroness rose from the bed like a monster from the deep. Anger filled every blue vein in her face to bursting. Her temple throbbed with the increased beat of her small heart. Charlotte moaned like an injured animal. She moaned until the noise bounced in on itself from the crimson walls. Her legs buckled beneath her. Her filmy body collapsed onto the bed. Her bowed head rocked side to side. The moaning turned to a demented chant. "Me Amour...me amour...me amour."

Charlotte's mind had turned. Enameling makeup ran from her eyes making her cheeks appear long and gaunt. Her face filled with hate. In a harsh voice she called out, "Sermonizing madman, clanging bell, divorce me like Lady Campbell, never!" The Baroness of Tweedmouth slid onto the floor.

"Oh, my Lord," said Eleanor. She dived for the woman.

She was struggling with the inert body when she felt a presence at the large window. She glanced up and almost dropped Charlotte's head as a muscled, naked back moved away. With distance from the framed glass, she noted that his tight buttocks bounced. The man was in a hurry. There was something about that walk. She needed to see him from the front, except that Charlotte was moaning, "I would be nothing, nothing," or some such rot and melting into herself.

She'd better get out. The proprietress was soon to be alerted, but Eleanor glanced at the boneless, moaning heap that was Lady Tweedmouth and felt at fault. Eleanor poured the red wine on the table into a crystal goblet. Wine spilled onto her fingers and then dripped from her hand. The afternoon delights had taken their toll. With her dry hand at the back of Charlotte's head, Eleanor put the glass to the woman's lips.

"Drink," Eleanor half shouted. The mumbling, vaporous Charlotte went limp. In catching Charlotte against her, Eleanor dropped the glass onto Charlotte's white negligee. Red spread though the fabric like a wound. The fast-spreading color appalled Eleanor yet fascinated her. She felt the need to rub at it, to clean it off.

She maneuvered around to pull Charlotte onto a sofa. The woman liked her sweets. Eleanor felt something in her back snap. In fresh pain, she took a blanket off a bed to cover the shocked body. It was hard to dredge up anything more than superficial pity for Charlotte Tweedmouth.

Eleanor guzzled from the wine bottle. The heat from the drink seemed to steady her hands. She breathed hard from both nerves and exertion. The smell of lavender mingled with burgundy gagged her. She took another drink and glanced at the window. They were all so naked.

The old cross-fertilizer, her husband, might have been happier here. She pulled open the door to her find the proprietor at it. Eleanor didn't pause to let the woman take in her wet, wine-stained, wild-haired appearance. Still, the manager managed a quick contemptible regard. While favoring her bad leg, Eleanor pressed past the woman saying, "Lady Tweedmouth needs a doctor. Her husband's funeral is tomorrow. Get the salts."

The woman didn't move—probably thinking Eleanor a mad woman and best not to touch. Eleanor made her damaged ankle take her weight until the front door. It was her mother in her that prevailed—energy in adversity. Chamomile flower meant energy in adversity. Eleanor couldn't remember a time when there wasn't chamomile spread about the house.

Eleanor limped outside. Fog, born of heavy rain and heated pavements hit her like a high concrete wall. Disoriented, she stopped. Her sight reduced, she noticed the hard thump of her heart. She turned what she thought was left with her back to the dress form toward the Gaelic League to find a cab. Her head was bowed to the rain. A body ran into her side at full speed.

"There you are, bitch!" a male voice said, striking at her like a viper. The voice was hoarse with rage.

Thrown sideways from the impact, her arms shot out for balance. Her attacker's hand snaked out, and grabbed her forearm. He spun her body, and then circled his long arms around her neck and waist. His strong hold tighten. He held her against him and against his hard erection. Coughing from the pressure on her collapsing windpipe. She slapped and using her nails, she dug at his grasp. Damn her long skirts. She bit through the white shirt on his arm and got to flesh. She tasted blood. He howled and let go and then grabbed for her again. She darted into the shroud of air. She thought of red grouse with their wildly beating hearts, hidden in the tall grass, being flushed into flight. She moved in the thick air, thinking of erratic flight. She needed to confuse him.

She had no way to tell if he were still after her. He knew her, had come for her. She hadn't gotten to see his face. Cold rains sluiced down her loose hair. He was insane. Had to be...the man at the window. She stepped too hard onto her damaged ankle. She fell, tearing her sleeve and skinning her elbow. Her heavy, wet, narrow gown grounded her for precious moments.

He must have heard her go down, heard her shriek. Eleanor peered through the sludge-colored air. Maybe she had lost him. She felt as if she were a blind woman. Hobbling forward again, her skirts flapped against her legs.

A hand from nowhere reached at her head. It missed, but she squealed. Stupid. The second time he had her by her roots. She screamed. God, was there no one about? She fell again. He dragged her down the sidewalk. By the neck of the back of her blouse, like a marionette, he raised her. His hand slapped over her mouth and over her nose, and then his arm snaked around and under her chest. He lifted her off her feet. His heart beat fast against her back.

He cut off her airway with his arm. She clawed at it. She felt her eyes strain in their sockets from the pressure in her body trying to breathe. She butted her head back and connected with something because he yowled and called her a bitch again. Oh yes, a bitch. She tried to hook her ankle around his calf. Off balance and stepping back, he fell off a curb. His grip loosened enough that she gasped for air. She fell with him. The man hit his head; Eleanor heard the dull thud. The fall must have dazed him as his hold slackened enough that she pulled away. Eleanor decided that like any intelligent being, she should get in out of the rain. With a sharp elbow to his midsection and a satisfying grunt from him, she stood. Rot in Hell.

In a windswept break in the fog, she ran toward ghostly buildings. Her body prickled feeling the possibility of the man behind her. With the dense air reforming, she groped the solidness of bricks and mortar, until she felt the smoothness of a door. Her hip found the knob. Once inside, she shut the solid door hard behind her and leaned against it.

She didn't move, letting the wood support her. The firmness against her spine gave comfort. To move away and feel just the insignificance of air around her, she'd have to stand alone.

She had lost him. He would be checking for her, but she had gotten away. She waited to open her eyes until her nerves lay limp in her body. When she did, on her right was the dusty dressmaker's form. In front of her was the same proprietress who had shown her the door. The stage glowed before her, and she laughed. The place felt like home—the proprietress—like family. Certainly the woman's frown resembled her mother's.

Setting the best smile she could manage, and standing on her last good leg, she felt as if the circus had come to London, and she was the trained monkey.

❧ 24 ❧

Anger is a short madness.
—Horace

Eleanor sat in jail. Her mother would be so proud. It smelled like fear and boredom. So the taxi driver had delivered her note. Faraday arrived like savior and judge. When she first saw him, or his eyes as he peered at her though the small square window on the door of her cell, her heart leapt. He was here.

When the door clanged open and he stepped in, he didn't smile for which she was grateful. Her damp back was clammy, and she knew she had ruined the silk of her blouse, her whole ensemble really. The straw at her feet was clean, but still, she was again a monkey in a very tight and fortified stall. Her ankle had swollen up like a rising loaf of bread. It was wrapped. She was wrapped. A veterinarian had been in to see her at least, she thought and then laughed to herself.

Faraday carried her to his motor. She wanted to lay her head on his shoulder, and she might have done it if the man didn't feel so stiff. His tight grip was killing her sore ribs.

He remained silent. Eleanor pulled at the gauze that wound her head, ankle, and elbow. She felt like a resurrected mummy. When he pulled to a curb Eleanor said, "It's your flat."

"You need to dry some more before your mother sees you. I'm worried about you. Have you seen the bruising on your neck? You were nearly killed, weren't you? "

"In broad daylight?"

Faraday got out of the car, slamming his door before coming around to open hers. "They had to carry Charlotte out as well. I promise you that we never laid a glove on each other. I offered her a glass of wine." Not even a chuckle from himself. She sighed. The road dirt was beginning to itch.

He helped her into the building and up the stairs. Down a creamy corridor of doors, he entered the last portal on the right and then threw his keys on a shadowy table. While he turned on the gas lighting, she stood at the door. She couldn't find the welcome mat.

Faraday shook his head. "You do know where you and Charlotte were?"

"Without doubt. I've seen the show there. It's quite revealing, very naked. Something Albert would love."

"Do you have to learn everything the hard way?"

"Well, I will not forget the lesson."

"You were arrested."

"One of their...men, thugs, attacked me."

Faraday sighed and tried to pick her up again.

She shrugged him off. Damn it, she was hurt. "I can walk."

"You can't."

"I can and did."

He hesitated, measuring her, then walked away.

Some lesson he's teaching me no doubt, bastard. The word slipped. She'd thought it, and it broke her heart.

The place was rich with the odor of men's cologne and leather. She gimped inland and saw a wall of books. On the walls, each individually lit, were paintings—scores of women in recline, men with solid chins, landscapes and urchins. He's going to have to get a bigger place, she thought. All the artists were unknown, except to Faraday. There was a square of wall just about the size of her mother's painting. She'd have to steal it for him so he could stop coming by. With nothing else to do, Eleanor lit the fire. Faraday reappeared with a tray.

She'd never seen him angry as he'd been this afternoon. She thought of all she had to tell him, the mortuary, leaving her mother at the milliners. It would all come out blacker than Reverend Peacock's socks. She giggled. Oh, do be serious. She thought of her mother and giggled again.

Faraday carried in a beautiful Belleek pot and two cups. Far cry better than his rental. She saw his cigarette box on his gleaming desk.

"May I?"

"If you throw one my way."

Eleanor settled by the fire. It was all going to come out. She might as well start. "Mother and I were in the village gathering some things for our trip abroad, when I left her there. I wonder if she's still packing or just taken to her bed. Maybe she has Owens beating the brush."

"No doubt he's praying that you're gone for good."

"No doubt," she said back even though Faraday hadn't spoken in a joking manner. She didn't want to tell him anything now. He handed her a cup. He then sat into a chair with his. He expected an explanation. She owed it to him. He had bailed her out, again. "Yesterday, Charlotte camped at my house. She was lying in wait to sic her solicitor on me. Look, I saw her getting on the train to London. She's not supposed to put her head outside her doorframe for six months minimum. If she were headed to her family law firm, I had nothing to lose.

"As Abbey Leix was empty except for Renard, I stopped by. I'd never get another chance like that. I interviewed Tweedmouth's valet who said that the deliveryman for the Baron's medications had changed and that the deliveryman had a bruise under his fingernail. I searched the balcony and found medicinal paper under the lounge chair. Lucky it's been so dry."

Why couldn't he say, yes, I agree, Eleanor, great job, Eleanor?

She had to look away from those lips she loved because with each word she uttered, the man's mouth was becoming more compressed. Oh, finish it off...the story...the relationship. Whatever it was, it is now over. God, what a muddle, what a complete farce. *This is why I'm alone. Why can't I think beyond my first thought? Because it is so mesmerizing, it is really like a bubbling spring. It's after you jump in that you find the bubbling spring is icy-cold.*

She felt like she and Faraday had only moments more to live as friends, but there was nothing to do for it.

"I analyzed the paper and found opium and aspirin." A little murmur of pleasure sifted through her with Faraday's surprise. "I also interviewed Renard. He hates the Baron. By the way, happy-go-lucky Haversack, chewed on me after you left the croquet party."

Faraday didn't say anything.

Eleanor could hear her own sigh in the quiet room. At least the fire was roaring. She remembered the kiss, how sweet it had been. That man was not in this room with her now. She lifted her chin, made her voice stronger. "There was another accident at a shoot yesterday, this one fatal. I suppose that you didn't make that shoot. The man was so suddenly dead, and you had said that these things never happen, so Letty and I went to the mortuary to check the dead beater." She left out that they had broken in there as well.

She remembered that two men were dead. The beater had been good to her. She had liked him. She had been there at the first attempt to kill him. She had seen him on the ground. No one had understood. No one had seen the accident for what it was, not even the beater himself. "My God," she said. "Not even the beater knew. He had thought that he was in this by himself." She stubbed out her half-smoked cigarette. "I have to see the beater's room. It's probably too late, but who knows. The balcony was still intact."

Faraday jumped. "Are you mad?"

"It was the same beater who had been shot before. This time he died. He's dead. He was bringing the opium. He's dead. How did he know about Tweedmouth's allergy? He wouldn't know. Someone, someone who knew, put him up to it...someone else who needed Tweedmouth dead. But the beater thought he was working alone. He didn't know that he was being set up. I have to get into the beater's room."

"It's on Haversack property."

"I thought as much. You have to help."

"I'm getting you home, and you are staying there. It's all become too dangerous for you. You have been attacked."

"And what if it was Albert who attacked me? He likes brothels of all sorts...Oh Lord..." The naked man had looked familiar to her as he walked away, not that she had seen Albert unclothed often. Had he attacked her, called her "bitch" again? "My God."

Faraday walked to a cabinet and took out a bottle. He poured what remained of Eleanor's tea back into the pot, and he replaced it with scotch.

"You can't go on playing with this."

'Playing' broke her heart. She wasn't playing; she wasn't a bitch.

"Your mother's right. You need to stop now. Your ankle has swollen to the size of an elephant's trunk. Your hair looks like it's been ransacked."

She finished her drink, practically licking the cup. She was going to need every drop of the false courage. It was going to be at least four hours in a car with Faraday being like every other man she knew. She already missed him so much. She had to turn her head away from him, so he couldn't see the tears. Oh God. Lord, Blinking-Awful, Haversack...and Olivia, and bloody Albert, and the Greenburgs, mad as anything now that their little boy was not in the will, and greasy Renard and crazy, lavender-infused Charlotte, her mother, and now Faraday bringing up the rear as friendly fire. Her body hurt.

When she realized that she was going to have to go to Owens to get into the beater's room, she poured herself another shot and tossed it back. It was so unfair. She let Faraday take her home. She ignored her mother, and she waited until dawn.

S he hobbled into Owens's office in the morning and found Olivia there. Had she broken a mirror she didn't know about? "I didn't think to bring garlic," Eleanor muttered. One good thing though, as she absorbed glances that would kill goats, her mother and Faraday would never think to look for her here.

She hadn't an opening line. She'd been trying to think of one all night, and now with Olivia they all seemed pointless and too informative. Olivia was holding a breakfast plate. Eleanor was grateful to see that plate that her heart leapt. "How is Louis? Eating?"

"You!" Olivia said. "My God, what right have you to be here? What right have you to ask? Patronizing, that's what you are. More intelligent? Pfftt. You're half-Paddy all dressed up. You're lucky you got Albert—a fine flesh and blood Englishman. But you eat flesh and blood."

The words pushed against Eleanor like a hot desert wind. Her face burned, and she stepped backwards. Leave them to their murder, her hurt feelings said, and their murderer. They are all alike. Looking at the hate in their faces, she realized that she'd have to move. Wrong or right about her hunch, the whole village was against her. What is so different, she wanted to yell at Olivia, murder, or rejoicing in it. What if you were killed today, Olivia, and no one cared? It was too close to any of them to let even one of them slip through. I'm sorry mother, Eleanor thought before she said, "I am here to see Constable Owens alone." The words tasted like parsley, bitter.

"She thinks she knows something. How grandly delusional. Don't listen to her. She has nothing. You'd be a fool to listen to her."

The one thing Owens hated was to be told what to do in his own office and by a female. *Bless, bless, bless you Olivia*. It was a short answer to a prayer.

Owens's first words were, "Not you again. You've got to be the most miserable woman alive. Can you not just put yourself out of your misery?"

Eleanor had to grovel. Grovel in front of the pea-brained Owens, the thought was not a moment in her brain when another trailed it, don't patronize. She glanced to the floor and huffed out a little air. All right then.

He was sitting, waiting—like a cat covering a mouse hole. "What is it that you think you know?"

She didn't think she knew...oh damn it. Olivia waited outside his office. The woman wasn't about to leave.

She'd never get Owens to understand. It was a waste of time being here. There was nothing to say that would help. She'd already tried, many times before. Her ankle hurt. He hadn't even asked her to sit.

"I need your help." If he'd noticed that she'd said it without patronizing him, and without instructing him, he didn't let on.

"Where's Lord Faraday?"

"He told me to stay at home. He thinks that I am at home." The truth was best, especially if it was demeaning to her.

"He doesn't believe in you?"

She swore he could hear her teeth gritting. "I don't know, but he thinks that I'm in danger. Someone attacked me yesterday."

Owens's eyes briefly lit.

"Unsuccessfully," she finished.

"No, I can see that," Owens said. "You have nine lives. How many has that been? Are we getting closer?" He pushed away from his desk and stood. "Good day."

"No please. Please, please listen." She rushed. "The beater was supplying Tweedmouth's opium and the beater's dead now. There was an attempt on his life the day Tweedmouth died, and again yesterday. This time, he was killed. I mean how often are there two shooting accidents in a row, the same person?"

Owens stopped his forward walking. He didn't know about crime solving, but he did know about sports.

She continued, "The deliveryman for the opium had a bruised fingernail. So did the beater. We are on the same side. I...we need to check the beater's room. You can't be popular keeping Louis in that cell." She had no idea what she'd do if he refused her now. Nowhere else to go. She had no idea where these rooms were, and which one was the beater's. She had no groveling left in her. The animals on Owens' shelves, that's what this felt like. She'd been killed and stuffed and mounted.

"I'll check it."

It hit her how often men lie to women. "There will be two sets of eyes, two brains if we go together," she snapped. It didn't matter even if he did go if he went without her.

"Lady Albright..."

She knew what was coming. It would never be solved. She'd be an outcast. Her mother was right. It would be like being in mourning.

He paused watching her. He was enjoying this. Maybe it wasn't over. Why not, he was probably thinking—as there is the potential for so much more embarrassment. She has nothing and maybe she didn't, maybe she wouldn't find a brass tack, but she was glad.

"Will that be the end of your person on my doorstep?"

"Never again."

"Do you promise on your own life?"

"It will be my last request."

"Good, because if it's not, I promise you that I will throw you into my jail next to your friend Louis and bury the key with Tweedmouth."

Olivia was gone by the time Eleanor left the police station with Owens. Olivia had raced home and now Lord Haversack was expecting Eleanor. Indeed the entire shooting party, her husband, that was still staying at Haversack's had been looking forward to her arrival. They smirked at her presence, confident in her failure. They'd all be there to watch her downfall. Haversack had been happy, giddy, to let her into the room.

Eleanor knew Owens was right. There was nothing in that room. She followed Haversack's man and Owens beyond the stables anyway, leaning on Faraday's stick and limping. The room, when she arrived, smelled acidic like unwashed men. The dead beater's room was quite empty, as empty as the hope left in Eleanor's body. Faraday was never going to speak to her again after this. In a way, she had betrayed him. She had made him look a fool, on a fool's errand. And Louis! Dear God.

She ignored Owens's smirk and gazed at the few objects in the room—a wooden bed, a small table, and almost under the bed, a chamber pot. Her heart fell to the floor at the witness of such simplicity. The search and her demise would be quick. Eleanor lifted the mattress. She searched for slits in it, for hidden packets of opium, for anything. The chamber pot was not empty. Disgusting.

She let the mattress fall back into place with a thump. Dust circled in the light. Her fate was sealed. She'd have to go back to her husband, if he would have her. She thought of sitting with her mother at breakfast forever. They'd all be right, so hold-it-over-her-head right every day. About to walk out the door, her mind's eye pressed forward the vision of a piece of paper that was also in the pot. Oh, give it up. You've even lost Faraday. She stepped into the rain.

"There's one other thing," she said as she blocked Owens from closing the door. She walked to the bed and, while Owens looked disgusted, fished out the chamber pot from under the bed. "Isn't this YOUR job, Chief Inspector Owens?"

"Not on your life. Just here to watch you make a fool of yourself. It's getting better and better."

Reaching down, she was relieved to find that what she thought was excrement was a cigar butt. "Oh, thank God." She pulled out the piece of paper that nagged at her mind and had turned her back—just a corner tear-off. Nothing was written on it. There was something stuck the fold.

Fool, she. It was nothing. Stupid. Owens laughed. She was grasping at straws, trying to avoid at any cost, facing them all with nothing. Egg on her face, her poor mother. Still the thing...there was something.... She turned it, something familiar about it...think.

"We're going, Lady Albright," Owens said. "Throw that thing back. Looks like a chunk of sick someone spit out into paper."

Eleanor started at the paper. Relief and exultation rushed through the length and breadth of her body. God bless chamber pots and baskets and paper. She danced the golden pot around the room. She was hugging the metal as if it was her last friend. It was.

"Who, in all this, can't afford to be the naked groomsman Bergami to the Baroness of Tweedmouth's Lady Campbell?" she said to Owens.

"What?" He said his face a picture of discomfort, even fear.

He thinks I've gone mad. Let him. "The Penny Press. Let's go back so I can make a complete report."

As she walked toward the main house, mud sucked at her shoes. It had started to rain again. The freshness reminded Eleanor of sitting beside her sweet stream. How good to have it all nearing an end, any end at all.

Wood warblers in beech trees cheered her. She itched to take a bath, to let light bubbles remind her of kinder things. Tweedmouth had not been kind, maybe not even one time in his life. So, legions of dark humans had been stepping on top of each other to end his life. One dumb thing had led to another and to another until the thing collapsed as a blue, broken man—a disowned man, a man who had lived life stupidly as if it were a fire within him.

Owens lagged behind her. She didn't care about him or her mangled ankle. The shot snapped her shoulder. It was a cross-shot and taken well in front. Eleanor felt the burn of the bullet's entry. Like the birds and the beater before her, she pitched forward into the muck.

❧ 25 ❧

Prisoner, God has given you good abilities, instead of which you go about the country stealing ducks.
—William Arabin

Faraday fell to his knees at Eleanor's side. When he had found her gone, her bedroom empty, he knew she'd be at the beater's hovel. One way or another, she'd be here, and he had come to get her. She was playing a dangerous game, a game she didn't know or understand. He had been too late. He had always been too late.

He lifted her head to his lap. She was glassy-eyed and dull-feathered. He clamped his hand over the blood spreading on the white ruffles of her shirt. He wasn't sure if he felt the rise and fall of a breathing chest. A piece of his mind prayed. Another piece of it cursed himself. The last piece worked on saving her.

With steady fingers, Faraday reached for Eleanor's throat and through her mud-stained, white skin, he took her pulse. It beat, while his heart had stopped, and the wound bled. "Send someone for a doctor," Faraday yelled to Owens, "and then start fanning out for that shooter."

For the second time, Faraday carried Eleanor. This time, he felt her weight.

Faraday ticked off the places the shooter might be. There would be no place on earth that the person who had done this would be able to hide from him. Eleanor's hand stirred. Her eyes opened and then closed again. "I will find him."

The bullet ended its life in Faraday's pocket. He took grave ownership of it. Owens had sent for his constables, all the while repeating that it could have been an accident. But in the face of two deaths, an attempted killing, and Faraday's anger, Owens's insincerity sounded shaken.

"She had a few last words," Owens said.

"Not last words," Faraday ground out.

Owens shrugged. "She said, 'Who, in all this, can't afford to be the naked groomsman Bergami to the Baroness of Tweedmouth's Lady Campbell.' You figure it out and just let me know."

Who indeed? Faraday intended to find out. He would have to tell Alannah first.

A clock behind Alannah's door struck seven as Faraday waited in the rain. He knew that even though he'd taken off his jacket, the blood on his shirt would give the game away. When Alannah saw him, she, without preamble, without words, walked toward the door.

"She's...she's resting," said Faraday. He put his hand on Alannah's shoulder to slow her. "Get Lady Darnley's rainwear." Faraday felt remorse as he followed Alannah's hurried steps to a Haversack carriage.

"Thank God you didn't bring that car," she said.

"She was shot in the shoulder," he said on the way. "It missed anything vital. Her room is guarded."

"Guarded?"

"Of course."

"This wasn't an accident."

"Someone thinks the investigation a threat with Eleanor at its lead."

Faraday absorbed the glare he knew Alannah would give him. "Eggs indeed," she said. The two were a matched pair, Alannah and her daughter. Faraday felt proud for both of them.

"The doctor has the best of hope. He does say full recovery."

"Don't give me false hope young man. What has been happening?"

"This morning she followed Charlotte to the Eleusian Institute."

Alannah looked long at the glove she had half pulled onto her hand. "My father used to watch the rich women come and go from there on his way to

Fenian meetings." She chuckled. He used to say that they didn't carry themselves with any joy. Faraday told her about the butt in the large picture window that could be Albert's.

"Wait until Letty hears," she said as she climbed into the carriage.

A joke...telling Alannah had gone better than expected. Still, the unapologetic day persisted. Faraday walked into Eleanor's room long enough to deposit Alannah and to talk to Owens. While riding with a calm Alannah, some of the anger that had been hitting him again and again like surf in a high wind had subsided. In a carriage with a man that singularly brings her heartache, heading to the bedside of her wounded daughter, she sat with her hands folded. He admired and liked Alannah even more.

"How many men do you have, Owens?" Faraday asked.

"I've got everyone out, and I've notified London. Only we don't know for sure who it is, do we? I've got a crew combing the grounds."

"Do you have a man searching Cornbury House?"

"You think he's here in the house?"

"It's more than a remote possibility. Do it, Owens. If I could take her anywhere else," Faraday fretted. "I've got to go back to London. If there is as much as a hair out of place on her head—"

Owens ruffled. "I've got a man at the door."

Things had gotten out of hand, Faraday thought. With Alannah deposited, he jumped into his car for the next trip—to London. Standing on Abbey Leix lawn that night under the full moon inspecting Tweedmouth's body, he had never expected any of this. In truth, he might have patronized Eleanor a little that night; she'd walked across the field with so much delightful intent. She knew the what, the where, the why, and the shooter had silenced her, too.

It continued to rain. On the way to London, Faraday wired The Yard for an inspector to meet him on Wigmore Street. He needed the connections Eleanor had but together. He needed to know whose butt she had seen.

Faraday arrived at the Greenburg drawing room like a shark to bloodied waters. If the leftover blood on his shirt startled Mrs. Greenburg, she remained within character and didn't comment.

"Where is your housekeeper?" Faraday asked.

"Why in the kitchen, of course."

"Is that the way it's going to be, Mrs. Greenburg? I suggest that you might rethink your approach."

Mrs. Greenburg smiled. She swooped her skirt to sit in a chair.

Faraday had known this wouldn't be easy, maybe even impossible. He was so fed up to the teeth with these women that his mouth hurt. He'd get what he needed, and then leave them to their miseries.

"I think that I'll arrest them all," said the inspector. "We'll do this from my office."

"Mama," Julia cried out.

Mrs. Greenburg remained unperturbed. "We have done nothing. I don't know what more we can say, here or there."

"Let me tell you what I expect you to say. Samuel Tweedmouth killed your husband in a duel. Emotions were high because your husband had been used. Besides, you were pregnant with Tweedmouth's daughter. You wanted to keep some control over the Baron who was worth millions by then. The Baron had injured your pride."

Faraday watched for a hardening to Mrs. Greenburg's smile or a tighter grip in her hands that lay together on her lap. She was still in control, almost mocking him. Julia, on the other hand, rocked and moaned. Her eyes had no resting place. He didn't care about them.

"Ask the maid to come in. We know that in any household the walls have ears."

The housekeeper had to be coaxed in like a threatened puppy. Her head appeared just above her collar. The girl knew her job was at stake. Faraday rubbed at his forehead and calmed his voice.

"Tell us the truth. Your employers are implicated, and you know too much. Either way, you will be scanning the classifieds for employment or watching out for your life. Have you seen or heard of the name Tweedmouth?"

"I saw it on a letter."

"That's all?"

"Didn't I hear Mrs. Lawrence say it?"

"Was she angry?"

"Yes."

"Did you know what she was talking about when she said the name?"

The girl didn't hesitate. "The boy."

Faraday relaxed a little. He continued to pinpoint the housekeeper's small frame with his eyes. Intimidation poured from him. The housekeeper wrung her hands on her apron. "How long ago did you hear or see the name?"

"Let's see, Mrs. Greenburg let me out that night to work on flower wreaths. It was May Festival time."

"Was anyone else here, maybe a man staying here? An American?"

"Yes, sir."

"When?"

"About five months ago, and from time to time."

"About the same time the Baron's illness got worse." Faraday dismissed her by redirecting his line of vision to Julia.

"Tweedmouth wanted to take over guardianship of Daniel, didn't he, Julia? He had your birth certificate changed to bear his name as the grandfather. In exchange, he'd leave Daniel everything—a considerable sum, hard to pass up considering the tarnish around this house. Maybe your mother thought you all deserved it. She had, after all, produced the first heir."

Julia glanced at her mother who watched Faraday.

Mrs. Greenburg appeared amused. Faraday knew from the set of her shoulders that she was relaxed. Faraday addressed Julia. "It was a botched job, poisoning with aspirin a difficult thing at best, a stupid job, a crucial day early. When you found out the will hadn't been signed, you must have been very angry." Faraday let the quiet settle. He waited and watched Julia. Through his gaze, he let her know that he knew everything. While he waited for her to worry, he wished for a cigarette.

"How could anyone be so stupid as to have a man killed on the wrong day?" said Mrs. Greenburg, redirecting Faraday's attention.

And now, the dragon. He didn't answer her right away. He knew he'd never get the truth from her, and no, he didn't think her stupid. She had to fill in the void before her daughter did. He wished he had been able to talk to the beater. The two had come so close to their goal. Now one was dead, the other, her goose cooked. "This beater was delivering a mixture of aspirin and opium to Tweedmouth."

"For pain?"

"Aspirin triggered severe asthma in Tweedmouth. I assume the plan was to keep him sick over time, so, in the end, the police wouldn't suspect foul play. It was a considerable risk, the timing, but worth it. Isn't it interesting that the onset of Tweedmouth's illness coincides with the letter on which your housekeeper saw the Tweedmouth name? The beater was your husband's relative?"

Julia's brow beaded with perspiration. Faraday knew he was going in the right direction. He thought of Eleanor lying in bed probably beginning to fever. These ladies, black-hearted as they were, hadn't done that. They probably didn't even know that the beater was dead.

"Your cohort is dead now, by the way."

Mrs. Greenburg glanced away. She was trying to hide either delight or surprise. Faraday wasn't sure which. She was awful, and he had grown tired of her.

"We have the body and his personal belongings. Do you want to claim them? While he was working flushing birds, a shooter killed him. Mrs. Greenburg, you may have begun the entire plot, but I suspect that someone superseded you. Tell me about this relative of yours. How did you come to know about Tweedmouth's problem with aspirin?"

Mrs. Greenburg shifted a little in her chair and arranged her dress to its advantage. She moved like she hadn't a care in the world. Faraday had met with many a hardened criminal, and this woman would vie with any one of them.

"How can you think we had anything to do with any of this? He had a lot of enemies. Mr. Greenburg's brother came here destitute. We helped him out as we could."

Faraday had to admire the speech. Its brilliance still crackled in the air. He marveled at her nerve and let her smug cleverness seem weightier than it was. Overconfidence sometimes worked as well as fear. Hard to wait, though, he heard his impatience in the questions he barked at them. He wanted to be gone and on the road back to Eleanor.

"What jobs has your brother-in-law done since his arrival?" asked Faraday.

"He drove a cab. He worked the docks."

"How did he end up a beater for Lord Haversack?"

"Was he? We did what we could for him."

Faraday had forgotten about Julia. No use in remembering her. Mrs. Greenburg would always stifle, would always answer for her. The mother and daughter were a united front. Let the dead beater take the rap. It didn't matter; Faraday had been setting up the evening for the next string of questions.

"Your brother-in-law. He's something of a flirt with a good face and body." Faraday pictured these two on the stand. The Penny Press would be at hand and drooling. Charlotte would have to go into hiding. "Did he work at a place called the Elusian Institute? I have the body and I can show it to the proprietress and to your maid." It was a bluff. Faraday knew the beater's face had been disfigured, but these ladies didn't know that.

Mrs. Greenburg considered. "If I said yes, would our cooperation be noted?"

Faraday noted that she didn't play feminine. She didn't claim unfamiliarity with the Institute. "Of course."

"I understand that he did."

Kindness all round, he thought. On the way to the street, Faraday asked the inspector to find a place for the housekeeper to sleep. Damn it, he still needed the last piece of the puzzle, "Do you know where the proprietress lives?" Faraday asked the inspector. "I need the beater's contact." Even though there would be no arrests on Wigmore Street tonight, Faraday knew that the Greenburg ladies were not celebrating; Mrs. Greenburg had lost her fortune twice. Faraday wondered if she'd paid the beater/brother-in-law for his services. Maybe his cut came from the unfettered inheritance they had expected. Too bad Tweedmouth couldn't die twice.

❦ 26 ❦

A loud laugh spoke the vacant mind.
—Oliver Goldsmith

Eleanor woke to pain that thumped like a muted drum in her right shoulder. The price one pays—the price seemed excessive. She didn't want to close her eyes again, to relax...to soak in laudanum-induced serenity. But she had to tell someone what she knew. She lifted her head and regretted it. In childhood, she had had food poisoning; she hated to vomit.

A bed supported her fragile body. The comforter lay over her like a mound of insulating snow. A faint, dancing glow from a dying fire lit the dark walls. She saw her mother in a chair. She must be home.

Her mind, cushioned by laudanum, circled inside her head. In the aftermath of a drugged sleep, her thoughts tried to reshape and gather. So many questions needed to be answered, but the heavy-handed drugs doused her thoughts; her wisdom floated.

These people...these people she had known all her life...the Charleses and Tweedmouths had seemed flimsy, too much time on their hands. But they were not. They were a determined lot. They needed to keep the status quo, however they could, with whatever means.

What was she thinking? She needed a drink of water. The dark shape of her mother snored in a chair.

It had seemed reasonable that Lady Tweedmouth would kill her husband. All of Eleanor's efforts had been to that premise. She had been wrong, in a way, just like Owens. Her dogged insistence had blinded her. Lying in bed, Eleanor felt all of the realities of life. She realized that walking in the village would never be the same. The players in this drama were now transparent, like windowpanes after a melted frost. While opaque, the Charleses and Tweedmouths had been easy to dismiss as something they were not.

Europe might be the thing after all. Time, season, the movement of life would stir the village back to a comforting density. She thought of being shot and wondered if she should be concerned. Fear wouldn't stick to her thoughts. The medication made her mind slick. Thirst clamored for attention. She glanced at her mother again. Alannah's hand now hung from the armrest. Her head tilted forward.

Too hot, Eleanor pushed at the comforter. She thought of Faraday, of water, and of heat. Thoughts rambled in her mind like an ill-written essay. She navigated in and out of foggy places. Murphy's Law she herself had been attracted to Charles once. He was funny, and charming. His smile moved dark clouds from the sky. That smile.

When Eleanor opened her eyes again, that smile was above her. The face behind it moved very close to her face and frowned. *Charles, sweet Charles, funny Charles—the Charles that had given Olivia American gum for her teeth. Charles the gum-chewer with the wide, bright grin, like a boy's really. Olivia had been chewing gum that day at the tea shop, but she is not the murderer, and not Albert either. All for the best. Divorce from a murderer just didn't sound that good, on top of all his other faults.*

She remembered the tilt of her mother's head. Opium-pillowed alarm moved through her. "My mother—"

"What does it take to kill you? You're like an evil cat with nine lives," Charles said.

His face appeared ill, so pale. Maybe he was a ghost. The room had brightened. He must have stoked the fire. She battled a desire for sleep and watched Charles shift about the area. He didn't talk again. He appeared uneasy, moving like a wind-up toy. He was not so beautiful without his smile.

Vague alarm helped her part the cotton wool that stuffed her head. She hoped that her mother only slept. She weakly called out anyway—risking the attention the sound would bring to her from Charles.

He did pull a chair to the bedside and sat. He smiled his smile. His beautiful smile that she'd never noticed before as having no warmth.

"I thought you'd just slip into death. You don't do that do you, slip away quietly?"

"My mother?"

"Sleeping, not that I've done her a favor."

There was no one to hear her scream. She hadn't the capacity for it anyway. He watched her. Charles's polished veneer glowed less in him tonight. Veins reddened his eyes. Eleanor realized that she had never been in a quiet room with the man. Charles always had people around him.

She had liked Charles, thought he had liked her, and he had shot her. Hunted her down and aimed a gun at her like she was a partridge that had flown into his sights. A sob cut her shallow breathing.

She closed her eyes and tried to fight the sorrow that clutched at her mind. He had played them all. It was easier to see it now...that his attention was all in the moment.

When Charles turns and no longer sees you, you are forgotten as if you were never there.

The bastard! Who was he... to shoot the bird at anyone that was in his way...play God...rearrange the rules in his favor? Wouldn't they all love to be able to do that?

"You killed the Baron of Tweedmouth for money. Gambling?" she said.

Charles laughed. "Quick mind. Always entertaining. Isn't that a woman's skill? No, you have no woman's skills."

With Charles's broadening, cat-got-the-bird smile, she understood with horrible clarity his need to destroy her. Still, if he felt mocked and exposed, she hadn't undressed him. He had done that himself. Everyone liked him. How good he had been at being liked. She had felt sorry for him. Now she felt sorry for Olivia, well maybe only a little. While watching Charles smile his unholy smirk, Eleanor remembered that his impromptu shoot had been opposite her mother's garden party. Not only had he embarrassed her mother, he had used the shoot to kill the beater, to get rid of any potential witnesses or blackmailers. How perfect he must think himself. Charles and his perfect gum-chewing, white teeth, that's how she had caught him, through his vanity.

"How could I have planned for the unreasonable that is you, Lady Albright? Only a woman would think the impossible."

"A new will had been written," Eleanor managed. "You knew. How?"

"Of course I knew. I knew everything about that house. Tweedmouth had a tongue like a wasp, always stinging with veiled truths. I figured out the clues he'd jab into the air and leave dangling."

Charles's lungs exploded their own hot air then. "You pushed and pushed. What for? Tweedmouth was hellish. Everyone knows that." He glared at her with layers of hate so profound that she was pushed into the cushiony softness of her bed.

Eleanor took in her mother again. Alannah hadn't moved.

"The most saintly man in the world is in a cell. You stupid woman. What's more, he believes he did it. I can't convince him otherwise without telling him about the aspirin. I didn't kill him just for me, you know. There was Louis. It was for him."

"There is no Saint Charles," she countered in a weak voice. "There is the new will, money lost to you through your friend if the money was out of Louis's control, and there was Charlotte's divorce. A trial about to begin, witnesses...your work at the institute. You are her whore."

He slapped her.

Eleanor felt it as an echo of light pain. "Damn you! Loser! Gambler! Bully! You need money from Louis, Charlotte, your marriage. It was you two together, Charlotte and you planning this."

"Charlotte!" Charles laughed. He stroked the skin from her ear lobe to the neck of her nightgown. With his anger under control, his sense of supremacy appalled her. His large personality demanded to be the center of attention. He needed to boast. Let him boast to her. She would use that. "You gave her quite a run. That bit was excellent. I thought, better yet, maybe you'd be successful, or she'd die of a stroke. Stupid women, both of you."

"I figured you out or you wouldn't be here. The beater, a fellow gigolo at the Institute?"

Charles's eyes narrowed. She braced herself for another slap. He leaned toward her instead. He laughed at her, with his mouth open, his too perfect, ugly, mouth.

She talked into his mocking noise. "You needed money. Charlotte picked you every time. The beater thought he was being clever, but he didn't know. You were her son's best friend. He told you about Daniel, and you told him how to kill Tweedmouth."

"Yes," he said, his hand smacking the mattress. "Everything would be gone with the signature of Louis's infernal father. All the money, gone."

"Louis throwing his father over the rail—"

"Idiot Louis taking his revenge. When I'd heard that Louis had confessed to punching his father, I felt like letting him rot. He couldn't be quiet. And you, you couldn't stop looking."

"The eggs..." Death stroked what was left of her energy. He leaned toward her with breath that was volatile. She was so tired.

"The eggs? Oh yes, the EGGS. That was Olivia. Her idea. Fun. Knew your mother would give you hell."

"You brought the last dose of opium, laced it with plenty of aspirin a day early, and you brought the water. The beater must have been distraught, his quarry died twelve short hours more, that's all he had needed."

His brilliant, gum-chewing smile glowed at full wattage. "Just before the will was to be signed. Breathtaking. You have to agree."

She wouldn't confirm the brilliance of the plan. She wouldn't encourage his joy. "The empty water glass...a small effort to confuse?"

Charles began talking about himself again. He couldn't seem to stop. He could brag into her already certain knowledge. The words sounded hollow. It wasn't the way he spoke, but the way she was listening, from inside a fish bowl. She tried to concentrate. She needed to watch him, to bide her time, and to summon her little energy.

"I've been walking around my own estate like a leper," he said. "You've done that to me—for trying to save Louis."

"Is he saved?" she whispered.

Charles startled. He squeezed her upper arm.

"Some are easier to save than others." He quieted himself some with effort. He considered her. "How beautiful." He stroked her cheek. "Beauty marred by a willful nature. The waste. Don't you see it, the waste?"

"We live...we must live...stupidly." She waited for him to react. She hated feeling impotent. He laughed. His emotional pendulum unhinged her.

"Louis, by Jove! Good one." He slapped his knee. "It's what one must do to live happily with the stupidity of others. The weak, the weak lose everything."

She closed her eyes.

He seemed to be unconcerned that all his plans had gone wrong, with Louis in jail, just as she had predicted. Louis couldn't inherit from the noose. Confidence that everything could be made right showed in his upbringing. He was entitled.

"You love to gamble." She opened her eyes.

"I love to win. There isn't any proof, you know," he said. "Without you around, I will convince them of that."

"The gum left in the chamber pot. You got the gum from him at the

Institute, from the beater. It's an American candy."

"I've always liked your hair, the color. I don't like dark hair, but yours... I've always wanted to unpin it." Charles spread some of its length over the pillow. "It's a common girl's hair, thick and unbridled. I met your Irish grandfather once. He called me a fat pup when he caught me shooting out of season on your father's estate. Now here you are." The smile cracked his face in half.

His glee chilled her. She wondered about Faraday. She wanted him here.

"You and your family ruin everything they touch. Faraday...ruined. It disgusts me."

Eleanor tried to keep her face bland. Animals...people...to Charles they both die the same way, conveniently. Her head would soon be a trophy on the wall in his library. She assumed that her hair would be flattering and her eyes glassy and an opaque blue. On the other hand, he might not want her scrutinizing him from eternity. No, it was going to be his head.

Charles unburdened was ruthless. The intensity that had always emanated from him felt magnified. He swaggered in his speech. He rambled on about being a savior, sounding much as Tweedmouth had sounded. Save her from the image of very small men posturing as gods.

"The probable, Lady Albright? Everyone but you thinks within the probable. The probable is that you are gravely ill and dosed with laudanum. A little more won't alarm anyone. Amazing how easy it is to get a person in a semi-wakeful state to drink."

Oh my God. Panic raked through her. No wonder she was failing. To pay for his gambling debts, he was watching her die. She wasn't going to let this man rant at her any longer. She had figured out what he had done, and how he had done it.

The fresh laudanum he had given her began to pull at her senses. In the strongest voice she could muster she said, "I am right. You gave him his last dose of aspirin. You killed him."

"I can't hear you." Charles propped his chin in his hands, his elbow resting on the mattress. He leaned in closer and whispered, "God is in his hell, and all is right with the world." He smiled again.

She used her anger and what was left of her strength to poke her fingers hard into the white orbs of his gleaming eyes. His hands went to his face as he jerked backwards. His head hit on the edge of a solid marble table. That wiped the damn, ever-present grin off his face. Chew on that! He howled and then when silent as a blessing. She felt the peace of the quiet of the room and then the peace of the laudanum.

❧ 27 ❧

The credit goes to the man who is actually in the arena.
—*Theodore Roosevelt*

On the long private drive to Haversack's house the last leg of a long journey, Faraday strained forward like his car. Thank God it hadn't failed him. He had failed her though. The light in Eleanor's window shone like a cheery beacon of stability. It cheered him. All was well. The engine turned off, Faraday slumped in his seat. Sounds of the road still hummed in his ears. Faraday's long frame still vibrated. He could have slept where he sat.

His damp coat steamed from the heat of his body. The rain and the cold of the night pushed him toward the door of the house. He whistled to keep himself awake. It was easy to whistle now. The beater and his friend Charles, the proprietress had described the two men to a tee. Tea, that's what's needed. There are times when tea is the most fortifying beverage on earth. This would be one of them. He'd drink it while checking on Eleanor, and then blissful sleep.

The aria he'd been humming died on his lips when an anxious footman answered the knock. "The policeman is on the floor in front of the door.

He's unconscious. Lady Eleanor's door's locked, and the spare keys are gone missing," the man said.

Faraday ran beside the servant while thinking that the long horrid day would just not end. Never, as they say, had so much gone so wrong so often. Damn Owens. He'd have the man's hide stuffed and mounted.

The policeman had fallen from his chair and been left there. "He's alive," the servant said as he stepped over him. "We haven't had the time to move him."

An absence of noise haunted Faraday. The living were rarely silent, the dead rarely noisy. Faraday hit his shoulder against the bedroom door.

"Solid," said the footman. "We tried. Mick's gone to get a crowbar."

Faraday pounded on the door, and then he threw himself at it again. It wasn't a door but a portal. Searching for some kind of lock pick, he ran from room to room. Nothing, so he kept body-slamming the door all the last seconds of the immortal wait. He'd not be putting roses on mother and daughter graves.

Mick and the butler arrived with tools. The door-jam splintered but held under their onslaught. Faraday took a crowbar and pried at the wood. The frame gave. Faraday pushed the door wide open. Alannah slumped in the wing chair. Eleanor lay on the bed. Mick rounded the bed and tripped.

"Jesus, Lord Charles is here on the floor. His head is bleeding."

"Is he dead? Is Lady Darnley?"

"Not sure."

Sod the bleeding Charles. "See to them," Faraday said as he leaned in over the bed to Eleanor. She was so still. Desperation clutched him. He grabbed her wrist. Her heart was faint. He shook her and called to her. He'd been at her side for the whole of this. He should have taken her seriously. He didn't know why he didn't. He would have to answer for her life. It crushed him to see her so lifeless.

"The mother's alive," Mick said.

"Eleanor, for the love of God, open your eyes." Her eyes fluttered and her lips moved. He bent to place his ear near the lips of her still-warm body.

"Lau..." She pushed air through parted lips.

"La...la...Jesus, laudanum. Make strong, cold coffee," he said to the maids peering in from the door. "Get a doctor here."

Eleanor lay in his arms like a worn-out doll. He carried her, holding her close. "Where's the bath?" Cradling her on the tile floor, he stuck his finger down her throat. The gag-reflex wasn't strong, but it brought up some of the poisonous liquid in her stomach.

A servant brought the coffee. With Eleanor propped up against his chest and them both sitting on the floor, Faraday gave her coffee with an eyedropper. "Drink." He pushed at her neck to help her swallow. "Talk to me." A doctor arrived. He took Eleanor's pulse and commented that it was good her eyes were trying to open. Faraday and the doctor walked her between them. Her shoulder bled. Her feet touched the ground every fourth step.

"Eleanor! Talk to me. What was the state of the groomsman Bergami's dress when the maid saw him in the passage going toward Lady Campbell's bedroom?" Faraday talked loudly into her ear. "And Lady Campbell was naked, spread out on the bed? You clever, clever girl. I remember the article. Charles couldn't afford to be named in a Lady Campbell style divorce. All of London would find out about his work at the Institute. I'd say at this point his lucrative marriage is dead." Faraday didn't know if the man himself was dead.

He continued. "The beater was careful with the aspirin, much to Charles's pique, I'm sure. The night before the signing of the will, Charles had to finish off Tweedmouth himself with a massive dose of aspirin mixed with the opium. The new will forced his hand."

He wondered how she had done it—figured out that it was Charles. He prayed she would live to tell him. When she said, "How's my mother?" he knew that he could put Eleanor back to bed and let her rest. "Good girl," he said while smoothing the covers over her with the sun coming up in the window behind him.

Alannah walked into the room. She looked the most refreshed of all of them.

"You look awful, Lord Faraday, she said. "What have you been up to? Go get some rest. Why is it so light outside? Why is Eleanor in here?"

Faraday sat with Lady Darnley while drinking the tea he'd wanted for what seemed like years. He tried to convince himself it was all over, but a kind of primitive superstition held him to the room, to the chair, to Eleanor's side. He watched the minute rise and fall of her breathing. She'd come too close. His fault.

Charles had always been a great hunter, but a bad gambler. He was smart, and he was expert at putting his prey off-guard, but Charles played short. Faraday would find out what happened in this room. When it all came out, as it would like lava pouring forth from an exploding cavity, the news would rock society. The local shooting season would now draw in. Faraday felt sorry for its loss. Oh well, he was going to have to go home anyway. His father wasn't well.

Faraday's anger was gone in the drama of the evening. He felt too tired to sustain it. In the chair next to Eleanor's bed, he woke from sleep once, when Lady Darnley covered him with a blanket.

❧ 28 ❧

I am obnoxious to each carping tongue,
Who says my hand a needle better fits
—Anne Bradstreet

Faraday was at Eleanor's doorstep the day after she and Alannah returned from Europe. They'd wintered in Italy. He'd received letters that her shoulder had healed, and her strength was returning over the five months she had convalesced next to the Mediterranean Sea. They'd sent him leather driving gloves.

When he entered the military-painted drawing room, Lady Darnley was at the window "Look at it out there." She let the curtain drop. "I hear you haven't had a fine day since Tweedmouth died. Oh."

Faraday laughed at the comment.

"A sunny day. Oh, you know what I mean."

"It has been a rainy winter. You were in the best spot. I had hoped to get my feet wet in the sunny Med, but my father's been too ill to leave."

"Is he better?"

He gave her a short nod. "He has weathered the worst of it, but he will never shoot again."

"I'm very sorry. I have always liked your father."

"And he, you."

Alannah walked over to the small painting of the girl beside the river and lifted it off the wall. "It's Eleanor," she said to him. "I suppose you have always known that."

"I will treasure it."

"I still don't approve, but I think you should have it. As it happens, she is at the river. It seems like she's always there, now. Walk down. She'd love to see you. You did bring a raincoat?"

E leanor sat under a huge hat with a coat buttoned about her. He watched her step forward and cast a fishing line out over the Windrush River. He had missed her.

"I suppose that you don't know that I love to fish?" she asked when she saw him next to her. "My grandfather and I used to fish a lot. I've missed it. I couldn't wait any longer." She paused for a moment. "Letty says that I'm a heroine."

"But you don't feel like one."

"No. I still feel mud splattered. Dealing with the meanest of spirits and the saddest of tragedies has quieted the victory march. I even feel sorry for Olivia. I hear that she's under a doctor's care, still. Seems odd that she would take it so hard. She always seemed more resilient, self-absorbed.

"She's got visitors day and night."

Faraday watched the corners of Eleanor's mouth turn up slightly at that.

"Ah, well then, I can cross her off my worry list."

"You were worried about Olivia?"

Eleanor shrugged her shoulders. "Maybe she did love him."

"It's Louis who loves him. The boy is standing by Charles and using Tweedmouth money for his defense."

"Well then as Louis says, *Inter spem et metum*—saints are not perfect, but keep coming back to God, in between hope and fear?"

"Are you saying that he is applying that to Charles?"

"Charles did say he was working for Louis's best interests."

"Tell me how you figured it all out."

She reeled in her line and cast again. "Fishing is deceptively simple, don't you think? A rod, a reel, bait, toss the hook in, the fish bite, but it's not. It's the very life of the fish and the fish wants to keep on living. There's nuance to the battle."

"Makes Owens sound more refined."

She laughed and reeled in. "If I hadn't encountered Olivia in a tea shop, I wouldn't have figured it out. She had wanted to make me squirm. Instead, she gave me the solution." Eleanor handed Faraday the rod. "She had gum in her mouth and had to expel it before she got to her table of friends, you see. Olivia very decorously spit it into a small piece of paper and left it on my empty dessert plate. She wouldn't have done that to another living soul but me. I found the same thing, chewed gum in paper in the beater's room in the chamber pot. Actually, they'd also stuck a piece in the bottom of our egg basket after they'd egged my mother's window. I didn't think of that until later."

"Olivia and Charles—"

"Egged our house."

He couldn't believe how joyful, even calming it was to see her again. "You are testifying tomorrow, in Charles's murder trial," he said. "Are you up to it?"

She locked her bait box. He carried the box and the rod and walked next to her toward the house. "As we live, we live stupidly," she said.

"Not you, you did figure it out," he said.

"And I used a sledge hammer to do it. Was Haversack right? Was I self-serving? I think about that. This was about people's lives."

"If I'd been more engaged—"

"No, you may have been right from the beginning. What has any of this accomplished?"

He shook his head. "No, I wasn't, and my uncle will follow you up."

"I hear that Charlotte was dragged to the courts to give testimony—as a hostile witness," she said.

"They don't come more hostile than Charlotte."

"I suppose that she didn't deserve having her brothel visits plastered all over the front pages. She must have loved Tweedmouth, just as she said. Even so, for Charlotte, and Louis, and Renard, the temptation to smother the man must have confronted them daily. They didn't act on it. They have my admiration."

"Charlotte?"

Eleanor made a wry face.

All the morning sitting in the witness box, she had to suffer the judge staring at her in stern disapproval. He was an older gentleman, not at all modern. He would be the first to complain about a woman's presence at any function. She heard rebuke in every word the judge directed toward her. She was after all the direct descendant of a viscount, and fashionable women don't shoot. They had to take into account her Irish ancestry.

Her backside hurt from the hard chair she had been sitting in for hours. The hushed courtroom smelled of men. The high ceiling seemed to suck up the heat leaving the room vulnerable to the chill, or maybe the room was cold from the blast of frigid, condescending words. A pettifogger in a dark robe and white, stiff wig asked her repetitive questions until she felt numb. None of the questions had been about science or even about facts in the case. Each one had been a personal attack.

At break over lunch, Faraday interpreted the judge's appearance as, "something that death couldn't alter."

"Certainly, the lord and masterful judge will die grasping Genesis," said Eleanor. "The judge should be on my side—a knight to the fairer sex and all that."

"Eleanor, do be respectful," said Alannah.

"Have I ever been anything but?"

B ack in the hard chair, Eleanor tried to brighten as the barrister, pulling at his goatee, began another hundred questions.

"Would you call yourself a trouble-maker?"

"Never. I suppose though, my lord, that no one else would agree with me."

Faraday and Alannah coughed in unison.

"You were under the influence of laudanum the night Lord Wallingford came to see you?"

Eleanor fixed her eyes on Faraday, who winked back.

"Yes."

"Your mind drugged, then?"

"Yes."

"When Lord Wallingford spoke about saving people, could he have been speaking about you?"

"No."

She tried to keep her gaze hard and directed toward the man who peppered questions at her. Truth couldn't be delivered with a weak mind or heart. She thought of Faraday in the crowd, wanting her to say what needed to be said.

"Hadn't you been shot?"

"He had shot me—"

"My lord." The barrister complained to the judge.

"Answer the question as stated, Lady Albright."

I thought I took an oath to tell the truth.

"I had been shot." She added in her mind, by that ass over in the dock. Who thinks the world of himself and even now thinks that I deserved to be shot.

"Had anyone seen the person who shot you?"

"No. He aimed low high, kept the gun moving, never checked."

The barrister glanced at her like she was something out of the realm of his understanding. He turned his head toward the jury as if to say, you see she is mad. Maybe she was or maybe she was the only sane person here. She wanted to jump up and point at Charles and say, that man shot me, and when that didn't kill me, he poisoned me with laudanum. He is not a good person. My husband is not a good person, and I'm tired of people telling me otherwise. I'm tired of how entitled they feel to mold the world exactly to their personal desires...at the expense of others.

The barrister began again. "You had hurt your ankle crawling in a window at a place of business in London? What place was that?"

She wanted to lick her lips but didn't. She glanced at the judge, the jury, the audience, they would love to hear the words brothel from her. And if she didn't answer—*you are in contempt of this court...answer the question as stated.*

"A business that provides male consorts for women."

"In fact, you have broken into two houses of business?"

"Yes."

"And you are in separation from you husband, living as a single woman."

"Did I conduct business with the establishment in London? Is that the question? If yes, I would have hardly needed to break in."

"You are a woman, separated from your husband. You had been injured. With no one in the room but your sleeping mother, you felt overwhelmed over your accident, and you were overanxious in your reaction. Most of your injuries are of your own doing, are they not?"

"Leading," called the barrister for the prosecution of Charles Wallingford. "And she didn't shoot herself."

"Granted."

The barrister for the defense crossed off a line of words on the paper in front of him before he continued. "Did anyone ask you to investigate the death of the Baron of Tweedmouth?"

"*Ignis fatuus,*" said Eleanor.

"Foolish, indeed." The barrister smiled at what he thought a capture.

"Indeed, sir, and should the foolishness be weighed, it would show to any reasonable person that Charles Wallingford is the most foolish of all. He was more pissed than sane, more egotistical than perceptive."

Faraday applauded her with a muffled clap.

The judge's hammer rained a staccato of dull sound into the air. Music to her ears. She had done what she meant to do, save Louis. She was glad, so glad it was not he in the docket. Let the court decide on Charles's fate, now that they could. Now that they could...Eleanor felt the smile on her face. *Bam*, she had gotten her bird, just this one flipping rich bastard.

THE END

Don't miss out on your next favorite book!

Join the Satin Romance mailing list
www.satinromance.com/mail.html

ABOUT THE AUTHOR

Julie G Murphy has a M.A. in Writing Popular Fiction from Seton Hill University and a certificate in short story writing from LongRidgeWritersGroup®. She taught English as a second language in Nagasaki, Japan, and has lived for two years in Ireland with her Irish husband. She also went to sea with him on British Petroleum oil tankers. She was born in Idaho, the granddaughter of Spanish Basques, and spent one year with Boise State University in the Basque country in Spain. *Flipping Rich Bastards* was voted first place by one judge in the Helen McCloy Mystery Writers of America Scholarship for Mystery Writing. From the four other judges, it was awarded two third's and a fourth. Julie has two other books with other publishers.

murphy_julie@icloud.com
Juliegmurphy.wordpress.com

 facebook.com/juliemgaldos